COME TO ME

CRYSTAL KASWELL

Copyright

This is a work of fiction. Similarities to real people, places, or events are entirely coincidental.

Also by Crystal Kaswell

Sign up for the Crystal Kaswell mailing list

From the Author

Five years ago, I started writing my first novel. After stumbling a lot and revising even more, I finished the early incarnation of this book. I published it in 2014 under the title *Rouse Me*.

At the time, I was still writing screenplays, still hearing "no one wants romance" or "no one wants stories about women" constantly. The very act of writing about a damaged woman finding love felt revolutionary. I had no idea what a "romance novel" was, but I knew I wanted to write a story about love that was romantic—my idea of romantic.

Then I wrote a bunch more books (including this one, a third *Rouse Me* book, and a dirty Cinderella story). Somehow, I lucked into my niche with my fourth book *Sing Your Heart Out*. By the time I started work on book three in that series, I knew I had my path.

I started writing damaged rock stars. Then damaged bad boys of all types. I found my voice… even if it wavered from time to time.

Then, I decided *Rouse Me* didn't reflect what I write

anymore. I took it down, with plans to rewrite it to bring it "on brand." Only it refused to fit neatly into the "Crystal Kaswell brand."

Last year, I published it anyway. And people liked it. A lot more than I expected. It wasn't my next *Tempting*, but it found readers and those readers wanted the rest of the *Rouse Me* series.

So… I reworked those too. It took awhile (it's been nearly a year now), but the entire trilogy is now available.

This series is a love triangle. It's about the hard choices and difficult moments that come with a relationship. And it's about how falling in love sometimes means falling apart before you piece yourself back together.

That's why the entire series is called the *Come Undone Trilogy*. This is book three, *Come To Me*. Reading books one and two is recommended, though it's not strictly necessary. Each of these books is a complete story, one trial and tribulation in the live of Alyssa and the man she chooses.

This book is a little different than what I usually write in terms of prose, subject matter, and hero. But it's the same, at its core. This book, like all my books, is about two damaged souls finding each other and helping each other heal.

This series still holds a special place in my heart as the books that started it all.

It's not for the faint of heart, but if you're ready to take the plunge, I promise to take you on a wild ride.

———

Please note this book contains material which may be triggering for some readers (including explicit descriptions of eating disorder behavior).

Chapter One

ALYSSA

L uke's face lights up when I step into the restaurant.

"I missed you so much," he murmurs in a low voice.

God, I missed him too.

I missed him holding me while we watch television, I missed arguing with him about the stupidest little things, I missed having him there while I drink my morning cup of coffee.

I missed the way he looks at me with those dark eyes.

Like he wants me so badly he can't wait to be alone. And might not.

It's been barely any time at all. Five days. One week of shooting on location, far, far away from Los Angeles.

But it feels like forever.

He wraps his arms tight around me, secure and warm. My body hums from the proximity.

It's as good as the first time he touched me.

"I missed you too," I whisper.

I bury myself deeper in his chest, inhaling him. He smells good. He always does. Like soap and Luke and my shampoo.

The obscenely girly honey scented shampoo I buy at Lush.

He brushes his cheek against mine; the beginning of stubble rasping against me lightly.

My whole body feels light, like I'm floating. It really does feel like it's been an eternity since I've been in his arms, since I've felt his skin against mine.

"How did you bribe Laurie into releasing you early?" he asks, his voice rumbling in his chest.

"I'm the star. I get to make all kinds of ridiculous demands," I half joke.

"Hmm. I'll make sure I use that to my advantage in the future."

I smile, breathing him in again, letting the feeling of being back in Luke's arms soak in.

"You're using my shampoo."

"And your conditioner." He squeezes me tighter then pulls back to look at me, his eyes soft. "It smells like you."

My heart squeezes in my chest.

"Barely. I only wash my hair once a week."

"It's close enough." He offers his hand, his palm flat like he's Prince Charming asking me to dance. I brush my fingers against it.

"I promised her a sleep over," I explain.

He raises a brow.

"She's a little old for that."

"Ah, but she's also incredibly abusive of her power. Reminds me of someone else I know."

"I do no such thing," he counters with mock affront.

"Then why is your assistant always booking my appointments?" I point out.

He raises a brow. "What's the point of having an assistant if she isn't assisting?" He sighs dreamily. "And thanks for reminding me I have my very own assistant."

Luke used to work with my ex, Ryan. They were partners in a tiny, two-man law firm. About six months ago, Luke sold his half of the practice to Ryan. He wanted to cut any ties with him forever.

Thank God.

Now, Luke works independently as a divorce lawyer. He really adores his job. He loves discussing the virtues of dissolving toxic marriages.

I bite my lip to keep from laughing at his expression. "You certainly didn't forget how to gloat in the last few days."

"It's a skill I'd never let die," he says seriously. Shifting his attention, he squeezes my hand and points me to the staircase. "Miss Summers, I'd love to stand here talking shit about your boss all night, but our reservation is for 7:00."

"Is that so?"

He nodes gravely.

"Yes, and I'd hate to be late to my anniversary dinner. It would be dreadfully embarrassing."

"So it would," I agree, smiling slightly.

He leans down and brushes his lips against mine.

They're so soft and sweet. Kissing him feels like home.

I'm so glad to be back.

I follow Luke upstairs.

He tried to convince me we should celebrate our anniversary at the restaurant where we shared our first meal, but I nixed the idea. Ryan still works across the street, and I don't want to ruin a year of bliss by running into my bitter ex-boyfriend.

Instead, we're at a secluded restaurant on the other side

of the marina. It's close to the water, close enough that we should have a gorgeous view of the sunset.

It's popular for that reason.

But today... it's quiet. Unusually quiet.

I frown, just then noticing it.

I was too busy taking Luke in before.

But I'm not in suspense for long.

When I get to the top floor, I see why.

There's space for 100 people.

But no one is here.

Light streams through the windows, bouncing off the clean hard-wood floors and the mostly empty room.

There's only one table set up.

One.

My jaw drops at the sight. It's so... perfect.

Luke knew I was dreading potential interruptions. Between *Model Citizen* taking off and my last film winning an Independent Spirit Award, I'm recognizable. Every few days, someone stops me to offer a compliment or, if I'm really lucky, a criticism of the show.

But not tonight.

Tonight it's only us.

Luke grins at my reaction. "I promised you'd like it."

I shake my head.

"I never doubted you."

The light from the windows falls over him. He looks so sharp in his black suit and royal blue tie, his dark hair falling in soft waves.

He had to wear a suit for work, but he doesn't usually go all out. I know it's for me.

"Stop objectifying me," he teases.

I sigh.

"But you look so good."

His eyes pass over my body. "You're not so bad your-self." He leans closer, his fingers on my upper back, his breath on my ear. "You know that's my favorite dress."

"Oh, this old thing?" I ask with mock coyness. It's a very sexy dress--smooth blue silk that clings to my curves.

Especially my chest.

"God damn, Alyssa. You are going to pay for wearing that."

I suppress a shiver at the heat in his eyes.

No one has ever made me feel sexier.

My response is more than a little breathy.

"I'm looking forward to it."

He pulls my chair out for me and sits across from me. There's a candle in the middle of the table, casting a soft light.

"I can't believe it's been a year," he marvels, his expression wondering.

"Me either."

It feels like the time flew right by.

"It's been the best year of my life."

"Me too," I agree. He's just... the best. So much more than I could have expected. "I just wish we didn't have to spend so much time apart."

"Yes." He offers his hand, and I take it. "I hate it too." He leans in closer. "I fantasize about just coming with you when you leave."

"You have a business to run," I murmur, wishing he could.

He shrugs.

"Sure. But it would be so much more fun to just say 'fuck it'. To quit and spend my life traveling the world with you."

"You'd get bored," I try next, my smile wider.

"Never," he scoffs. "I could never get bored with you."

"You love your job."

"Yes." He leans in close. "But I love you more."

I feel my cheeks flush.

I know it must be true--we've been together for a year.

A year ago, I dumped Ryan's sorry ass to be with Luke. We've been through a lot together. But it's been fucking amazing.

I was never a romantic person. I'm still not, not really. But, being with him... I finally get it. I understand pop songs, greeting cards, proposals written in the sky.

He's so damn sweet. He's smarter than anyone I know, driven, funny. So sexy I sometimes can't stand it.

He's also an insufferable tease and there are moments in the middle of an argument where I want to just scream.

I wouldn't change him for anything.

He's perfect.

"What are you thinking, Ally?" He searches my face.

I shake my head. "It's nothing."

He tilts his head, giving me a look.

"It looked like something."

"Just that I love you," I say. "That's all."

His face lights up with a smile.

God, that was it. The first time I saw his face light up like that, I was hooked.

"Go on."

I laugh, rolling my eyes.

"In your dreams. Your head is already too big."

He shakes said head, a wicked glint in his eye. "No. My dreams of you are never that tame."

My temperature goes up a couple of degrees.

"Mr. Lawrence," I whisper, making a show of looking around. "This is a family restaurant."

"So it is."

"But... I wouldn't necessarily ask you to stop."

His eyes darken.

I feel my heartbeat quicken.

I know that look.

"Would you ever ask me to stop?"

I bite my lip. We've been so busy--I've had early call times and he's been home late--that we've barely touched each other in the last two weeks.

Tonight can't come soon enough.

"We'll see," I say.

This time, his smile is too sharp, too hungry to be at all innocent.

I can't look away.

"Ally... you're going to be in agony tonight." His finger traces a line across my palm, oh so lightly. I feel that small touch... everywhere. His gaze is knowing as he continues. He knows exactly how he affects me. "In the most delightful agony. You're going to beg me to do anything to release you from it." He brings my hand up to his mouth, kissing my palm softly. "And... I just might."

I still haven't fully caught my breath when the waiter arrives.

————

DINNER IS AN AMAZING, THREE COURSE AFFAIR-- A FRESH salad with plump tomatoes, seared sea bass with braised kale and roasted yams, and a plate of chocolate dipped strawberries.

Yum.

The sun sets, until the only light is from the stars outside and the candle flickering between us. I tell Luke about all the irrelevant details of my trip--the oppressive sunshine in Arizona, getting dragged to townie bars by the other cast members, Laurie scolding the director of the week for getting too invested in his shots.

It's exactly what I didn't know I wanted.

After dinner, Luke insists on driving. "It's a surprise," he tells me.

I don't know what to expect, anticipation building.

My heart melts when I see where we end up.

The bookstore. The place where we had our first real date.

Just like the first time, we walk around the aisles, our fingers lingering on the crisp paper. We find a corner upstairs, in the non-fiction section, and steal a long, deep kiss.

It's been so long, and there's so much need pouring from both of us. His hands brush against my thighs, all the way to the edges of my dress. I moan into his mouth.

"Not here," I say hoarsely.

"Of course not here," he agrees. He nods to the movie theater across the street. "Not when I have a chance to repeat one of my favorite-"

"We're not going to luck into an empty theater tonight."

He draws back, feigning offense.

"Miss Summers. What do you take me for--some kind of pervert?"

His eyes twinkle mischievously.

"What do you have planned?" I ask, suspicious of that look.

He just smiles, squeezes my hand, and leads me to the theater.

Inside, the theater is the same as it was before--fluorescent and almost empty. That's not a huge surprise--there's a new, cool movie theater across the street. One that serves dinner and drinks and has couches that beg you to push the limits of decency laws.

Of course, I don't need any extra motivation.

My body has been flooding with want since I first felt Luke's arms around me.

He was right. This is already painful.

But I'm not shying away from more. It's going to be such delicious agony.

We buy tickets to a film that started five minutes ago. The usher assures us that the trailers are still rolling, that the theater is nearly empty. He looks at us like he knows what we have planned. Are we really that obvious?

I whisper in Luke's ear. "Are you sure this is wise? What if someone recognizes me?"

His hand slides over my waist, until his fingers are pressed against my bare back.

Jesus. My skin tingles with an electric current.

There's no way I can sit through a two-hour movie before getting his hands on me.

He brings his mouth to my ear, his breath hot and heavy. "I am dying to make you come."

I must have a stupid look on my face, because he's grinning again. It's that confident look of his, the one that says *I know how much you want me. I know how good I am at filling you with desperate, achy need. And I'm going to do it. Then, I'm going to release you in a torrent of ecstasy. But not until you're begging and pleading.*

"But we could always go home. Traffic has cleared by now," he offers.

But there's no doubt in his voice. He knows we aren't going anywhere.

He knows I need him now.

I shake my head. "No. I like that other plan."

He presses his lips into my neck. I already feel it--the

rush of want between my legs. "Good," he whispers. "I've been daydreaming about it all damn week."

His lips are on my neck again, a harder kiss. We're in the middle of the lobby. The surly teenager at the concession stand is staring at us, but I don't care.

I close my eyes and lean into his kiss.

He takes my hand and leads me into the empty theater.

It's dark, but I can just make out a few people in the back-middle rows. The very back corner is empty. Is it the same corner, the same theater where we...

"It is," he responds to my thoughts. "But I don't want you thinking about that day when you scream my name. I want you so filled with pleasure that you're practically incoherent."

Jesus.

I nod. "I'm... on board."

His hands skim my waist as he follows me into the row. I sit next to the wall. It's the farthest corner of the theater. If anyone looked, they would be sure we were doing something...

Just like last time.

My heart pounds in my chest. Someone might see us, but I don't care. I almost want someone to see us, to see how damn good he is at delivering on his promises.

Luke lifts the arm rest and presses his lips into mine. It's soft at first. He moves slowly. His fingertips circle my knees and slide up my thighs, inching closer and closer to the edge of my dress. His kiss intensifies as his hand slides under my dress.

I clench my thighs, soaking in the feel of his skin on mine. God. He's about to... Almost... It's been so long.

This is already torture.

His tongue plunges into my mouth as he presses his

hand against my panties. Every sense in my body turns on all at once.

I can hear his soft, heavy breath, even with the air conditioning on full blast and the movie launching into some loud action sequence.

He keeps his hand flat against my panties, another one of his horrible, wonderful teases. I flood with want, squirming in my seat, kissing him harder and harder.

Then, he runs his fingers over my panties. It's so light and gentle I can barely stand it. "Luke," I groan. "Touch me."

But he keeps at it, his touch still light and slow and soft.

"You look too damn beautiful like this," he growls. He kisses me, as hard as I was kissing him. His tongue swirls around mine as he slides his hands under the fabric of my panties.

Jesus Christ. My body burns from his touch.

It's been too long.

I kiss him back even harder as he rubs me with long, slow strokes. His hand is so soft and hard all at once, and I arch to meet his touch.

But I need more.

I pull my dress to my waist, pull my panties out of the way. I don't care that someone could see. All I care about is him touching me, him delivering on his promise.

And he does. His soft touch gets harder, faster. I am so wet and desperate and full of need. He whispers in my ear, "I want to watch you come because it's the most beautiful thing I've ever seen."

I grab his shoulders, digging my nails into his back as he rubs me. I get closer... and closer... and closer. Clenching as I fill with pleasure. And then his lips are on my neck, and my nails are on his skin. The pressure builds. It's too much. It's so much. It feels so damn good.

He rubs me, harder and harder, his kiss is harder and harder.

And then everything in my body... releases.

I groan, "Luke," and he does nothing to stop me.

I'm sure someone turns, someone sees, someone notices.

But I can't bring myself to care.

Chapter Two

LUKE

Alyssa is relaxed on the drive home.

She doesn't even protest when I promise we can pick her car up tomorrow. Instead, she curls up in the passenger seat, her head on my shoulder, her arms wrapped around mine.

"You seem tired," I observe.

"Don't even start. I'm not that tired," she returns. Her lips curl into a smile. She crosses and uncrosses her legs, the hem of her dress sliding up her thighs.

I try and keep my eyes on the road, but it's hard. This is the first real date we've had in weeks.

We've both been busy. She's always gone when I wake up, and when she gets home, she barely has time to memorize her lines before she crashes on the couch.

She tries to stay up with me, lying next to me on the couch during one of my *Law and Order* marathons. But she always falls asleep in my lap by the time the jury comes back with a guilty verdict.

I also used to be vigilant about getting out of work by six p.m., but I've been leaving work later and later.

"What are you thinking?" she asks.

She's tired. She must be--she's been working 14hour days for months. But she's as desperate as I am to make this night as amazing as it should be.

"You only have two weeks left of shooting."

"Thank God. I can't wait to do nothing," she sighs.

"Well, what if you did nothing with me?" I glance over at her.

"What do you have in mind?"

"Three days in San Diego. I'll take Monday off."

I've been thinking about what to do that's low key enough to still feel relaxing.

"What's in San Diego--besides the drug store where you used to buy eyeliner?"

"You won't let go of that, will you?" I laugh.

She leans in closer.

"At least tell me--did you wear black, brown, charcoal? I could see you in an electric blue or a shocking pink. Something from Urban Decay."

"Oh yeah?"

"Mhmm. You could pull off a lot of color. Or a black. Some nice, dark lines to draw even more attention to those gorgeous eyes."

We stop at a light, and she presses her hands against my cheek. I feel a rush of warmth.

It's so good to be next to her. I never get sick of the feeling in my body, that sense that I'm home.

The sex is fucking amazing too.

"You're obsessed." I smirk, turning towards her.

"It's true." She smiles, looking into said eyes. "I wonder what would have happened if we met as teenagers."

"I already know. You would have thought I was a rich snob."

She tilts her head to the side, considering.

"You would have thought I was a burned-out loser."

"No way in hell," I scoff. "I would have seen you in the school play and been transfixed. And, after, when I went to tell you how great you were, you would ask me what brand of eyeliner I use. Boom—we'd be best friends."

She laughs. "Definitely."

"But when you found out the eyeliner was only a three-week phase, you'd get bored of me."

"Was it really?"

I shrug.

"Maybe a month or two. But no more."

"You're destroying my fantasies here," she groans.

"Miss Summers! I was underage."

"And a virgin too, I bet," she says with more than a touch of sarcasm, rolling her eyes.

I grin.

She's not wrong. I wasn't a late bloomer.

"And I'm the pervert?"

She nods. "We're both perverts. That's why we're so perfect for each other."

Absolutely perfect. I squeeze her hand. "So, what do you think about San Diego?"

"Laurie is probably going to throw an end of season party."

I shrug.

"Ditch it."

She smiles. "Okay. But I'll be exhausted all weekend. I won't want to get out of bed."

"I wasn't planning on spending much time out of bed. Except to eat amazing Mexican food, drink loads of tequila, and lounge on the hotel's private beach."

"Private beach, huh?"

"Mhmm."

She nods. "Okay. But I don't know if we'll even make it to the beach. Or if we'll have the energy to lounge."

I adjust myself in my seat.

"Miss Summers..."

"Don't worry. You'll get a taste soon," she teases in that husky voice.

It's so fucking hot.

At the next stoplight, she kisses me.

It's a hungry kiss. One that makes my already hard cock throb.

She must be waking up.

"Thanks, Luke," she whispers, pulling back. "I need something like this. I haven't had enough of you lately."

"Yeah," I agree. "But I don't think I could ever have enough of you."

Smiling she kisses my cheek, snuggling into the side of my neck.

It's sweet.

But I need more than a kiss on the cheek.

I need to be buried balls deep in her yesterday.

We can't get home fast enough.

We pull into the driveway and I wait impatiently for the garage to open.

Alyssa's eyes watch me with the same hunger I feel.

In only minutes, we'll be alone in our house.

And naked and sweaty as quickly as I can manage it.

Though it's not strictly our house.

Technically, it's my house. After the agony of Samantha buying me out of my half of our house, Alyssa refused to share a mortgage.

My ex-girlfriend was willing to resort to whatever emotional manipulation it took to get her way. Alyssa bends over backwards to ensure she doesn't have leverage.

I wish she wouldn't be so damn careful. I'd trust her with much more than a mortgage.

"Well, Mr. Lawrence. I do believe you have a promise to live up to."

I turn at Alyssa's low voice.

She brushes her lips against mine, sliding the straps of her dress off her shoulders.

Fuck.

No more waiting.

Chapter Three

ALYSSA

An urgent message from my agent greets me when I finally get to my dressing room. "Darling, call me back. Trust me. You will die when you hear this."

Corine is always going on about some terrific opportunity.

I don't want to complain too much. It's good. She's doing her job, earning her 10 percent. But her opportunities are usually awful parts as the sexy wife or the naked murder victim in the newest blockbuster that's in the works.

I know a 100-million-dollar movie is a big step up from a cable comedy. But she should know by now that I'm past the point in my career where I'm willing to play the hot chick.

I check the time--just after seven. Corine left this message three hours ago. She's probably still at work.

I better get this over with so I can spend my night with Luke interruption free.

Even if we're not going to do much more than watch TV.

I take a deep breath.

It's a weeknight. We're supposed to be relaxing. And I'm the one who always insists on TV. I'm too tired for anything else, and I have lines to cram.

I close my eyes. I'm almost done. Eight more days and we'll be done shooting. Eight more days and I'll be in San Diego with Luke, doing something much, much more exciting than watching TV.

Alright, I need to just do this. It might really be a great opportunity.

I sit down before calling her back, already preparing how I'll say no to this one.

"Darling," Corine purrs. "How is everything? Are they treating you well over on *Model Citizen*?"

"I'm fine. Just tired."

"Hmm, that is to be expected with a project like that." I can almost hear her deciding that's enough with the niceties. "Do you remember what you said when you met me?"

"You remind me every time we talk," I sigh, tilting my head back. "I said I wanted to play Ophelia in *Hamlet*."

"Yes, well, Ophelia is pathetic. Killing herself over an indecisive loser like Hamlet." She makes a disapproving noise that makes me smile. "I've got a much better opportunity for you."

"Better than Shakespeare?" I drawl.

Yes, I'm skeptical. But she's given me reason to be.

"You grew up on the East Coast. I'm sure you dreamed of New York City."

That catches my attention.

My throat goes dry.

Of course, I grew up dreaming of New York City. Everyone around me dreamed of getting an apartment in the village and "making it."

But I choose LA. It's warmer, cheaper, farther away from home.

Win, win, and big win.

"I'm listening," I respond cautiously.

"And, as an aspiring actress, you no doubt wanted to appear on Broadway?" she continues, her tone smug.

I swallow. "Broadway?"

Who wouldn't want to be on Broadway, with her name in lights on a marquee, performing in a historic theater every night?

Broadway. Of course I fucking want to be on Broadway.

The air leaves my lungs as I think about it.

Broadway. Broad-fucking-way. It's not possible. I must be dreaming. There's no way I'm going to have a part on Broadway. I can't compete with full-time theater actors and those parts don't go to B-list TV stars.

They go to serious film actors. The kind who win Oscars.

"And, darling, I know how you adore Tennessee Williams."

"What?" I gasp, my heart pounding.

"Ah, so do I finally have your attention?" she croons.

"Yes. God, yes. Tell me."

"Do you remember Kyle Lee, the producer from that movie... *Golden State,* wasn't it?"

"Yeah." We met once during production and had a thirty-minute conversation about my largely irrelevant character. He was nice enough, but it didn't seem like I made an impression.

"He's got some sort of family connection and he's in charge of a revival of *A Streetcar Named Desire.*"

"If you're fucking with me, I swear..."

"Never," Corine reassures me. "He wants you to play Blanche."

My heart skips in my chest.

Blanche DuBois.

He wants me to play Blanche DuBois. One of the best fucking characters in American theater. He wants me to play Blanche DuBois in a Broadway revival of *A Streetcar Named Desire*.

There's no way this is real.

"Corine, I swear. If you're just leading me on here…"

"I have the contract right here." I hear papers shuffling in the background.

"What?" That's too fast, too easy.

"Well, Mr. Lee is lacking in the organizational department. He wants you in New York as soon as you're done with *Model Citizen*."

"But that's in eight days."

My stomach drops at that important piece of information.

"I know. It's sudden. But it's Tennessee Williams, Alyssa! You won't get this chance again."

Like I don't know that.

"Did his first choice drop out?" I ask.

"He fired his Blanche this afternoon. You're his first choice for a replacement."

"What happened?"

"Artistic differences, drug addiction. Who cares? You're a TV actor. You're not getting another chance to appear on Broadway unless you learn to sing and dance."

Corine is always so supportive.

"I want to," I offer carefully.

She groans.

"Don't tell me-- your boyfriend wouldn't like it?"

"You know I'm not with Ryan anymore."

"Yes. I found out through the gossip blogs. But your tone tells me this new guy is still holding you back somehow." She sighs. "You're a stronger woman than this. You shouldn't let men run your life, Alyssa."

"I'm not. I want to spend time with him. If he knew, he'd tell me to take it. He'll actually be upset if he finds out I turned it down."

"Really?" Her voice hums with delight. Another angle she can use to try to convince me to agree.

"Don't even think about it," I warn. "I want to do it, but I've barely seen him for the last two months. We've been so busy." I shake my head, not finding any way around this. "I need a few weeks off. We have a trip planned..."

"So come to New York instead," she urges. "It's only a six month engagement."

That's quite a run for a revival play. And too long to be away from Luke.

"I can't," I murmur, regret filling me. "I'll miss him too much."

"I'll tell them you're considering it," she says firmly.

"Corine, no. Not this time."

"Darling. It's Wednesday. I'll promise them an answer by Friday evening."

"I'm not going to change my mind," I tell her, just as firmly.

"Sure. No pressure. Sleep on it. Dream about the Tony you'll place on your mantle."

I shake my head.

I can't dream about anything. Six months is far too long to be away from Luke. Things are so good right now. It's not worth taking the risk.

Not for anything.

———

I'M RELIEVED WHEN LUKE ISN'T HOME.

It gives me time to compose myself so he doesn't immediately know I'm hiding something.

God, I shouldn't be so secretive. He's not Ryan. He's not going to hold it against me.

But he'll get so excited. He'll offer to come with me and completely throw the six months he's spent building a business out the window.

Or he'll be devastated when I tell him I can't take it.

It might be worse if he didn't offer to come with me. What if he was okay with six months apart? I know he loves me. I never doubt that... but passion does fade. Even Luke's.

The buzz of my phone jolts me into awareness. It's Luke. *I'll be home in ten.*

It's just a part. It's no big deal. There's no reason why I have to tell him.

And there's no reason why I shouldn't tell him. Not if I trust him.

I resolve to play it by ear and step into the shower. That should ease the ache growing in the back of my head.

It almost works. The pounding water drowns out my thoughts. And it's warm enough to relax my achy muscles.

Only eight days and I'll be in San Diego with Luke. I'll be spending the weekend rolling around in bed, reacquainting myself with every delicious part of his body.

I hear the front door open.

You know... we don't have to wait until this weekend. We can get started early.

I turn off the shower and meet Luke in the living room.

He stills, giving me a slow once over. One that warms me from the inside out. "I like your outfit."

His voice is deeper, my effect on him clear.

I smile, taking a step closer.

He looks like he wants to pounce on me. But he doesn't move. "Did you eat at work or do you want in on my delivery order?"

"I'm in."

He slides out of his jacket and hangs it off a chair, still watching me. "Is everything okay?"

Damn it.

"I'm naked and you ask if everything is okay?"

He nods. "I'd love to throw you on the bed and have my way with you." He scans my face, frowning slightly. "But you seem upset."

I shake my head. There's no reason to bring up the part. Not yet. "I'm tired. That's it."

I bite my lip at the evasion.

But it's close enough to the truth. Right?

"You'll be on vacation soon. Though, I must admit, you won't get much rest." He slides his arms around me, his eyes on mine. "Are you sure nothing is wrong?"

I nod.

He rubs my shoulders, still watching me closely. He's still worried. "Didn't you take a shower this morning?"

"I wanted to relax."

I try not to sound defensive about it. I mean, he's right —something is wrong.

"Ally..."

"You go crazy when I don't talk to you?"

He raises his brows, not buying into that line of conversation.

I sigh. I know he really does want to know the stupid things on my mind.

"Can you promise you'll react as calmly and coolly as possible?" I ask, giving him a strong side eye.

I can't take his excitement, not when I've already decided not to take the part.

"Last time I checked, you weren't a fan of promises from Luke Lawrence."

I crack a smile at that.

"That's true."

He smiles back, smoothing my hair.

"But, I do promise. What is it?"

"It's not a big deal."

"Uh huh. You want to wait until we order dinner to tell me about this teeny tiny thing?"

I nod, my shoulders slumping.

"Alright. And, I imagine that you—unfortunately—want to get dressed?"

I shake my head. "No, but I probably should. Unless..."

"Not right now, Ally. You're clearly stressed out about something." He kisses my cheek. "But later, if you're still awake and you're still up for it."

Fair enough.

I disappear into our room and spend what feels like forever changing into my pajamas.

It is a big deal. It's a huge deal.

And Luke's perfectly capable of crushing me with his reaction.

Chapter Four

LUKE

Alyssa joins me at the dinner table after hiding out in her room forever.

She keeps pressing her lips together, squeezing her hands together.

She's a nervous wreck.

I wish she had an easier time talking to me.

"I ordered from the Indian place," I let her know.

"It's so over-priced," she protests.

"I don't care. I know you like it."

She smiles, though whatever is weighing on her dims it.

What could it be?

I offer my hand and she takes it. Her skin is so warm, but she's shivering.

"Ally, what's wrong?"

"It's really not a big deal." She presses her lips together again. Her gaze moves to the floor.

Sure it isn't.

"Are you sure about that?"

"Yes." She presses her fingers into the table. "And I'll tell you. But I don't want to be talked out of my decision."

"Okay." What the hell could she be talking about?

Her eyes stay on the floor as the first sentence comes out in a rush, almost in one word. "I was offered a role in a play in New York and I turned it down." She fiddles with her tank top as she pulls her knees into her chest. "That's it. No big deal."

For an actress, she really is a terrible liar.

"What play?"

"Just an old play."

"Just an old play my ass," I say mildly. "If anyone cares about some old play it's you."

She really does read the most awful, English major shit.

She smirks, but it only lasts a second. Then she's back to that same serious expression. "It's not a big deal."

"Nothing is a big deal to you."

She clears her throat. "*A Streetcar Named Desire*."

My heart sinks. No. "You turned down a role in *A Streetcar Named Desire*?"

"Yes. And it's not a big deal. An actress was fired and I'd be the replacement. But it's too sudden. I'd have to leave the minute I finished shooting here." There's no pause between her statement and her hiding behind a glass of water.

She's not shutting this down that easily.

"Which part?"

She shrugs like it's not a big deal.

She was offered a part in her favorite play. And it's no big deal?

"Come on, Ally. Who do you think you're kidding? We both know you could spend the entire night talking about the themes in any depressing work of American literature."

"It's not depressing," she immediately counters.

"Oh yeah?"

She sighs.

"Okay, maybe it's a little depressing. But why is that such a bad thing?"

"You're just proving my point."

She uncrosses her legs. "I know." She frowns, clearly trying to figure out how to get me on board with this decision. "It's a great opportunity, and under different circumstances, I'd love to do it. I'd love to do it if it was in Los Angeles and I could come home to you every night."

Shit.

"Ally..."

She holds up a hand.

"No, don't Ally me. Right now, I'd rather spend my time with you."

I need all the information here.

"What was the part?"

She looks at the ground. "Blanche."

My stomach drops with an almost audible thud.

I know Alyssa would kill to play Blanche.

"Ally..."

She folds her arms. "You promised."

"Okay. I won't try to talk you out of it."

She stares at me like she doesn't believe me.

She shouldn't. This is a terrible decision.

"I won't," I lie.

If I push now, she'll close down.

I need to be sneakier.

The tension in her expression eases. "Okay. Thank you. Why don't we set up for dinner?" She stands and fetches plates from the cabinets. "Do you want a drink?"

"Water."

She pours herself a generous glass of tequila.

I eye it.

"Are you sure you're okay?"

She nods. "Tired. I really can't wait to be done with filming so I can relax."

"So you're not turning down the role because of me?"

She sighs.

"Can we not do this?".

I move towards her. Slide my arms around her waist.

She looks away, but she leans into me, her body relaxing as I hold her tighter.

"I won't be upset if you take the role."

She eyes me warily.

"Okay."

"And I don't want you to reject it because of me."

"I'm not." She slides her hands around my neck. "I'm rejecting it because I want a break. I'd rather hang out with you."

"But the Alyssa I know would kill for a chance to play Blanche DuBois."

"Usually." She leans into me, wrapping her arms around me. "But I don't have the same priorities I used to have. I'd be away for six months. That's too long to be without you."

"Ally..."

"You promised."

I shake my head.

Fuck.

"I could come with you. For a while at least. I could visit every weekend."

She shakes her head. "This is what I want."

"Are you sure?"

She nods. "Positive."

Our food arrives. Alyssa promptly changes the subject, but something is still off. She's too desperate to talk about anything else. She even asks about boring legal technicalities.

I try to shake it off. This conversation isn't going to change her mind. And I want to respect her decision. I do.

But my own baggage won't let me.

I can't help the nagging feeling in my gut that I'm holding her back. I'm my asshole father, forcing my mother into this tiny box, refusing her desire to be something besides a wife and mother.

It's bullshit. I'm not forcing Alyssa to do anything.

But I also can't let Alyssa give up what she wants for me.

And I know Alyssa. There's nothing she loves more than tragic literature. She reads Sylvia Plath like it's Pulp Fiction. And, for God's sake, she's obsessed with plays. Despite her undying love for her Kindle, she has an extensive collection of paper plays highlighted and annotated to death.

There must be a way to make her realize she needs to at least consider this.

It means too much to her not to.

I sit down next to Alyssa. "I was just thinking."

"You look cute thinking."

"I've never given *A Streetcar Named Desire* a proper read. You must own a copy."

"Don't start."

"But it sounds sexy with the desire and everything."

She rolls her eyes, but there's a tiny smile on her lips. Perfect. She's getting excited.

"There are a lot of sexual themes," she admits.

"Do tell." I wag my eyebrows at her.

"Please. Like your PhD mother didn't explain Brando's performance to you."

"Yeah, but I don't remember."

"You don't fool me, Lawrence. I know what you're trying to do." But her lips are curled into a smile. She likes talking about this kind of thing.

I move towards her. "Miss Summers, I meant what I said. I just want to learn a bit more about theater from my favorite teacher."

"You could start with an acting lesson so I'd buy that story."

She rolls her eyes, but she's laughing. I have her exactly where I want her.

I sit next to Alyssa, my body facing hers. "You don't have to believe me. But you do have to humor me."

"I have to do nothing."

I shrug.

"But you want to."

She folds her arms. "Maybe."

"So what about this desire?"

"Go read Spark Notes."

"But there's no chance Spark Notes will end with you on top of me."

That gets her attention.

She shakes her head, but her voice is low and throaty. She's not opposed to the idea. "You're shameless."

Sure am.

I press my lips to hers.

She kisses back hard, hungry.

"See, you're teaching me so much already," I say, feeling a little breathless.

"Jesus." She frowns at me. "You aren't going to stop, are you?"

I shake my head.

"Fine," she sighs. "You win." She tilts her head back, looking up at the ceiling. Composing her thoughts. "Well. It's been a little while since I've looked at *A Streetcar Named*

Desire, but I'll explain it as well as I can. Blanche is obsessed with being the object of desire. She's always flirting with men and taking great delight in dressing provocatively. There's a scene where she comes on to a young man. But she's got this Virgin/Whore thing going on. When she tries to seduce a proper suitor, she pretends like she's this chaste, honorable woman."

Her face lights up as she explains it to me, her passion for the play so clear it makes my heart ache.

Why the fuck is she shutting this down so hard?

"That sounds like a fascinating character."

She rolls her eyes. "You're so obvious." Her eyes turn to mine. Her defenses fall away, leaving her raw and open. There's no pretense to hide behind anymore. "I can't leave you for six months, Luke. It's out of the question."

She's scared.

I nod. I need to tread softly. "I'll respect your decision."

She gives me a skeptical look.

"Uh-huh."

"But I do demand to hear more about this play. It sounds awfully sexy so far."

"It is," she confirms. "But in a tragic kind of way. Stella, Blanche's sister, is super-hot for Stanley. That's Stella's husband. But he's abusive. He beats her."

I grimace.

"That sounds awful."

"And he rapes Blanche."

"That's even more fucked up." No wonder she likes this play. She only likes the most awful, tragic shit.

"It's basically what pushes her over the edge. She ends up in a mental institution."

"So it ends on a positive note?" I ask hopefully.

She shakes her head.

"She's completely divorced from reality by the end, lying to herself to get by."

Dark.

Not my cup of tea, but Alyssa's eyes light up talking about it.

She'd be in heaven being in this play.

"That sounds like a complex and interesting thing to play."

She throws her hands up in exasperation.

"Jesus Christ!"

"Okay, I'll stop." For now. "But I really do support you if you decide to take it."

Her eyes soften.

"I miss you too much already."

"We'll figure it out," I offer, injecting the words with confidence. "We can figure anything out together."

She looks away. "Well, Corine did make me promise to sleep on it."

Thank God.

"Okay."

"Don't look so happy. I'll think you're trying to get rid of me," she warns.

"I'll be miserable without you. But I'll be more miserable knowing I prevented you from something you clearly want so fucking badly."

"I'll think about it." She presses her lips to mine, a soft flutter of a kiss. "Now.It's later. Are you up for it?"

I know part of the reason for this is just a subject change.

But fuck. I'm only a man.

"Hmmm. I might be convinced."

She swings her leg over my lap, grinding her crotch against mine. "I might be interested in convincing you."

She kisses me, firmly.

I slide my hand under her tank top, going with it this time. My fingertips make their way to her chest.

She groans, her hands digging into my shoulders, her body arching into mine.

Shit.

I'm convinced.

Chapter Five

ALYSSA

"Alyssa!" The director of the week yells in my general direction.

Oh no.

It's my line. What the fuck is my line again?

I offer an apologetic smile and he shakes his head.

I'll be the first to admit I'm not perfectly focused. It's Thursday. It's late. I've already been working on the show for 40 hours this week. Maybe 50.

But that's no excuse.

I shake my head at myself. I know better. Zoning out for five minutes doesn't sound like much, but five minutes is a gazillion dollars in production time.

The director walks over to Laurie.

Shit. Laurie only comes to set if there's a problem.

Everyone else is doing fine. That means I'm the problem.

Laurie whispers something to the director.

He nods, giving her a look as he steps back.

"Take five everyone," he shouts.

There are a few groans from crew members. It's

already seven and this is the last scene of the day. We'll be done as soon as I get my head in the game.

The crew scatters and Laurie motions for me. Ugh.

I meet her at one of the fake walls. I'm in costume--the skimpiest pajamas the world has ever seen, no fucking shoes or socks-- and the cold concrete floor saps the energy from my body. How can it be so cold so late in the spring?

"Alyssa Summers," Laurie says in her best stern I'm-your-boss voice. "What's happening?"

"Sorry, I'm a little distracted. But I'll get through it."

She lowers her voice, stepping closer.

"You've flubbed this line five times."

"I know. I'm just tired. I'm dying to be on hiatus."

She sighs.

"Me too," she agrees. "But..."

"But I have to bring it while we're still here. I know. I know. I will. Just let me get some coffee."

She shakes her head.

"What are you so distracted about? This isn't like you."

My chest is tight. "Nothing. Nothing important."

She stares at me. It's friendly, but it's a demand too. "Right."

"Really."

She looks up in exasperation.

"Jesus, how does your boyfriend deal with you? You're impossible!"

"Why don't you call him by his name?" I ask, avoiding the issue.

She shrugs. "I better not get any calls from Luke asking what's wrong."

"He calls you?" It doesn't sound like Luke to ask anyone for help.

"It's happened." She motions to a set PA, a poor 20-year-old texting on his cell phone. "Alan, bring Alyssa and me some coffees. Make a fresh pot. And plenty of sugar in both!"

"And almond milk," I call out.

"And almond milk!" she yells.

She smirks as he rushes off to run her errand.

Hmm.

"Is that part of his job?"

Her face lights up. She's reveling in her power. "Hell no. But he does it. So what do I care?"

"You're such a humanitarian."

Laurie's eyes narrow. She pushes her mass of curly hair behind her ears. "I am your best friend."

"True."

"And your boss."

"I almost forgot. It's been minutes since you reminded me."

She folds her arms. "You should tell me what's going on. In case it's a problem."

Uh huh.

"Is that my friend or my boss talking?"

Laurie clears her throat. She's not sure. Finally, she just shrugs. "Both. I'm concerned."

"It's not a big deal," I reassure her. "But I was offered a role."

She gasps, opening her mouth to ask a bunch of questions. But she closes it again, trying desperately to wait until I'm finished.

I appreciate the restraint.

Deep breath. I have to prove this isn't a big deal. "Nothing that will conflict with this show."

"Thank God."

When I don't keep going right away, she leans forward, impatiently gesturing for me to go ahead.

"It's a play in New York."

I meet Laurie's gaze. Her eyes look even more intense framed by her bright red glasses.

I press my nails into my palms. "The lead in *A Streetcar Named Desire.*"

Her jaw drops, her eyes almost bugging out of her head. "Alyssa Summers! You have to take that! You'll have so much cache!"

"Boss Laurie?"

She nods. "But friend too. That would be amazing, and you'll be killer in it. You'll knock it out of the park." She inches even closer, almost whispering. "I'm sure you're sick of playing Marie fucking Jane. I know I'm sick of writing her."

I smile.

"I'm posting that on Twitter."

She rolls her eyes. "Why don't you want to do it?"

I let out my breath in a huff.

"It's six months on the other side of the country."

"So? It's Broadway, isn't it?"

"Yeah," I say. It is Broadway. It is amazing. But it's also too much time too far away from Luke. "But I don't want to be away from my boyfriend for six months."

She waves a dismissive hand.

"He'll buy you a vibrator and talk you off every night."

"Laurie!" Though, I must admit... I'm not exactly opposed to the idea.

"It's not worth the risk," I try.

"What risk? He's crazy in love with you."

The "you idiot" is silent but heavily implied.

"Yeah, but..."

"But nothing. You should do it. If you want to." She grips my arm. "I'll visit you constantly. I'll show you around all the cool parts of the city."

"You lived in New York?"

"Please. I'm a Tischie," she informs me proudly. I stare at her like she's crazy. "NYU Tisch School of the Arts. Oh, never mind. I can show you a killer time—a killer totally appropriate for grown-ups time."

"But what if it takes too big of a toll on our relationship? What if we don't stay close?"

It's a real fear. And I know it isn't unfounded.

"Not in a million years."

"It's possible," I insist. "This is why all these Hollywood marriages break up. People are off shooting halfway around the world and they fall out of love." Just saying it breaks my heart a little. "I don't want that."

"So, you'll work at it."

"I'll miss him. We'll fight. Resentment will grow. I can't do it."

Laurie furrows her brow, considering my words.

"But can you really say no to the lead in a Broadway revival? Really?"

I bite my lip. "How can I say yes?"

"Just... do it. Just call your agent and say yes. It will be the best six months of your life. It's New York, for God's sake!"

I shake my head. I wish I had Laurie's optimism, but it really isn't worth the risk.

Not to me. Not if I could lose Luke.

———

I GET HOME LATE, BUT LUKE IS STILL IN HIS SUIT.

He looks like he's been waiting for me.

He greets me at the door with a long kiss.

I feel calmer already. Right now, I need to be in his arms, need to feel his body around mine so my stupid brain will shut up.

The last time I tried to take a life-changing role, I put my entire life in disarray. Sure, it ended well.

But my life needed changing then.

Right now, everything is good. I can't mess it up.

Luke pulls away, his dark eyes still on mine. He smiles. "I got you something," he announces.

"Really?"

He nods, disappearing into the bedroom and returning with an over-sized hot pink gift bag.

He moves closer to me again, until his body is flat against mine.

God, he feels so good, so hard and safe. I wrap my arms around him, savoring the feel of him. He smells good, not like my honey shampoo but like Luke.

"Go on," he urges, handing me the hot pink bag.

What is it?

I tear out the purple paper decorating the bag and reach inside. I feel something slick and thin. It's a poster. One of those matte posters pasted on cardboard.

What the hell?

I pull it out of the bag.

My heart skips a beat as I see it for the first time.

It's a mockup. The poster for the original Broadway run of *A Streetcar Named Desire*--a silhouette of a debutante against a gorgeous red background--with my name replacing the original Blanche.

My heart starts to pound in my chest. My mouth goes dry. Even my lungs feel empty.

It's a mockup of the poster with my name.

This could be real. I could be on Broadway. In a fucking classic.

I could be the star.

Luke watches me, his eyes hopeful. "You like it?"

I nod stupidly.

He really wants me to do it. Maybe I should be annoyed--he's trying to convince me despite his earlier promise--but I'm not.

I love it.

He wants me to do this. He's willing to do the work.

Maybe... if we're both willing to work at it. Maybe we can get through six months.

"Ally, if you don't say anything I'm going to think you hate it."

"I love it," I whisper.

"Really?" His eyes light up. He's so excited for me. "So will you take the part?"

"It's such a long time," I hedge.

"Fuck, we can do it. Look at how much we've been able to get through."

He's not wrong about that. But...

"I'm not even sure I can survive six months in New York, alone. I'm not that far along in recovery."

"You've been doing amazing with your recovery. I think you can do it."

I shake my head. New York City is the land of temptation. There's a trigger food on every fucking block. I've been in recovery for my bulimia for almost two years now, but I've had help. "I don't know if I can do it without you."

He slides his hand along my cheek. "I think you can. You're not giving yourself enough credit. It's going to be difficult, but we'll get through it."

I grip his hand, holding it there.

"But what if we can't? I'm not willing to risk this relationship. Not even for Broadway."

"Trust me," he murmurs. "You're everything to me. Everything that matters. We'll make sure we check in, stay as connected as possible." He brushes my hair behind my ears, glancing at the gift. "You look so excited. You want to take the part, don't you?"

I have to admit it. It's too obvious.

Clearly, nobody is buying my act anyway.

"Yeah."

"So do it. I want you to do whatever will make you happy."

Maybe... I can.

Oh my God.

I nod, filling up with the almost painful excitement I wasn't allowing myself to truly feel.

My head is bursting with visions of how it'll be--my name on the marquee, standing on stage to a standing ovation, Luke visiting me in my tiny little New York apartment.

But I still can't quite shake some other images too-- lonely nights alone, missed calls, ignored texts.

The two of us growing apart.

But if Luke and I both make sure that doesn't happen...

"Okay," I say, feeling a little dazed at the roller coaster of emotion. "I'll do it. I'll take it."

Luke pumps his fist into the air before picking me up and spinning me around.

I laugh, kissing his happy smile.

But I still feel like it's an enormous risk.

Like this might be the very thing that takes our nearly perfect relationship and burns it to the ground.

Chapter Six

LUKE

Alyssa is distant all week.

I want to pry her feelings out of her, but she's going through a lot. Giving her time to process seems like a good idea.

Time moves quickly. It's all travel plans and living arrangements. A friend of a friend has a sublet that lines up perfectly with Alyssa's schedule. It's furnished. It's clean. It's in the middle of the quiet, safe financial district.

I almost tell him no--Alyssa would much rather live in some fourth floor walk-up in the village; a place with "character" and drug-dealer neighbors--but my need to protect her gets the best of me. I'll feel better knowing she's in a building with a doorman and security cameras on every floor.

It's like we're in a dream as we prepare.

We pack. We drive to the airport. We try and fail to sleep on our red eye flight.

And then we're in a cab, on our way into New York City.

Alyssa rests her head on my shoulder, her hand locked

with mine. She's not as used to thriving on a night of awful sleep.

She looks at me when I shake her gently, groggy and irritable. I point to the skyline. Her jaw drops and her eyes go wide. "Jesus Christ," she breathes.

She moves towards the window, sticking her face against it like a kid on a road trip. "That's... it's... it's so... Oh, my God, Luke. That's fucking New York City!"

I laugh, happy to see her excited.

"It fucking is."

"I'm going to live there for six months." She smiles, her face filling with delight. She's waking up. "I'm going to be a New Yorker."

"You're practically one already."

"Spoken like a true Californian. Do you have any idea how different suburban Massachusetts is from New York City?"

I shrug.

"As different as suburban San Diego and Los Angeles?"

"Not even close."

She looks so happy. Thank God I convinced her.

Her jaw drops. "Jesus. That's really a skyline. Makes downtown LA look like a joke."

"Are you going to come back to California complaining about the coffee?"

She chuckles.

"Maybe if I was spending six months in Portland or Seattle."

"Then it will be the weather--you'll be sick of sunshine."

"Once again, spoken like a true Californian."

"Please. Southern Californian. It gets cold in San Francisco."

She shakes her head, practically buzzing with excitement. "You're only making my case, honey."

I smile. "Then you'll complain about the pizza."

"I don't eat pizza," she reminds me.

It rolls off her tongue like it's nothing, and I try to treat it the same way. So what if she doesn't eat pizza? She's been better a long time. She'll be okay in New York.

I take her hand. "There are too many things you can learn to hate about L.A."

"Like its utter lack of personality. Or its terrible public transportation. Or maybe it will be all the shallow assholes," she lists off the top of her head.

"We could move to New York."

She glances at me.

"You just started a business."

"I could take the New York bar. I could start a business here. Expand."

She shakes her head. "You're getting ahead of yourself."

"Maybe. But I like getting ahead of myself. I like envisioning us as some bi-coastal power couple."

She cringes, sticking out her tongue. "I am not going to be half of a power couple. That sounds horrifyingly public."

"I think it's an interesting option."

"Let's just survive these six months before we entertain any more crazy ideas."

Seems reasonable enough.

But crazy can be fun sometimes.

She leans back into me and I wrap my arms around her, pulling her close.

We spend the rest of the drive absorbing the scenery.

There's a lot to take in.

When we finally cross the bridge into the city, I'm in

awe. Spending so much time in Los Angeles, it's so easy to forget how a real city feels.

This is a fucking *city*. The slate gray streets, the bright yellow taxis, the dark blue of the Hudson River.

We stop at a building on Water Street.

It's a nice place--as sleek on the inside as it is on the outside. Everything about it is shiny, clean, and new.

Alyssa bites her lip, clearly not in love with the place. She throws me an *of course you want me to live here, you rich snob* kind of look.

I'm fine with the look if she's safe.

A security guard greets us. It's early, barely 7 A.M., but he's incredibly chipper. Nothing like the prototypical angry New Yorker. He makes small talk before handing over the set of keys.

"This is a very selective building," he informs us.

Alyssa smiles politely, playing her part, as usual. When the guard isn't looking, she turns to me and raises her eyebrows.

"It's a safe neighborhood," I murmur.

She shakes her head, but there's something sweet about her expression. She appreciates my concern.

We take the elevator to the 23rd floor and take a long hallway to its end. It's a corner apartment. It must be as nice as promised.

I open the door.

"Jesus Christ." Alyssa's eyes go wide.

The view is amazing-- we can see half the city beyond the floor to ceiling windows.

The apartment itself is small. There's a main room with a couch and a TV. A tiny kitchenette. A small bedroom with a very nice king-sized bed. The bathroom has a very spacious shower/tub combo. I have to stop myself from asking Alyssa to christen it.

She's already half asleep on the couch after the quick tour.

"How about coffee?" I ask.

She grins. "Such a sharp mind. I knew there was a reason I liked you."

———

AFTER COFFEE, WE SPEND THE MORNING TOURING downtown.

Wall street, Bryant Park, the famous charging bull statue, even City Hall. I ramble about the eight million scenes of *Law and Order* that took place on the steps of City Hall. Alyssa humors me, nodding along like she's enjoying my speech.

We move to the park across the street. She slings her arms around my neck, raises to her tip toes, and kisses me.

I forget where we are or why we're here, taking over the kiss.

"I'm starting to rethink my sightseeing plans," I mutter.

She leans in towards me until we're only inches apart, her body soft and pliant against my own. "We have a whole day and a half. And we're missing out on that San Diego hotel experience."

She presses her lips into mine. It's harder, more needy.

I slide my hands under her t-shirt, over the soft skin of her lower back, and pull her closer. She moans lightly, her body melting into me.

We're only a ten-minute walk from the apartment, but it feels way farther.

I feel her hands on my skin, under my t-shirt. "Ally," I groan. "We're in a public park."

"I know," she says. And kisses me harder.

Alright then.

When we break, she's flushed. Panting. I can imagine her lying on her back like that. "Damn. That's what I get for trying to torture you."

"Trust me. It's still torture," I return, adjusting myself with a wince.

"Revenge is so sweet. Even when it hurts." She takes my hand. "Do you want to go back to the apartment now?"

Yes.

"No. Let's finish all the errands first. So we don't have to leave."

Her lips curl into a smile and she nods.

We rush through a host of errands-- the drug store, K-mart, lunch, another cup of coffee--and end up at Whole Foods. I fill her cart with fruit and vegetables, but she shoots me a *mind your own damn business* look and removes everything I loaded.

"You don't want apples?" I ask.

"I do."

"Then why put them back?"

"Just let me do it, okay?" She stares at the apples, really examining them. Finally, she packs a dozen into a plastic bag and places them in the cart. She slips into the rhythm of shopping, picking up bits and pieces here and there.

I bite my tongue a dozen times to avoid offering suggestions.

She's always painfully distant about recovery, and she mostly refuses to discuss anything related to food.

"You're hovering," she says.

"I'm not hovering. I'm just here."

"But you look so concerned."

"Am I not allowed to be concerned?" I ask.

She sighs. "I'm not a vase that's going to break."

She's prickly, but I can see it's because she's afraid. And trying to hide it.

"It's okay if you're scared of being on your own. I'm scared too."

She cocks a hip.

"What are you scared about?"

"I don't like being without you."

She turns away, her fingers digging into the cart. "This was your idea."

I feel a flash of irritation that I quickly control.

"I only helped you realize how much you wanted this. You're happy, aren't you?" I point out.

There's definitely excitement there, mixed with that fear.

"Yeah, but..." She lowers her voice. "What if I can't handle being here alone. What if it's too much, too soon? There's a street cart on every corner. A trigger food on every corner. This is going to be so stressful. I'm going to be tempted."

There it is.

"So, you'll call me."

"Yeah..."

"You will call me." It comes out as an order.

That's a mistake.

Ally draws back.

"I'll do what I want to do. If I want to call you, I'll call you."

"If you don't want to call me, call your sponsor, talk to your therapist. But I'm going to miss you too. I'm going to be lonely without you too."

"That's not the same."

"Maybe not." I agree, switching gears. "But you've been in recovery for almost two years. Borrowing trouble isn't a good idea."

"Yeah," she sighs, accepting that truth. "Technically it's been two years."

"Two years. And it's been almost a year since you've purged, right?"

"Wow. You said purge without cringing. That's serious progress."

"Ally."

"Okay, you're right. Sorry. I have been doing well with recovery. I'm just... I'm scared. You can reassure me all you want. But I'm still going to be scared."

At least that's honest.

"Okay."

I rub her shoulders and she leans into me. "I'm terrified," she admits. "I can barely shop for groceries by myself. How am I supposed to survive six months alone?"

I slide my arms around her. "I know you can do it. You're one of the strongest people I know."

She pulls away, shaking her head. "Maybe."

"Ally. Don't beat yourself up before you've even tried."

Her demeanor softens, her defensive stance dropping away for now.

"Let's finish this and go back to the apartment, okay? It was a long trip and we're both tired."

I agree.

She's right. It's not a good idea to talk about this while we're both not at our best.

———

THIS IS SUPPOSED TO BE THE CITY THAT NEVER SLEEPS, A place brimming with life.

But on a Saturday afternoon, the financial district is dead quiet. And it's mocking me.

Alyssa is back on the defensive, and she shows no signs

of letting down those walls. I rack my brain for subtle ways to nudge her out of hiding, but I've got nothing.

She's in a new place. She's overwhelmed and under slept. It's fair that she's upset.

Doesn't make it any less frustrating.

I wait until we're back in the apartment to broach the subject. "Ally, talk to me."

She rubs her face.

"Can we just not talk for a little while? I'm exhausted."

"I need a little time to not think about anything."

I nod. Fine. "Can I say one thing?"

She smiles.

"Sure."

I wrap her in a hug, pulling her in.

"I love you. And I promise I'm not trying to get rid of you."

Her smile widens.

"Yeah?"

"Yeah. If I could, I'd stay in New York for every minute that you're here."

She kisses me on the cheek. "I love you too." Extricating herself gently, she heads into the bathroom and steps into the shower, shutting the door behind her.

I hate this.

I could have been selfish. I could have asked her to stay with me then felt guilty every day I failed to get home by 6:00.

Fuck. I'm obviously being ridiculous now.

I need to get out of my head or this spiral is just going to get worse.

I look towards the bathroom.

If Ally really wants to clear her head...

There's a much better way to do it.

Chapter Seven

ALYSSA

C an I do this?

The hot water pounding on my back does nothing to relax me. I try and take a deep breath but it feels rough and shallow.

I need to be stopped. I'm acting like a child, pushing my boyfriend away because I'm scared.

He's trying to help. It's not his fault I'm so incapable of expressing my feelings.

I'm afraid of doing this alone. I'm afraid to be without you for six days and now I'm supposed to do six months?

Don't leave. Stay. Say fuck the business and stay. Or ask me to change my mind. Ask me to stay with you in Los Angeles.

That's what I want to say.

But I would never put him in that position. It wouldn't be fair.

Maybe I should have put my foot down. Yes, I want to be in this play. And it's a great opportunity. It might be one of the best things I'll ever do.

But it's still so hard to do it without him.

I lean my head back, letting the water soak my hair as the anxiety rises.

I shake my head at myself in frustration.

This is ridiculous. I need to calm down. This is a lot all at once, but I can do it. And I can enjoy the next 24 hours.

Twenty-four hours with Luke, twenty-four hours until he's gone, and I'm here all by myself.

I repeat my mantra, a cheesy new-age therapy technique. *I will keep my head up and my heart open.* I whisper it three times, taking a deep breath between each. It's silly, but I feel a little calmer.

Maybe I can do this.

I close my eyes and listen to the water pounding on my neck. It's warm and hard and steady. *I will keep my head up and my heart open.*

I will talk to Luke.

I won't lock him out.

But not now, not yet, not until I have a better handle on this.

When I open my eyes, I squint at the light in the room.

Deep breath. Ground yourself.

I am Alyssa Summers. I am in New York City, my home for the next six months.

I can do this.

Whatever this is.

The door creaks open but I don't turn towards it.

"I'm not ready to talk yet," I call out.

"I'm not interested in talking." Luke's voice is serious, low and deep.

I bite my lip.

He wants to not talk with me. God, I hope he means what I think he means.

"You know, Ally," he continues. "I almost can't decide if

I want to step in the shower with you or if I want to enjoy the view."

Yes.

"There's a better view in here," I say hoarsely.

"So, there is."

My heart pounds against my chest. When did it get so damn hot in here?

He opens the shower door, the steam escaping into the rest of the bathroom.

Damn, he looks so fucking sexy. His hair is messy and his skin glistens with a faint layer of sweat.

Sometimes I forget how irresistible he is. Every part of him is perfect--his sculpted shoulders, his strong chest, his perfectly chiseled abs.

The tattoos that add that edge I didn't know I liked before him.

My breath grows heavy.

I need this. I need this so fucking badly.

He slides his boxers to the floor. Jesus. He's hard already.

He steps inside the shower, shutting the glass door behind him. Fuck, he's so close and I want so badly for him to touch me.

His expression is intense.

"Please don't tell me you're only here for the view."

He grabs my hips and presses me against the tile wall. His grip gets tighter, rough and gentle all at once.

He moves closer, his body pressing against mine.

It feels almost too good.

The tile is cold against my back and his body is hot against my front as he brings his lips to mine. His kiss is possessive, his lips sucking on mine. I reach for him, gripping his back, trying to get closer.

I want more.

"Fuck me," I groan.

He doesn't say anything, but he brings his lips to my ear. I press my fingers harder into his back.

He sucks on my earlobe, softly at first. Then harder, his teeth scraping against it. He starts to move his hands. Over my hips and stomach. Up to my chest.

The sensation is so different than usual, so much hotter and wetter. Desire shoots through me, straight to my core.

Fuck.

"Luke," I moan, arching my body into his, until I can feel his cock against me. I grab his ass, pulling his body towards mine.

But he grabs my hips and pushes me against the tile again.

"Not yet," he whispers in my ear. He takes a long look at me, his eyes filling with delight. "You're too fucking sexy, Ally."

He cups my breasts, his expression getting more and more intense. I'm desperate with want, almost shaking. I kiss him, hard, my tongue plunging into his mouth. He responds with the same ferocity; kissing me hard, sliding his fingers over my nipples. I groan, and he responds with a harder touch. Every stroke of his finger sends another pang of desire through me. My sex clenches. "Luke..." I moan. "Please. Fuck me."

"Soon," he croons, pressing his lips against my neck. My collarbone.

Almost. Please...

Then he brings his mouth to my nipple. At first, he only brushes it with his lips. It's so light and delicate, I can barely stand it. I dig my hands into his hair. He does it again.

"Don't stop," I groan.

He slides his tongue over my nipple, his hand sliding between my thighs. I start to shake.

I need him inside me. I need him to fuck me.

But he doesn't stop. He lavishes my breasts with attention, rubbing his wet thumbs against one nipple while he sucks on the other. I feel pangs of want in my sex, a building tension. I could almost swear I'm going to come from this, that he's going to suck me to an orgasm.

"Luke," I groan.

He responds by sliding his tongue over my chest, tracing the outline of my nipple. He flicks his tongue against me, soft then hard. Then harder and harder, until it almost hurts.

He strokes my inner thighs, so, so fucking close.

I could scream with sweet frustration.

Finally, he stands and kisses me. It's so much harder than before, so much more intense. He reaches for the shower head.

Fuck. It's detachable.

He moves closer to me, presses his lips to mine again. Then it's his entire body, hard against mine. I wrap my arms around him, kissing him harder and deeper.

"Turn around," he says. "Hands on the wall." He plants a soft kiss on my neck. "Can you stand?"

I nod.

"Not now, Ally. Will you be able to stand when you're coming so hard you're shaking?"

"Hold me."

He moves behind me and places a hand firmly on my hip. I lean into him, pressing my back against his chest, my ass against his cock. I close my eyes, quivering with anticipation.

I feel the water streaming onto my stomach. "Tell me if it's too much." He kisses my neck again. "Too hot or too cold." He slides his hand around my hip, resting it just below my belly button. "Or if it feels so fucking good you can't take it anymore."

No way in hell.

I groan, arching my body into his. He brings the shower head to my shoulders and works his way down. It streams over my chest, the lightest pressure. He slides his free hand over my nipples as he moves the shower head across my chest. I close my eyes, leaning into him to inhale the sensation. It's so warm and soft, somehow touching me everywhere all at once.

He brings his lips back to my neck, sucking this time. His touch is so light, lighter than the water. A tidal wave of want surges through me.

He moves it down, slowly, along my stomach down to my inner thighs. Closer and closer...

And closer...

My thighs buzz with pleasure. How the fuck can water do that?

I turn my head to meet his mouth and he kisses me deeply. His hand slides down my torso until it's inches away from my clit. He moves the water closer and closer, until it meets his hands.

And then it hits my clit.

My sex clenches, a dull ache. Luke moves his hands over me, spreading my lips apart. He moves the shower head up and down, over every inch on me.

I squirm, my hands digging into the hard, tile wall. He does it again, and again. It's a sweet, warm pressure like nothing I've ever felt before. It's everywhere, warming up every part of me.

I close my eyes and inhale the sensation. Luke brings his mouth to my ear, sucking hard on the lobe.

"Luke," I groan.

The water streams over me, so warm and soft. The pressure inside me grows, tighter and tighter.

I lean into him. His breath is heavy, strained. He moves the shower head over me again and again and again. It's almost too good, too intense, too much to take.

"Fuck," I say. "Don't stop."

He does it again and again, moving faster. The water streams over me, hitting every nerve in my cunt.

My body buzzes with pleasure and I get closer and closer and closer. One more time and the pressure is so much, so intense, so fucking good.

"Luke," I groan as an orgasm rushes over me. I press my hands into the walls, pushing my body against his. His cock presses against me. He's still hard.

"Fuck me," I order. "Fuck me now."

He brings his mouth to my ear, sucking hard on my ear lobe. Then he slides inside me.

Jesus Christ.

He grabs my hips, thrusting into me slowly. "Mhm-mm," he groans. "You feel so fucking good." He scrapes his teeth against my neck, his nails digging into my thighs.

"Fuck me," I say.

He thrusts into me again, deeper this time.

I sigh in relief. It's so much sensation--the water from the shower head against my clit, his cock filling me, his hands on my body.

I groan, arching to meet him as he moves harder and faster. I lose track of anything I thought five minutes ago.

I'm only here, with him, our bodies joining.

I arch my back, pushing against the wall to give him better leverage. He pushes deeper inside me, so deep it almost hurts. My sex clenches. Pleasure floods my body, radiating to my chest, my ass, my fingers and toes. Every part of me feels so fucking good, and every part is begging for his touch.

I lean back into Luke, my back rubbing against his hard chest. He's wet, slippery, and his body feels so good against mine. He nuzzles my neck and tilts my head back, kissing me hard.

"Come for me," he murmurs. "I want to hear it."

Breath leaves my body. I turn back, one hand against the wall, the other on the shower handle. I move it up and down, the water rubbing my clit, pushing me closer and closer to the edge. Luke runs his hands over my body, only his slick fingertips. Then he brings them to my breasts. He plays with my nipples, rubbing them with slow circles. He thrusts into me, harder and deeper, and I get closer and closer.

I close my eyes. Jesus. He kisses my neck again. Then it's teeth, a hard scrape. His touch gets harder, rougher. He thrusts into me again and again, and I fill with pleasure. Almost. Almost.

An orgasm washes over me. I groan, dropping the shower handle and grabbing his thigh. He kisses my neck, thrusting into me harder and faster. His breath gets heavier, harder, deeper.

He sinks his teeth into my neck and groans. He's almost there. I press my hands against the wall, arching into him.

He groans one more time, and then he's coming, his cock pulsing inside me.

We stand like that for a moment, our breath slowing.

Then he turns me around and we kiss until we're both soaked to the bone.

———

THE NEXT TWENTY-FOUR HOURS ARE BLISS.

We kiss. We touch. We fuck. We break for dinner, for drinks, for a few hours of sleep. When we're both too exhausted to move, we lie on the bed, our bodies tangled up in each other.

We don't talk. We don't listen to music. We don't watch TV. Instead, we listen to our breath and heartbeats.

I have no sense of time. No sense of tomorrow or yesterday or anything except Luke and I in this apartment. I don't even know how many times we have sex, how many times I come from his cock or his hands or his mouth.

It's perfect.

But it's only perfect for so long.

At six a.m., his phone rings with an alarm. We pull ourselves apart. I push away any feelings of concern.

I still have him a little longer. I want to savor every last minute that he's here.

I watch him get dressed. He's slow about it, putting on a show for me. He steps into his boxers, making a point of stretching his arms over his head. He smirks as I take in every perfect inch. "I appreciate your enthusiasm, but you don't need to put this image in your spank bank. I'm happy to send you pictures."

"My spank bank?"

"Don't you think about me when you touch yourself?"

"Oh. Sometimes."

His lips curl into a smile. "Don't tell me you're shy now."

"I'm going to miss you," I say, skirting the subject.

His expression softens.

"I'll be back before you know it." He lets me pull him onto the bed. I kiss him, trying to sink into him. My hands slide to his jeans. But he stops me. "I wish I could."

"You could stay." It's a moment of weakness.

"You'd be okay with that?"

"No," I sigh, dropping back onto the bed. "I'd hate myself for making you quit your job."

He cups the side of my face.

"I know exactly what you mean."

"I know," I murmur, kissing his palm. "That's why I'm not asking."

He smiles slightly, his eyes sympathetic.

Reaching down, he offers my bra. But I shake my head.

"No underwear."

"That's just cruel," he mutters, watching as I slip my dress over my head. "That's all I'm going to think about the entire flight."

I laugh.

"I can't believe you've got anything left in you." I pull him close, enveloping him in a hug. His arms are so safe, so warm, so God-damn comfortable.

"I love you," he offers. "More than anything."

I close my eyes.

"I love you too."

For a minute, I feel like everything is going to be okay.

But then, we're in the hallway. In the elevator. On the street, hailing a cab.

He's kissing me goodbye, a long, sweet kiss.

Then he's in the cab, and it turns a corner, and I'm standing on a street corner all alone.

I'm in New York City all alone.

And soon he'll be 3000 miles away.

Chapter Eight

LUKE

The next few days aren't the best.

Work consumes me. I barely have time to call Alyssa to wish her goodnight. And the three-hour time difference isn't doing me any favors.

She calls late one night, late her time anyway. I'm still at work, but I answer without hesitation.

"Hey."

"Hey yourself."

"How is everything?"

"I'm too tired to talk much right now," she says. "But I can't wait any more."

I smile, leaning back.

"Miss Summers, you're being awfully mysterious."

She laughs. "I got you something. It's in my room, under my bed." She yawns. "And now I'm too damn tired to think. So, I'm going to fall asleep picturing you with the present."

So, it's a sexy present.

"What if I'm desperate to talk to you after I find it?"

"I guess you'll have to stay desperate."

———

I GO INTO ALYSSA'S ROOM, ANTICIPATION BUILDING.

The mysterious gift is all I've been thinking about since the phone call.

When I look under the bed, there's a small wrapped box.

I pull the wrapping off to find a gourmet honey set. There's a card attached that reads: "think of me when you're licking your lips."

I turn the card over and there's another message. "Check the iPad. There's a new folder. I know you'll find it... very interesting."

Damn. Where did I leave the iPad?

It doesn't take me long to find it, not with how motivated I suddenly am.

It's sitting in the middle of the couch, its glass screen as innocent as could be.

I unlock the screen and open the pictures application. Sure enough, there is a new folder. Alyssa's Special Secret Folder to be Opened Only by Luke.

My fingers hover over the screen.

This is going to be good.

I tap it.

Wow.

It's better than I imagined. Pictures of Alyssa. A slide show of sorts. She starts off fully clothed but loses layer after layer until it's just her in lingerie-- the most gorgeous black lace lingerie I've ever seen. It hugs her body beautifully, barely covering her chest or ass.

But this isn't all of it. This is only photo 15 of a 50-photo set.

My blood flows to my cock. There are 35 more pictures

of my gorgeous girlfriend. They are here for me to savor at my leisure.

And these aren't tits and ass photos. She's looking at the camera, looking at me like she wants to fuck me. She trusts me enough to give me these pictures. She trusts me enough to leave me with photos that could cause major damage to her career.

She trusts me.

I abandon any intention I had of waiting. I need to see these, to see all of her.

She slides out of her bra over three pictures. And it's just her, a coy smile on her face, her hair hanging over her eyes, her hands digging under her panties.

Then, she's out of her underwear. She looks so fucking sexy. So confident.

But it gets even better.

In the next picture, she's touching herself.

It's not shy or coy or demure. She's looking at the camera, at me, as she fills herself with pleasure. It's a demand or a dare or maybe just payback for every time I've tortured her.

I don't know, and I don't care. It's hot as hell, and there's more of it. A dozen pictures of her, every part of her, while she brings herself to ecstasy.

My breath catches, heavy and strained. It's a dare, right?

I'm not about to let a dare go unanswered.

Chapter Nine

ALYSSA

My phone greets me bright and early. Seven A.M.

Somehow the sun is already high in the sky, the streets below me already filled with people.

As I swipe away the ever so tempting snooze, I see a silver lining. A new message from Luke.

Alyssa Summers, you are the devil.

I grin. So he found the present. I must admit, it was terrifying to take those pictures and even scarier to leave them waiting for him. But it's so worth it knowing he enjoyed them.

But two can play that game. Check your email. Should be a very interesting link in there.

Fuck.

I rush to my computer and open my inbox. There is an email from Luke, a sweet, little email just begging for my click. But can I do it now? I have to exercise, shower, and eat breakfast before I leave for rehearsals.

And it's not like I can call him now. It's 4 A.M. on the West Coast.

Maybe I should wait.

But my heart is racing, and my breath is shallow. Hell, I feel a lightness in my chest, a growing need between my legs.

It might be nothing. Luke didn't necessarily send me several dozen pictures of his amazing body, naked.

My heart thuds against my chest.

Fuck the gym. I'll go after rehearsals if that's what it takes. Or I'll skip breakfast. I have to see this now, even if I wait until later to...

I click on the link. It's a private website, password protected. There's a hint in the email. *I have an image in my mind of my favorite person covered in one of her favorite things. You could say I licked my lips at thought of her. I can't help but envision my tongue against her skin, lapping up every inch of... well, I'm not going to give it all way.*

My mouth waters. God, I'm already shaking, already wet. I try my best guess:

AlyssaSummersHoney

It works.

I close my eyes. Deep breath. I've sent Luke a few sexy pictures here and there, but never like the ones I left on the iPad. And he's never replied. God, I bet he looks just as good on screen as he does in front of me.

My eyes open of their own accord.

There are pictures, yes. But there's also a video.

Holy fuck.

I press my fingers together. There's a video of Luke. A video. A fucking video.

I look at the pictures first. They're amazing, out of this fucking world. Luke's chest, his shoulders, his amazing as all hell abs, his entire torso all the way down to the soft hairs below his belly button.

My legs rub together, my sex clenching. His body is so

damn amazing. I could never get tired of looking at it. But this video... is it really?

I swallow. We've talked on the phone before, but we've never... I've never even seen a man touch himself. Any other guy, it would be awful, weird, creepy even.

But, God, the thought of Luke stroking himself, looking at my pictures, coming thinking of me... I can barely breathe.

I press play.

It's our bedroom, our bed. It's dark. It must be late, after he got home last night. He steps into frame, his gaze flitting towards the camera. Then he smiles, that million-dollar smile of his.

He's in his suit, like he just got home from work.

A corporate fantasy come to life.

He takes it off slowly. First the tie. Then an eternity at each button. He moves slowly, deliberately. Like he would if I was there, watching him. He undoes his belt next, sliding his slacks to the floor.

My mouth waters. I never get the chance to gape at him quite like this. There's so much else to take in when he's here, but this is different. I have plenty of time to gawk.

And I do.

His body is a fucking work of art, and he moves so expertly. It's pure masculine sensuality.

He hooks his thumbs in his boxers, slowing even more.

I bite my lip, moving closer to the screen.

Over his hips... down... lower...

Then, they're at his knees.

God damn.

I blink, my nails digging into my thighs. It's not a close-up or anything. It's all of him--from his shoulders to his knees--naked and ready for me.

I can't look away.

He starts to stroke himself.

God, I wish that was my hand, that I was in bed with him. I wish I could feel him, hard under me.

I wish I could be the one making him come.

But I already am, aren't I? This is practically a dedication. He was so fucking hot looking at the pictures I sent him that he had to respond.

This is how he feels about me.

This is how much he wants me.

And it's so fucking hot watching him touch himself.

Maybe he's not there. Maybe it's not live. But I have to come with him.

I slide out of my boxers—his boxers actually—and drag my laptop to the bed.

There's no teasing. I'm already wet and needy and completely desperate.

I touch myself as I watch him. And I don't stop until I'm there, until I see his body careen towards an orgasm, his eyes closed, his lips pursed as he mummers, "Alyssa."

———

My mind is preoccupied all morning.

But the second I step into the theater, I am all business.

I am Alyssa Summers, amazing actress, successful TV star.

Okay, I am Alyssa Summers, cable TV actor, but that still counts for something.

Ellen is already there. She's sitting in the audience seats, drinking a cup of coffee. "Hey," she greets me, even and calm.

Ellen is a force of nature later in the day. But before lunch she's quiet, almost shy.

She plays Stella, my character's sister. And she is a million times more pleasant than my usual fake sister, Naomi. "You run here or something? You look a little flushed."

So I'm that obvious. "No. I just..."

She smirks.

"Doing the old walk of shame, huh? I knew you had it in you."

"No, I... I have a boyfriend. In L.A."

She nods like she gets it. Then, she shakes her coffee cup. It must be empty. "I'm in desperate need of cup number... too high of a number. I'll buy if you tell me all this juicy dirt about you cheating on your boyfriend."

"I'm not." I bite my tongue. I can't exactly reveal I spend the morning touching myself to his dirty pictures.

"Leave her alone, Ellen." We both look over to see Nicholas, the male lead in the play. He's a handsome, brawny blond. Could easily be cast as Thor, both on stage and on screen. But, much more telling, he's only been sweet and welcoming. His attention shifts to me as he draws closer. "Don't mind her. She thinks that just because she can't make a relationship work on Broadway, nobody can."

"Fuck off, Nicholas," Ellen sighs, rolling her eyes.

"It's okay. I don't cheat." I look over at Ellen. "Tried that before. It was too much of a headache."

She laughs and pushes herself to her feet. "I knew I'd like you."

Nicholas smiles, stepping back. "Glad to see you can hold your own." He glances over at Ellen. "See you both at rehearsal."

"See you."

Ellen waves over her shoulder as she leads me outside the theater.

The sunshine is already blinding. New York may be cloudy half the year, but when it's bright, it's damn bright. The sun bounces off every inch of glass and concrete, landing right in my eyes.

"Have you heard the rumors about Kyle and our director?"

"I try to avoid rumors," I say.

"So, don't spread this one. But supposedly, they're sleeping together." She sighs, tossing her coffee cup in a trash can. "Though... if you don't like gossip, you should probably get the hell out of the New York theater scene. It's nothing but drama and everyone is fucking everyone." She looks at me. "But you have that boyfriend. In L.A."

I nod.

"And this run is six months?" She shakes her head. "That's rough. I've never made it..." She taps her fingers like she's counting. "More than two weeks."

"We've been together a year."

"Sorry. I didn't mean to suggest you and your..." Ellen smacks her palm into her forehead. "I'm really sorry. Maybe Nicholas is right. I'm probably freaking you out."

"A little," I admit.

I have enough anxiety about this all on my own already.

"Sorry," she repeats. "I'm sure you and your boyfriend-"

"Luke," I offer.

"Like *Star Wars*?"

"I think like the Bible."

"Well, I'm sure you and Luke like the Bible will be great. He sounds nice."

I raise a brow.

"Biblical?"

She laughs, her nervousness abating somewhat. "He

must be great if you're committed to not fucking someone else for six months."

We make small talk through our coffee and end up ten minutes late. Nicole, the play director, reminds us to get here earlier next time, but she doesn't dwell on it.

The first few hours of rehearsal are tough. The other actors, especially Ellen and Nicholas, are seasoned theater actors. They know their lines inside and out. I'm finally off book, but I'm still struggling to really make the words my own.

By the end of the day, I have a little footing.

Nicholas gives me a discreet thumbs up when I nail a line I've been having trouble with. I smile back, appreciating the gesture of support.

I'm still out of my league, but I'm not quite so overwhelmed.

I can do this.

I can absolutely do this.

———

THE WEEK PASSES QUICKLY. ELLEN INVITES ME OUT MOST nights, but I decline. From the way she talks, I can tell she's not exactly a bastion of moderation.

I talk to Luke for a few minutes before bed every night. We're both too tired to say much, but it feels so good to hear his voice.

I spend the weekend rehearsing in my apartment. I know Luke would mock me or tell me I work too hard, but he doesn't understand how out of my league I am. I was in a few plays when I first moved to Los Angeles, but it's been years since I've seriously done any theater.

When I finally call it a night, I realize I haven't eaten dinner. I barely ate lunch. But it's nothing. No big deal. I've done enough recovery that I don't have to obsess over every single thing I eat or don't eat.

Come Monday morning, I am ready to kick ass and take names. I get to the theater half an hour early, bursting with energy. I am finally up to speed. Finally where I want to be. I understand Blanche-- she lost everything she cared about. Her secretly gay husband killed himself after she caught him with another man. She's an outcast, but she denies it to herself, hiding behind a veneer of superiority. She claims to put great value in sexual roles and manners, but it's a lie she tells herself, to help herself understand why life failed her so utterly. She's insecure, desperate, terrified of losing her only value in the world-- her beauty.

The only thing that lifts her up is attention from men. It doesn't just make her giddy. It reaffirms her belief that she deserves to exist.

People read Blanche as weak, as pathetic sometimes. But she's not. She's a woman in an awful situation, doing everything she can to hold it together. But her real self keeps sneaking out.

I put everything in rehearsals and the director praises my dedication. I'm proving my competence. Finally.

Ellen invites me out once more, but before I can refuse again, Nicholas steps in.

"Come on," he murmurs. "You've clearly been working hard. It's good to do something else, give yourself some room to breathe. And I'll be there too—I promise to keep you safe from Ellen's party mode." He grins at me as Ellen scoffs.

"Whatever. But he is right about getting out once in a while," Ellen agrees. "It's not healthy to just live and breathe the theater. It can consume you. Gotta let off some steam."

They convince me. And I know Nicholas isn't off the rails like Ellen, so I feel a little more comfortable going.

They keep me busy all night.

We go to an amazing restaurant in the village, swig way too many cocktails, and meet Ellen's weird, artsy friends for an off-off Broadway play. The star is great, one of Ellen's ex-boyfriends. We meet him for drinks after the play and he picks my brain about acting in Los Angeles.

Ellen insults him. It's traitorous to even think of moving to LA. Talking about it is practically treason.

"If you're lucky, the money's better," I point out.

Nicholas laughs, elbowing Ellen.

"She's got you there."

She huffs, sitting up straight.

"I'm not in it just for the money."

"Well, I like money," her friend interjects. "And acting. Why do they have to be mutually exclusive?"

That sets off a whole other round of debating.

Nicholas makes sure it doesn't get ugly, steering the conversation expertly.

I was right to come on a night that he was going out too.

And, like a gentleman, he even makes sure I get home safe.

"Thank you," I murmur when we reach the door to my building.

"No problem." He gives me a friendly hug before stepping back and continuing down the sidewalk. "See you tomorrow."

I wave, stepping inside.

It's beyond late when I finally fall into bed.

So late I forget to call Luke.

Chapter Ten

LUKE

I don't think much of it when we miss our first call.

We were never going to make it six months talking every single day. Not with the time difference on top of our hectic schedules.

It doesn't feel great, but it is what it is.

I bury myself at work. I run until I'm dead tired. I clean the damn house to keep my mind occupied.

Finally, some time around ten, Alyssa texts me.

Give me one minute. I want to get into something comfortable.

Shit.

I'm going to have a miserable time resisting her if she goes straight to dirty talk and slipping her clothes off.

I open my laptop and accept the incoming chat invitation.

The video pops on screen. It's a little box of Alyssa, in her bedroom, in that giant bed. She's wearing a tiny tank top and it clings to every one of her curves. She smiles, catching me checking her out.

Not that I'm trying to be discreet.

"Ah, so this is what it feels like to be you," she teases.

I nod sagely.

"Yes."

"This is so weird. I can't even remember the last time I did a video chat." Her voice is slightly slurred, like she's had a few drinks.

"I'm not sure that I ever have."

"Like you didn't have some college girlfriend who begged to see you naked over break," she scoffs.

I shake my head. "You're the only girl I'd ever get naked on camera for."

She blushes, biting her lip. I can see she didn't expect that answer. "I really, um... enjoyed that video you sent me."

I grin.

"Enjoyed, huh?"

She laughs. "Yes. I did *enjoy* it."

I want to keep going in this direction. But I want to talk too.

"How are you, Ally? We've barely talked all week."

She shrugs.

"I'm... busy."

"Well, how was dinner?"

"You know. It was dinner." She grimaces slightly, shrugging.

"Tell me anyway."

"Why? It's boring."

"It's not boring to me," I protest. "Did something happen?"

"A dozen people from the production went out to dinner. And we had drinks. Ellen and Nicholas claim it's a tradition. To get drunk before the first day of Previews, I mean."

"And?"

"I had a few drinks."

"What did you eat?"

She throws me a side eye. "This again?"

"Humor me."

"I don't know. I ate food. Some kind of salad. It was very healthy and wholesome and exactly what I should be eating."

She's always resistant to talking about her recovery, but this is something else. Something more. "Ally, what's up? You're defensive."

She sighs.

"You always think I'm defensive."

"Talk to me. I want to hear it."

"There's not much to say. I've been busy. I've been... less than perfect about my recovery work. But it's fine. I skipped lunch twice. And... I got scared. When I got the urge again, I called Angela. It hasn't happened since."

My stomach drops. Angela is her sponsor.

She skipped two meals. But it's a good sign that she reached out for support.

She clears her throat, and I bring my gaze back to the little image of her on screen. "It's really not a big deal," she reassures me. "I've just been nervous during rehearsals. Makes it harder to eat."

"I'm glad you reached out for help." I say carefully. "You know you can talk to me too."

She shakes her head.

"Luke, it's not a big deal."

"It sounds like a big deal."

She folds her arms. "Sorry. It's just... I'm trying to handle this the best I can, okay?"

"Why do you have to handle it on your own? Why can't you talk to me about it?"

"I just... it's hard to talk about." She shrinks further into herself.

"You don't have to talk to me. But I'd really appreciate it if you did. I'd rather know what's going on than worrying about it all the time."

She takes a deep breath. "You'll think less of me."

"I won't."

"How do you know?"

"Because I love you. Because nobody's fucking perfect. Least of all me."

She cracks a smile at that.

"Excuse you. My man is perfect, I'll have you know."

I wish I could hold her right now.

"You can trust me."

She presses her lips together, searching my eyes before nodding slowly. "Okay. But I don't know where to start."

"Why did you really skip lunch?"

"It was an accident the first time. I was too busy. But then I liked it. It felt familiar. Comfortable." She presses her fingers together. "I know it's stupid. I've been in recovery a long time. And I didn't even usually restrict. But everything with this play is so overwhelming and every time I try to tell you how scared I am, you tell me I can do it."

I frown.

"That's bad?"

"No, not bad. But it doesn't make me feel any less terrified," she explains.

I nod, trying to understand.

"Tell me about it."

"I fight this panic when I get to rehearsals. I want to lock myself in the bathroom. I'm so out of my league and I've never done anything like this. Not on this scale. I can't get on stage. Not in front of two thousand people who are waiting for me to fail."

I can only imagine being in that position.

"It must be miserable to feel like that."

She nods. "I really don't know if I can do this, but how am I supposed to function with all of this doubt drowning me? I can't."

"You can't run away from it."

"I have to. That's the only way I can get through this."

"I know you hate when I try and play therapist."

She nods. "Yeah."

"So what if you started seeing someone again?"

She blinks a tear away, her eyes on the ground. God, I wish I was really there. So I could hold her and kiss her and promise everything would be okay.

"It's not that I don't want to hear it," I reassure her.

"Okay."

"You can talk to me. About anything. Tell me every ugly thought you have. I'll listen."

She shakes her head. "Not right now. I have to get through this first."

Dammit. We were off to a good start. "Are you sure?"

"I'm going to go," she murmurs. "I'm really tired."

"Ally."

"It's not a big deal."

"That's bullshit. You just said that you're drowning in doubt."

"But I'm used to it."

A long silence passes. She's sitting there, alone in that little apartment, the New York skyline filling the room with light. And I'm here, in our living room, nothing around me but grass and pavement.

"Do you remember what you said to me after I punched Ryan?"

She smiles. "That you're a hopeless idiot?"

"Besides that."

She shakes her head.

"You told me I don't have to handle everything alone. That you want to be there to share the burden with me."

She nods.

"I do."

"So let me share this burden with you. I want to be there for you too. This isn't a one-way street."

Her shoulders drop.

"I can't, Luke. Not right now. I can't. I'm sorry. But there's too much. I can't afford to fall apart now."

"I'll be here to help put you back together."

"You won't be here. You'll be in Los Angeles. You have no idea how bad it gets."

"But Ally-"

"I'm sorry, but I have previews and Laurie is visiting Monday. I have to get through this first," she insists.

I rake my fingers through my hair, taking a deep breath.

"Fine. On one condition."

She groans. "Condition is a fancy way of saying promise."

"Alright. Then you have to make me a promise."

"I could hang up this call right now."

"But you won't."

She frowns. She hates it when I'm right. "Fine. What's the condition?"

"If you feel like you're going to fall, if you feel like you're too overwhelmed, you call me. Okay?"

She sighs.

"Okay," she agrees. "I—thank you." She closes her eyes. "I love you, Luke."

"I love you too."

She nods her way through a goodbye.

I hate seeing her like this.

But this isn't a battle I can fight for her.

Come To Me

———

WHEN I BOUGHT THIS HOUSE, THE FACT THAT LAURIE lived so close was a complete coincidence.

But, right now, I'm glad that we're so damn close to Alyssa's best friend.

I get dressed and run the three blocks to Laurie's house. There's a light on in the living room and a low roar that sounds a lot like TV. She's home.

I knock on the door, but Laurie doesn't answer. A man does. He's tall, good looking, wearing classic black glasses. Exactly Laurie's type.

"Hi. Can I help you?" he asks.

"I'm a friend of Laurie's."

"I knew you had a booty call," he calls out over his shoulder. It's jovial. So, they aren't an item. Just friends.

"Shit. At eleven. Only person that could be. Does he have a lovesick look on his face? And is he just so fucking hot you want to scream?"

The friend laughs. "I wouldn't know." He turns back inside, to where Laurie must be sitting. "You describe me like that when I'm not around?"

"Come in, Luke," Laurie says in a louder voice. "It is Luke, right?"

"Yeah," I confirm. The friend moves out of the way to let me inside, shutting the door behind me.

It looks like it always has-- a big couch, a bigger TV, a little bit of mess everywhere.

"This is Zack," Laurie says. "He's a college friend of mine."

"Nice to meet you," I say politely. Zack and I shake hands.

"And this is the guy I was telling you about. Alyssa's boyfriend."

"Oh, *that* guy." He and Laurie share a smirk. "Sorry. Laurie is a terrible gossip."

"You begged for gossip the minute I picked you up," Laurie points out, laughing.

There's something different about her. She likes this guy.

"I'll apologize on her behalf," Zack offers. "Laurie has always been rude. Ever since college."

Laurie rolls her eyes.

"So what's up, Luke? I'm guessing it's about Alyssa."

"I could have stopped by to say hello."

"At this time of night, yeah." She pats the couch and Zack sits next to her. "I don't have any information if that's what you're after."

"But you're visiting this weekend."

"You know, I have a telephone. And I also have a life outside of the drama hurricane that is you two."

"Me, drama? Don't be ridiculous."

She sighs. "I'm not spending my hiatus time trying to fix your problems. Get on with it so I can reject your idea."

"I'm worried about her."

"Did you talk to her?"

"Yes, I talked to her. But she's nervous and there's only so much I can do here."

She throws her hands up.

"So, go visit her."

"I will." I plan on it. "But I can't get away from work until next week. And since you're going to be there already..."

She narrows her eyes at me.

"What do you want me to do?"

"She said she skipped some meals."

"Really?" Laurie asks. Her expression fills with concern.

"It slipped out like it wasn't a big deal."

"But that's a huge deal!"

Preaching to the choir.

"Why do you think I'm here? All I want is for you to check on her," I explain. "See if she's lost weight. She's talking to her sponsor, but I'm still worried."

Laurie looks at me. "I'll check on Alyssa because I care about Alyssa. But I'm not going to spy and I'm not going to give you a report."

I tamp down on my frustration.

"We have the same goal. I'm not you're adversary here."

"I do like you, Luke." She rubs at her face. "But you need to grow up. If you want to check on Alyssa, do it yourself. I'm not a tool you can use to make your relationship better. Alyssa is my friend too, and I'll do what I think is best for her."

"I would. But I have obligations here too. Making an impromptu trip right now isn't in the cards." I wish it was. "All I want you to do is check on her."

"Fine. But I would have done that anyway. And I'm not stupid. I know that if she's slipping in her recovery, I'm over my head. I would talk to you and try to work something out together."

I can work with that.

"Good."

"I wouldn't try and manipulate you into doing what I want," she says pointedly.

Zack interrupts. "Don't you spend enough time being a hard ass at work?"

"Shut the fuck up," she snaps back. "You have no clue what this guy is like."

"He seems sweet."

"No."

"It's nice that he's concerned about this Alyssa girl," Zack continues doggedly.

"Please. Like you know anything about relationships. You haven't had a girlfriend in about eight million years," Laurie remarks.

"And you haven't had a boyfriend in nine million years."

Laurie smiles. She's definitely got a thing for Zack. She looks at me. "Fine. I can see Zack's point. Alyssa does love you very much and you do appear to have her best interests at heart."

"You think?"

"See! This is why he's so difficult to talk to," she complains. "But, I do agree. We should be partners in this mission. Not adversaries."

"You two are ridiculous," Zack observes.

Laurie ignores him.

"I want her to be healthy as much as you do," she says, meeting my eyes. "And, I'll call you with my findings when I'm back in LA." Zack clears his throat. "Or sooner if there is something to talk about." She turns to Zack. "Is that good enough?"

"Perfect." Zack turns to me. "You want to watch with us? We're marathoning *Battlestar Galactica*."

"That's okay."

"You'd like it," Laurie says. "It's way better than *Law and Order*."

"I'll pretend I didn't hear that."

"But it's a scientific fact," she insists. "All the lawyers on it are greasy jerks."

"Thanks," I mutter.

Laurie smirks, very proud of herself. "You should see President Roslin. She's-"

"As much of a head bitch in charge as you are," Zack interjects.

"Shut the fuck up! It's rude to call your friend a bitch, especially when she's kindly letting you stay in her spare room." She sticks her tongue out at Zack. She looks back to me with a hint of concern. It must be bad if Laurie is concerned. "I'll walk you out."

When we're out of earshot, she whispers to me. "I really do want her to be okay, and I will hold it against you if you fuck that up."

"Right back at you."

Chapter Eleven

ALYSSA

The high-pitched ring of my doorbell wakes me.

Laurie.

What is she doing here so early? She's supposed to come over after her big, important New York meeting.

The doorbell rings again. And again. Yep, there's no mistaking it. That's definitely Laurie.

"I'm coming," I yell, rolling out of bed.

I drag myself to the door, squinting to block out the brightness. It's too early to be this bright.

Laurie greets me with a smirk. "I know you normally reserve that line for your boyfriend." And then she jumps —yes, jumps—into my arms. Like a damn puppy. "Girl, I missed you! It feels like it's been a century."

"I figured you and Luke would be happy to be rid of me, since you both colluded to get me here."

Laurie shrugs, sheepish. "You're not glad you're performing on Broadway?"

I have to grin at the reminder.

"The theater isn't technically on Broadway," I correct.

She's waves that away.

"Broadway means neighborhood. It doesn't necessitate a Broadway address." She enters, shutting the door behind her. She's not carrying any luggage, just a purse and a truly beautiful take out cup of coffee.

"What happened to your meeting?" I ask.

"Had it early. The producer had to be on location today. We met at six A.M.," she shakes her head. "Horrifying, right?"

I nod. "What's the verdict?"

"I don't think it's happening. He wants to take the feature in a different direction, more 'four quadrant.' You know, code for we can't have a romantic comedy with a female protagonist as we'll turn off the dudebros who don't like these kinds of movies anyway."

"Hmm. You sound kind of bitter."

She sighs.

"More like annoyed. I'm crazy lucky. I've been working as a TV writer since a few years after college." She takes a long look at me. "Alyssa, I can't lie. You look terrible."

"I didn't get to bed until three."

"I'll make you coffee." She moves to the kitchen, searching in vain for the coffee maker and beans. Laurie makes terrible coffee, even when she uses great beans.

Too many years of forcing underlings to get it for her.

"That's okay."

"Girl, I can tell I'm not getting more than a peep out of you until I get some caffeine into you."

"But your coffee making skills... leave something to be desired."

"Do not even!" She folds her arms. "Fine. Then we'll get it out."

"You want to go out?"

"Yes."

"You know the TV is here." I look over at the living room.

"I do more than watch TV. I go to the Paley Center."

Crickets.

"It's a museum about TV... never mind. It was supposed to be a joke." She shakes her head. "I want to show you around the village. With plenty of stops for coffee and food." She puts particular emphasis on the food, like she's also worried I'm not eating.

Great. Another person who thinks my business is her business.

Okay, I know that's not fair to her or to Luke, but, right now, I don't care. I'm tired of being on the defensive.

"You sound like Luke."

"Don't get too hot and bothered over it."

"It's too early for bad jokes."

"Good thing I only tell good ones."

She pours herself a glass of water while I get dressed.

I check my phone for any contact from Luke. There's nothing new. Why would there be anything new when it's six A.M. in Los Angeles? He probably went to bed before I did and he's probably sleeping right now.

Then again, he's not exactly a sound sleeper. It's perfectly plausible that he spent the night working or watching TV on the couch or taking another dirty video for me.

I check my email again, just in case. There's nothing.

"What's the weather like?" I ask.

"Typical late spring shit. Gray and muggy. Jeans and a t-shirt would be fine."

I take her advice and pull on a pair of skinny jeans and a fitted blue t-shirt. It's an outfit I can disappear in.

In the kitchen, Laurie slurps the last drop of her coffee drink and tosses it in the trash can. "Damn, girl. You really do wear clothes. Now, let's get some coffee before we both fall asleep."

————

WE MAKE IT ALL THE WAY TO THE VILLAGE BEFORE WE acquire coffee. That's four stops on a crowded subway car. Nearly half an hour of my brain flailing in a torturous caffeine-free state.

When we finally sit down at some little cafe that "absolutely has the best coffee in the city," I am in heaven.

It's such a quaint place. Most New York restaurants are tiny--the tables are packed so tightly they're almost touching--but this one is especially cozy. The walls are painted pink and there's a huge clock on the wall that says "it's time for tea."

I take a picture with my phone and send it to Luke. He'd kill to get that clock in his house.

Well, maybe not. It wouldn't exactly fit with his sparse *I'm not going to decorate until you agree the house is ours not mine* decor.

I shake my head. I don't need to deal with anyone's attitude today. I don't need anything but the giant mug of coffee in front of me. It's damn good coffee--strong and nutty with hints of cinnamon. I squeeze honey onto my spoon and bring it to my lips, letting the sweet substance coat my tongue. I could really put this honey to good use under different circumstance...

"Are you going to order food or are you just going to make love to your coffee?" Laurie asks.

"You should know better than to get between me and coffee."

Laurie watches me lick every bit of honey off my

94

spoon. I raise my eyebrows--a real you've got a problem kind of look. She shakes her head.

"I wish someone loved me as much as you love that spoon."

"It's not the spoon. It's the honey." I squeeze more honey onto the spoon, this time stirring it into my coffee. Then, I add a little almond milk, and the drink is perfect-- sweet, creamy, rich.

"So you and Luke use that when you fuck, right?"

"I need three coffees before I can even think about answering that question."

"He seems like he'd be kinky."

"Oh yeah?"

She nods. "Definitely."

"And what does he seem like he'd be into?" I ask, curious to hear her answer.

Laurie screws her nose. "I can't even think about it, or I'll get madly jealous that no one is that into me. God. He's so lovesick. Every time I look at him, he's about to burst."

"I thought you were done talking about our sex life."

She laughs.

"Not like that." She stirs sugar into her coffee.

"When did you see Luke?" I ask.

She shrugs like it's no big deal, but she doesn't fool me. Something is up. "You like eggs? This place has amazing omelets. Amazing."

I don't think about what I like. I eat food I know won't mess with me mentally or physically.

"I eat oatmeal."

"Fuck oatmeal. Get something good. Your BFF is visiting you in New York City. You need to celebrate!"

I narrow my eyes. "Why do you care?"

"Okay. Order whatever makes you happy. You like oatmeal, order oatmeal. It's not like oatmeal is the most boring, awful breakfast food. And it's not like you could have oatmeal at home for 25 cents any time you want."

"Maybe I like oatmeal."

"Okay, fine. You like oatmeal, you want oatmeal. Whatever. I'm sure you still have to watch your weight."

The waitress returns and I butt in before Laurie can order. "We're not ready yet, but can we get more coffee? And more almond milk? Thanks." I turn back to Laurie, folding my arms. I'm not going to start with this. Not today. Hell, not any day.

"At least you like the coffee," Laurie mutters. She shakes her head, slightly irritated.

I'm not about to open this can of worms.

"I really do like oatmeal."

She taps her fingers against the table, her jaw tensing. Then she shakes her head as if to say forget it. "So tell me about the show. I want to hear everything."

"There isn't that much to tell."

"Are you kidding? There has to be some gossip. Are any of the actors horrible?"

"Sorry to disappoint you, but no. Ellen is a little off the rails with her partying and the loud type, but she's only been welcoming. And Nicholas, the actor who plays Stanley, keeps her in line for the most part. He's a great actor too. I've learned quite a bit. Between the two of them, I don't feel like an outsider at all."

"Uh huh." She tilts her head, watching me. "Is he hot?"

I laugh.

"Is that all you care about?"

"That's a yes."

I shrug, a little uncomfortable.

"He's not any hotter than Zack. Who also conveniently stayed in your house." I raise my brows at her.

Laurie stirs her coffee and takes a sip. "Damn. That

really is good coffee. No wonder you were going all *When Harry Met Sally* over it."

Of course, Laurie has to relate everything to some movie or TV show.

"Coward," I say mildly, shaking my head. She can dish it out but taking it is a different story. "How is everything back home?" I ask.

"Same old, same old. I had a few meetings, watched a ton of TV, went hiking a bunch all by myself." She fakes a pout. "Showed Zack around LA. He's one of those I'll never leave New York guys."

"I never heard about Zack before this visit."

"Don't worry. There's room in my heart for both of you."

She's trying too hard to keep it light.

I grin.

"So, you like him like him?" I push.

"No way." She folds her hands together like she's negotiating. "You can meet him tomorrow, actually. After I see your show."

Oh no.

"You shouldn't see it."

"Why don't you want your friends to celebrate your success?"

"If I was an accountant and I got a new job, you wouldn't come watch me work."

"I'm going to see it and you're going to be amazing," she says firmly.

I'm not going to get anywhere by pushing this.

"Okay."

One more reason to be nervous.

I finally take a look at my menu. It's huge. Two dozen different kinds of omelets with a dozen different sides. Then, there are pancakes and waffles and all sorts of other things that will put me into a guilt inducing carb coma.

What's wrong with oatmeal? Why the fuck does everyone object to me eating oatmeal?

I glance up from the menu to catch Laurie staring at me. The second our eyes meet, she looks away. At her menu. "Damn, they have more stuff than I remembered," she remarks, suddenly absorbed by the words.

Deep breath. Sarcasm does me no good here. It only convinces her I'm defensive.

So I nod and look back at the menu until I find something besides oatmeal. Something that doesn't suggest obsessive health, restriction, or indulgence.

Something that will get her off my back.

When the waitress returns, with coffee thank God, I order the veggie omelet, no cheese, with wheat toast, no butter. Laurie hangs on every word like I'm reciting Sylvia Plath instead of ordering breakfast.

Laurie orders chocolate chip pancakes. With whipped cream. When in Rome, I suppose.

We hand the menus to the waitress and I turn all my attention to my coffee. To its creamy, robust embrace. The caffeine is finally making its way to my brain.

Good. I'm braced for an all-out attack.

I'd much rather avoid it. But I don't think it's in the cards.

"You want to talk about food, right?" I ask. Might as well get it out there.

She shrugs. "What makes you say that?"

I lean forward. I don't want to dance around this.

"Can we get this out of the way so we can enjoy the rest of our day?"

She purses her lips, considering it. "Okay. I am... a little concerned."

"About?"

"You have a history and you're alone in New York and I'm pretty sure you've lost five pounds."

"I have not."

"Well, your tits don't look quite as huge." She looks down at my chest.

I laugh. "So you're checking out my tits?"

"Always." She shifts in her seat, clearly uncomfortable. At least that makes two of us. "Just put my mind at ease. Convince me you're doing awesome and that you'll tell me if you have a problem."

I frown. Why is it my responsibility to always convince everyone I'm okay?

"That's not very convincing."

"I'm doing okay," I say. "Not awesome but okay enough."

"Can I do anything to help bring you up to awesome?"

I shake my head.

"Let me deal with it on my own."

She nods. "I don't want to ruin our day. I want to have fun dragging you to all the places I went to in college." She smiles. "And I have awesome plans tonight. You like burlesque, right?"

I relax a little.

"I love burlesque."

"Great, because I already bought tickets to this amazing performance. It's totally famous in the performance art community. And that is all going to be so much more fun if I'm not worried that you're planning your next binge."

"I'm not."

"Are you sure?" she asks.

"Yes. As long as you lay off with the don't order oatmeal shit."

"But oatmeal is so..."

"Jesus Christ. Did I miss some kind of memo where all the cool kids decided to hate on oatmeal eternally?"

She nods. "You haven't been cool in a long time." She takes a long sip of her coffee, formulating some response. "So are you really okay?"

"I really am."

She sighs, her shoulders relaxing as her lips curve into a smile. "Then I'll stop."

"Good." I take another long sip of my coffee, trying to taste every note of the flavor. To think about something besides this conversation.

Laurie is always protective, but this isn't like her. There has to be some reason...

There can only be one reason for this.

Luke.

He must have put her up to this. I bite my lip. I'm sure he meant well, but I'm sick of it. I'm sick of everyone looking at me like I'm about to break.

"Laurie," I start.

She must hear a warning note in my tone because she immediately starts to babble, trying to fill up space.

"You know there are male performers in the show. I think they're gay, but they're still hot."

I'm not being deterred that easily.

"It's not like you to bring up my eating."

She doesn't know where to look.

"Oh, well, you know... I was concerned."

"You were or Luke was?" I push.

She slides her cup around the table, looking down.

"We both were."

"You two were talking about me?"

"I ran into him."

"Where?"

She clears her throat. "He stopped by to say hello."

"'Hello and can you spy on my girlfriend'?"

She doesn't answer that. Which is an answer.

"He's worried about you."

"He should talk to me."

I can't believe he did that.

Laurie brings her attention to me, her expression irritated. "Don't take this the wrong way, but do you actually let him talk to you?"

"Of course I-"

"Do you tell him when you're upset? When you need help?"

I bite my lip.

I do. Sometimes. I may not go into lurid detail, but I talk to Luke about how I feel. More or less. "Sometimes."

"Well, there's a reason why he's worried. I'm not saying you need to tell him every tiny thought you have, but he's obviously not getting enough. Maybe you could tell him more to ease his mind."

"You're never on his side."

She sits back in her chair.

"I'm not on anyone's side. I want you two to live happily ever after together. But it isn't going to happen if you don't talk to him."

Damn it. I hate talking about this.

"Maybe."

"Think about it. It would be a shame to lose someone who loves you so much," she implores.

Does she really think I'm pushing Luke that hard? Does she really think I might lose him?

I frown down at the table.

It doesn't feel great to have my fears spoken aloud by someone else.

The waitress returns with our food, and I push the thoughts away.

Laurie is here and we're going to have fun. We aren't going to sit in this little cafe wallowing.

I refuse to do that.

Laurie slides her fork into her chocolate chip pancakes, bringing a large bite to her lips. She closes her eyes, clearly savoring the taste. "Oh my God, Alyssa, you have to try these." She clears her throat, catching herself. "If you want."

"Okay."

"Really?"

I nod.

I can do this. And I don't want her to worry.

I take a bite of the pancakes.

It's a tiny bite. But it's something.

They're good. Sweet with a rich cocoa flavor.

Laurie practically squeals over my taking a bite, and I know she'll leave me be for the rest of the day.

I no longer merit concern.

Now I have to figure out a way to convince Luke of the same thing.

Chapter Twelve

LUKE

Your plan has been exposed. Your operative cracked like a walnut and it really didn't take much. I have her under my control now. It was smart recruiting someone from my side, turning her into a double agent, but perhaps I can turn her into a double-double agent (whatever the hell it's called). I'll keep her in your good graces. You'll think she's working for you pretending to work for me, but really she's working for me pretending to work for you working for me. Don't worry if that sounds confusing. I don't read Tom Clancy.

I'm staying late at work when I receive Alyssa's paragraph of a text.

So Laurie "cracked like a walnut?" I'd prefer if she had used a light touch to make sure Alyssa is okay, but anything that gets Alyssa to open up is fine by me.

I read the text again and I can't help but smile. Only Alyssa would throw parenthetical asides into her tipsy text messages.

I call immediately.

She picks up with a breathy, "Hello." She's tipsy, definitely, but not drunk. "I'm sorry, I can't talk." That's the understatement of the century.

"Why not?"

"The show is about to start. Cell phones off. I'll call you when I get home." There's a long pause, like she's thinking. Or maybe like she's going to say more. "I love you. I'll talk to you later."

And then she hangs up.

Well, that was unsatisfying.

I manage to shift my focus back to my work for hours, until I have nothing left to do. It's past late, almost midnight, and I've yet to eat dinner.

Maybe Alyssa was honest about skipping meals. She forgot.

Fuck, I hope so.

I'm about to head home when my phone rings.

I'm more than a little disappointed when I see it's just Laurie.

"Hello," I answer, my voice short.

"Don't take a tone with me," she warns. "I did what you asked."

"Yeah, and I've already heard you weren't all that delicate about it," I return. "How is she?"

"There's a lot going on, but she's holding it together."

I don't like the sound of that. "And she's eating okay?"

"Her eating is the least of your concerns. You two seriously need to communicate. And not, you know, go between your mutual friend."

"Does that mean I've been promoted from annoyance to friend?"

"I guess," Laurie mutters. "I'm going to go. I'm tired. But I figured you were worried after those weird texts."

"You saw them?"

"I may have snooped after she fell asleep." She sighs.

"Listen, Luke. You need to get over here as soon as you can. She misses you like crazy."

Laurie is right. I wanted to surprise Alyssa last week, but one of my client's court dates changed, and I couldn't get away.

There's no way Alyssa will ask me to visit. She won't want to interfere with my life.

Hell, I can make it happen now. "I can get there next weekend. But don't say anything. I want it to be a surprise."

"Can or will?"

It's a fair question.

I log back onto my computer and pull open a travel website. "I'll have tickets in less than five minutes."

"That's going to cost a fortune."

"I'm not worrying about money if Alyssa needs me."

"Ugh! You're too sweet. It's sickening." She huffs out a breath. "This is the last time I get involved in your business. The absolute last time."

Leave Sunday, return Tuesday. I'll have to move around a few appointments, but that's fine.

"Thanks, Laurie."

"Yeah. You're welcome. I guess."

She can be as grudging in her words as she wants. I know she cares.

We hang up, and I read over Alyssa's texts.

Worry gnaws at me. But at least I know exactly how soon I'm going to see her now.

————

CURTAIN IS EIGHT O'CLOCK, BUT I ARRIVE AT THE THEATER as soon as the doors open--7:30.

My mother didn't take me to plays often--there weren't

a ton of opportunities in San Diego--but when she did, she always arrived early to marvel at the inside of the theater.

And this place is a marvel. Gold walls, red chairs, soft yellow light everywhere. I drink a glass of wine, barely able to contain my anticipation. This is the first time I'll see Alyssa on stage.

She's going to be fucking amazing.

I take my seat, fiddling with the flowers I brought for her. They're roses, vibrant red roses. It's an obvious choice, I know, but they remind me of her. Strong and delicate, with a stray thorn that might prick me if I don't approach carefully.

Not tonight. Not this weekend. This weekend will be perfect.

The theater fills. It's the official opening week of the play, and it's a packed house. Alyssa is probably a nervous wreck about it. I'm tempted to call her and wish her luck, but I'm sure she's "in the zone;" the way she gets when she locks herself in her room to memorize her lines.

I don't want to mess up her zen right before she goes on.

The lights go down and the play begins. There's a short scene--the two male leads shooting the shit--then Alyssa steps on stage. She stares into the blindingly bright lights coming from the balcony. Her eyes pass over the audience.

They stop at me. Her mouth drops open, and her face shifts.

Shit. Maybe I should have given her warning.

For a split second, it's not Blanche, it's Alyssa, and she's shocked to see me. But she shakes it off almost immediately, slipping back into character like a pro.

Her posture changes. It's longer, sultrier, more confident and more insecure at the same time.

She's fucking amazing.

I almost can't believe she spent so much time tearing her hair out, stressing over how to play to the back of the room. Because she's nailing everything. She's easily as good as the seasoned actors she's sharing the stage with.

I forget my plans for the rest of the weekend. I forget everything except watching her on stage, moving and speaking and living with effortless grace.

Intermission comes and goes quickly, and I'm back in my seat, drawn into the world of the play. It's as gripping and beautiful and tragic as Alyssa claimed, and when it ends, I'm on my feet applauding.

She's so ridiculously good.

An usher taps me on the shoulder as people filter out of the theater. "Miss Summers has requested you come backstage." I grin and follow him, feeling kind of like a cheap groupie at a rock concert.

She's got her very own dressing room.

The usher points me to the door and I knock.

"Get your fucking ass in here," Alyssa calls through it. She pulls the door open and scans my body with bright eyes. "You fucking... why didn't you tell me?"

"This is more exciting."

I offer the flowers and her face lights up. She grabs my hand and pulls me into the room, slamming the door behind us.

She tosses the flowers onto the vanity and presses me against the door. Her body is so soft against mine.

I'm desperate to slide her robe off her shoulders, to touch her until she purrs.

But not yet.

Instead, I slide my arms around her, pulling her close. I feel her hands on my waist, her head against my chest as her body melts into mine. "You have no idea how glad I am to see you," she murmurs.

"Same." I bury my face against her hair.

She hugs me tighter. "I better wash my makeup off or I'm going to ruin your suit." She pulls back, wiping a tear from under her eye. "You look hot as hell in that."

"I look hotter in nothing." I tease. She blushes, pulling her robe around her shoulders. "If you're lucky, you might get a look tonight."

She raises her brows, a smile tugging at the corners of her mouth.

"If I'm lucky?"

I nod. "I'm not easy, you know."

"I know." She grins and takes a seat at the vanity. "How was your flight?"

"I worked the whole time. I didn't want any distractions this weekend."

She fiddles with her makeup remover, pouring it onto a cotton ball. "This is so disgusting. You shouldn't watch."

"You were amazing."

She smiles, basking in the praise.

"I won't object."

I chuckle, leaning against the door.

She washes off her makeup then slips out of her wardrobe. She makes a point of lingering in her bra and panties before she pulls on a low-cut cotton dress.

Damn. Maybe she did know I was coming.

I move closer to her, wrapping my arms around her as I kiss her neck. Mhmm. She smells so good. "I'm going to take you out to dinner."

She glances at the clock.

"It's tenthirty."

"Have you eaten?"

She shakes her head. "Let's not get into that."

"We don't have to discuss it in detail. But I would like

to feed you before I use up every last ounce of your energy."

"Every last ounce, huh? We'll see." She offers her hand and I take it.

"Now you're just baiting me."

She laughs, tugging me along.

We make our way out of the theater, through the back entrance where no one will spot her.

We eat at a nearby restaurant, a deli known only for being open late. Alyssa orders a salad and a cup of soup and she eats all of it without comment or protest. She doesn't even make a fuss about me watching her.

"Tell me everything about the play," I order.

She does. She talks about every little thing until our last scraps of food are cold. She's so animated, so passionate, I can't stop staring at her as I soak in every word. I've never seen her so excited.

Not while she was clothed.

———

AFTER DINNER, WE CAN'T GET TO THE APARTMENT FAST enough.

Our cab feels like it's crawling at a snail's pace. Alyssa is sleepy but that doesn't stop her from slipping her hands under my suit jacket and dragging her lips against my neck.

Fuck.

I want her so fucking bad.

When we're finally in the apartment, Alyssa slides my jacket off my shoulders and gets to work on my buttons. She presses her lips into mine; a soft but hungry kiss. She moans. "I missed you so much."

I press my hands into her back, pulling her closer. She

kisses me harder, deeper, her body melting against mine. "Let me... get into something more comfortable," she murmurs. "You could do the same."

"Comfortable how?" I smirk. It's fun to pull this out of her, to get her to admit how much she wants me.

"You know how," she returns. She moves to the bedroom. "Give me five minutes." She bites her lip, eyes on mine as she shuts the door behind her.

Five minutes until a few scraps of silk are wrapped around her body like a bow around a present. Until I peel that bra and panties off her and run my hands over every inch of her body.

These are going to be the hardest five minutes of my life.

I strip to my boxers. Alyssa is in her bedroom, nearly naked, desperate for my hands on her body.

I wait for her to say "come in," to taunt me the way I always taunt her, but there's nothing. Finally, I can't take it anymore.

I open the bedroom door.

And Alyssa is lying there, in that unbelievably sexy silk lingerie, fast asleep.

I take a moment to enjoy the stellar view.

My little seductress is completely exhausted.

Moving quietly, I pull the covers over her and get in bed, wrapping my arms around her and tucking her in close.

I'll have plenty of time to torture her tomorrow.

Chapter Thirteen

ALYSSA

The smell of coffee wafts into the bedroom.

My boyfriend is making me coffee.

I'm already smiling before I open my eyes.

And then it hits me.

Oh no.

I fell asleep last night! After revving things up, I came in here and... passed out.

And somehow managed to stay asleep in this utterly gorgeous silk lingerie.

Great. Nice one.

Groaning, I cover my face with my hands, imagining Luke waiting for me to come back out.

Well.

I drop my hands.

It happened. There's no use crying over spilled milk.

And hey—I'm already dressed to kill. All I need to do is wash my face and brush my teeth and I'll get Luke right where I want him.

By the time I rush through the bathroom, I'm feeling better.

Luke is in the kitchen, sipping a mug of tea, wearing nothing but his navy boxers. He has a shit eating grin on his face.

He's not going to make this easy.

He looks me over slowly. "That's some outfit for breakfast."

I give his body the same once over.

"And yours?"

He brushes his shoulders and chest like he's smoothing his shirt. "You like it?"

I nod. I do like it. And I'd like it even more if those were my hands on his body.

Luke stands and moves towards me. He places his hands on my shoulders and runs his fingertips over my collar bone. His lips are inches from mine and my body hums from the proximity.

He brushes his lips against mine, as softly as humanly possible. His hands slide down my shoulders.

I lean into him, grabbing his waist.

He kisses me harder, sucking on my lips.

Then, the microwave beeps. Luke pulls away, his face lighting up with a smile. "Your breakfast is ready."

"Fuck breakfast."

"Sounds painful." He slides his fingers over my spine, his touch soft and delicate. "Unless you have a banana you want to put in your oatmeal?"

I fold my arms. "I hate you."

He smiles and kisses me again, hard, a kiss that says you're going to wait. "We have a full day ahead of us. You'll need your energy." He pulls away from me, finishes fixing breakfast, and takes a seat at the kitchen table. His gaze returns to me, passing over my body again. "You look amazing."

Not amazing enough, apparently.

"Don't pout, Ally. I'd love to fuck you right now."

My teeth sink into my lip and I reach for something, anything to grab.

"But, first, I'm going to torture you all day. Until you're so wet, so ready that you think you might die if I don't fuck you properly."

Jesus Christ.

"How does that sound?"

"Umm..." I stammer, trying to wipe the shocked look off my face. "I can live with that."

"Good." He smiles and pats the seat next to him. "Your coffee is getting cold."

I fold my arms across my chest. "I'll change first."

"I wish you wouldn't."

His eyes pass over my body. It's a look of pure desire, and it sends electricity buzzing through my body.

Fine. If he's going to torture me, I'll torture him too.

"I'm taking off my underwear and I'm not putting any on."

He smirks. "I like the way you think."

I go back to the bedroom and pick out the sexiest outfit that is still weather appropriate. Thigh high socks, ankle boots, and a short, V-neck dress.

A really, really short V-neck dress.

It's perfect.

When I return to the kitchen, Luke looks at me like... well, like I look at him.

"You're going to pay for that," he says in a low voice.

I feel that voice down to my toes.

"Good."

I join him at the table, and we talk about little things over breakfast. He asks about the play. I ask about his current cases, but he insists he wants to keep his mind off work. So I request the same.

This weekend—well, this Monday and Tuesday—is going to be about us.

———

Luke and I are tourists all morning.

We start at the MoMA, making our way through rooms of famous pop art and truly strange installations. He takes me into the staircase and runs his fingers over the edge of my dress.

It's a small thing, something no one else would notice. But it wakes up all the nerves in my body.

We eat lunch at a quaint Japanese restaurant, and Luke keeps his mouth shut when I order nothing but sashimi. The fish is amazing, fresh and melt-in-your-mouth tender, and I almost relax, even though Luke is making a point of not watching me eat.

We linger in the restaurant, drinking green tea and catching up on all the little details of the last three months.

After lunch, we take the subway to one edge of Central Park and start making our way to the other end. It's quieter than I expected. And more of an oasis. If I don't look up, I can't tell I'm in the middle of the most populated city in the country. All I can see is long grass lawns, clumps of deep green trees, and little man-made lakes.

We walk quietly for a while, soaking in the scenery and the pure ecstasy of being three inches apart instead of three thousand miles apart.

Finally, Luke breaks the silence. "I've been thinking..."

"That doesn't sound like you."

He stops and pulls me towards him. Our bodies connect, his hands on the small of my back.

"I think about you constantly," he murmurs, his eyes on mine. "You have a vice grip on my thoughts."

I shake my head, my teeth sinking into my lip.

"I think about you too." There's no way I can stop, even this far away from him.

He leans closer, until I can smell his earthy aftershave, feel his breath on my cheeks. "I've been thinking about the future."

The future.

Anxiety starts to rise again.

My face flushes as I struggle to find an appropriate response. "What about it?"

"I have an amazing vision of the immediate future--how I'm going to tear that dress off and lick every inch of your body."

He brushes his fingertips across my neck and jaw, resting his palm on my cheek. I turn into the gesture with a quiet sigh.

"You know I'm not good with the future." I know that's not what he wants to hear.

"Ally... do you see anything at all?"

I shake my head. I don't want to deal with this right now. "I can barely see getting through the next five months," I say, trying to keep things light.

"You will." He brushes a hair behind my ear and brings his hand to my chin until our eyes are locked again. "And then we'll have the rest of our lives to spend together."

I bite my tongue. It should sound amazing. It does. But there's something about it, something that makes my knees weak and my grip shaky.

Luke pulls me closer, only for a moment. I close my eyes and press my lips into his, trying to pour everything I'm feeling into him.

I can't explain it. I can't even figure it out myself. But I need him to know how I feel, how much I love him.

Our kiss breaks and he meets my eyes once more, his sweet, sincere.

But then he frowns slightly.

"Are you okay?" he asks.

I nod. I'd rather we never discussed if I was okay again.

He runs his hands over my arms. It's so easy, so natural. I feel like I could melt. But I stand firm as he takes my hand and continues our walk. "What do you want to happen next year?"

"I don't know. I guess I want to survive."

He shakes his head.

"Ally, I know you have higher aspirations than that. You don't get to be a TV star or a Broadway actor by only aiming to survive."

"Career is different. I'm sorry, but I really don't know."

He nods.

"Well, let's try to see if you can get some kind of idea then. Close your eyes."

I don't want to.

"This is silly."

"Do it anyway," he insists. He pulls me towards the side of the path, under the shade of a blossoming tree. "Now, close your eyes."

I do as I'm instructed. If this is what he needs, I'll try.

"We'll start with something easy. Think about tonight. What are you going to do?"

A smile creeps onto my lips. "You know what I'm going to do tonight."

He chuckles.

"I want you to imagine it vividly. Every touch, every kiss, every caress."

I'm sure I'm blushing.

"Do you see it?" he asks, his voice close.

"Yes."

"Now, let's move a little further. Let's try next week. Can you imagine what you'll do next Monday, on your next day off?"

"No." I try, hard, to imagine where I'll be next week, but all I can see is that apartment. I'll probably be lying in bed, dead tired, barely able to read my Kindle.

"You're thinking something. I can tell."

"I'll be in the apartment reading."

"That's a start." His voice is deep and soft, but there's an urgency to it, like there's something he's getting at.

Of course there's something he's getting at.

I'm not an idiot. He's asking about my future, but really, he's asking about our future. If I think we'll be together forever.

There it is again, that scary word. Forever.

I hate forever.

"How about next year. This time, next year, where will you be?"

I open my mouth to object, but I resist the urge.

Where will I be next year? What do I see? I'm not entirely sure. There are hints of something-- Luke getting home from work, slowly stripping off his suit, torturing me. We're in his house, our house, I guess. And we're going to eat dinner. But there's still a fuss, still all these questions, all this tension. We still can't manage to eat a damn meal without it becoming an interrogation.

Is that the future we're hurtling towards?

I open my eyes. "I don't want to do this anymore."

Luke squeezes my arm gently as he moves closer. "What is it?"

"Whatever this is, this self-help vision game, I don't want to do it anymore."

His frown deepens.

"Why not?"

"Because I don't like it. Why is this something we have to talk about right now?"

"Our future together?"

I nod. "How about we just let it happen instead of over-directing it?"

"One question every few months isn't over directing." He runs a hand through his hair, his expression filling with concern. Great. I'm a matter of concern again. "I love you, Alyssa. And I never doubt that I want to be with you. Do you doubt you want to be with me?"

Shit. I could lie.

Or I could be honest. He deserves that.

"On occasion."

He releases a heavy breath. Like he just got punched in the gut.

"Okay. That's fair. You know what a fan I am of reasonable doubt."

I suppress a laugh. "That's only vaguely related."

He smiles slightly.

"True. But it made you smile."

"Luke, you're killing me here."

"I know." He searches my eyes. "But I won't be able to think of anything else until you tell me if you see a future together."

"We've been together for a year."

"That's not an answer."

"Are you going to keep sending my friends to check on me?" I ask. It's not an answer, not really, but it will deflect him until I can figure out what to say, how to explain the thoughts careening around my brain.

"You sounded shaky. I needed to know you were okay, even if I had to hear it from her."

He doesn't sound at all apologetic about it.

"Why don't you ask me?"

He sighs.

"Would you tell me?"

"Maybe." I look up into his knowing eyes. I have to look away, have to bury my head in his chest.

"I love you, Ally. I'm not going anywhere."

"Even if I close off and shut you out?"

A moment of silence. And when he does respond, he doesn't answer the question.

And that fact isn't lost on me.

"You still haven't answered my question."

My heart clenches in my chest.

"Can I think about it?" I ask. I don't know if it'll help, but it'll at least get me out of this conversation now.

"Fuck, Ally." He lets go, takes a step back. Looking away, he rakes a hand through his hair. "You can't even *think* about our future?"

"I..."

Can't even finish that sentence.

We stand there for a while, listening to the sounds of the park and the city around us.

Eventually, he takes my hand and we keep walking.

He lets it go.

But I'm not an idiot.

It's not gone.

That conversation isn't one I can delay forever. No matter how much I might want to.

Chapter Fourteen

LUKE

Alyssa can't answer my question.

It's a simple question. It should have an easy answer.

Either she sees a future together, or she doesn't... I'd think, by now, she sees something.

But she clearly doesn't want to say what it is.

So, we walk.

We walk through the park silently, both of us locked in our respective heads.

This is no good. This is not how things should be.

I keep my mouth shut, my hands in my pockets. I'm not going to keep trying to pry an answer out of her.

I may as well have stayed in Los Angeles for how close we are right now.

I glance at Alyssa. She's wearing a frown. Pressing her nails into her fingers.

I run a hand through my hair. Maybe we need a little time away from this subject of conversation. Maybe it's good to walk quietly, like we're...

No. It's not good. It's fucked up.

I pull my hand out of my pocket and offer it to Alyssa. She says nothing, but she wraps her fingers around mine. Her skin is soft and warm, and, for a second, I feel like there's some way to get past this.

Then I feel a drop on my forehead.

Rain.

And, out of nowhere, it's pouring.

"I thought we were past this phase," she says in a low voice.

I move closer. "What phase?"

"The one where you sulk because I won't tell you what you want to hear."

I take a deep breath, trying to summon patience.

"You think this is sulking?" I shake my head. "You're so wrong. The problem isn't me. It's you. You act like I'm your fucking enemy instead of your boyfriend."

"Because you act like you're interrogating me."

Interrogating?

"Now that's overly dramatic. If I had this all on the court record, I could prove how wrong you are," I mutter. "But it wouldn't do me any good, would it?"

She sighs.

I'm so over this right now.

I squeeze her hand and take a step towards the street. "Come on. Let's get out of here. Get somewhere dry."

"I don't mind the rain." She pulls her hand away and keeps walking. The rain is heavy and cold and the sky is gray around us.

"Ally!"

She moves faster, nearly running. She's going to fall, hurt herself.

She'd probably do it just to get out of this shitty conversation.

I run after her, grab her arm to stop her. "Fine. You don't mind the rain? Then, talk to me in the rain."

She jerks out of my hold.

"Why does everything have to be such an ordeal with you? Why can't we have a day together without it turning into some conversation about our future?"

"That isn't fair," I growl. "I'm not the one with the weird hang-up here. I'm not the one dragging my feet in our relationship. What the hell are you waiting for?"

She crosses her arms.

"It has nothing to do with you."

"Bullshit. You agreed to marry Ryan."

Any hint of pleasure drops off her face and she stares at me like I'm the root of all her misery. "Are you jealous of fucking Ryan?"

I don't even know.

"You saw a future with him. You don't see one with me. Maybe..." My fists curl into tight balls. My jaw clenches. Every muscle in my body is stiff and tense. I can't say that.

"For a smart guy, you can be such an idiot," she mutters.

I can barely hear her over the pitter patter of the rain on the sidewalk.

Her eyes are intense as she glares at me. "Do you know why I agreed to marry Ryan?"

"He convinced you that you'd never survive without him."

"Yes, but there's more to it than that. It wasn't a happy thing. I knew I was giving up any chance of ever being happy, really happy. I knew I was giving up the future I wanted. And I definitely knew I'd never have the kind of love we have. At least, the kind of love I thought we had." She turns and walks away again.

Shit.

"Ally, wait."

She stops but she doesn't turn to face me. "Why are you bringing up Ryan?"

I shove my fists back into my pockets.

"I hate that you loved him."

It burns to say it. I hate that I care.

"I didn't. Not the way I love you." She finally turns to face me. She's soaking wet, dripping actually, and her expression is anything but happy. "Can't you see that?"

I know that.

I do.

But...

I nod and take a step towards her.

"This isn't going to work unless you see that." She moves towards me. "Do you?"

"Alyssa... you're everything I've ever wanted." I lift my hands to reach for her but let them drop again. She needs to hear this first. "You're sweet, sincere, caring. I love how pretentious you are. I love that you're tied to your Kindle. I love that you read awful shit like Heart of Darkness and lock yourself in your room to perfect your lines. But none of those things are my favorite thing about you."

I can see her softening slightly.

"Yeah?"

"My favorite thing about you is that you look at me like I'm the only thing in the world better than a perfect cup of coffee."

She laughs. It's a tiny thing, but it fills the whole, dreary park with warmth.

"I love you, Luke. I love you so much."

"If I love you and you love me, why are we failing so horribly at talking to each other?"

She wraps her arms around me, burying her head in my chest. "I don't know. And I don't know why I can't see this future you keep talking about. But I do want to be with you. More than anything."

She rises to her tip toes and kisses me.

Her lips are soft and wet. Her skin, her hair, her clothes are wet from the damn rain that keeps falling on us. Her lips part and she slides her tongue into my mouth. It's equal parts hungry and sweet.

I run my hands over her back and she nearly moans. She's melting in my arms.

There's only one appropriate course of action.

I slide my hands to her ass, pressing my body hard against hers.

She feels so good to touch--her perfect breasts, her round hips, her firm ass--but I fight my urge to rip off her clothes and fuck her right here.

Not yet. Not until she wants it as badly as I do.

I squeeze her ass, digging my hands under the edge of her dress. This time, she moans into my mouth and slides her fingers around my neck.

Her back arches, her crotch shifting into mine.

Blood rushes to my cock.

I can feel her against me, through the thin, wet fabric of her dress. God, I need to feel her against me, to feel her around me.

I need to be inside her.

When our kiss breaks, she's flushed and panting. She looks so fucking sexy like that, like she needs me more than she's ever needed anything.

"Fuck me," she says. "I don't care if it's here. I don't care if someone sees us. Right now, I don't even care if I get arrested. I need you, Luke. I need you so fucking bad."

I respond with my arms around her waist, my lips on her neck. She gasps and moans and melts completely into me.

I take her hand and lead her into the bushes. The grass is wet, slippery, and Alyssa nearly trips. So I take her into my arms and carry her past a scattering of trees, to a patch of grass where no one can see us.

I lay her on the ground. She squirms and arches her back. Her dress rides up her legs and I suddenly remember that she's not wearing any underwear.

She's a fucking genius.

I kneel over her and trace the outline of her collarbone. She bites her lip, her eyes fluttering closed as she turns away.

"Luke," she groans.

Right now, she's mine. She's all mine.

I trace the neckline of her dress. Her skin is soft and wet, and my fingers slide over her with almost no friction. She squirms, reaching for my arms.

I pull her dress aside, exposing her breast, and bring my lips to her neck. Her nails find my back.

She digs her hands into my shirt and groans.

I kiss her neck again, lower this time. Rain runs off her skin, but it still tastes like her, like Alyssa. I run my tongue along her collarbone and brush my fingers against the inside of her knee. She squirms, again, her back arching, and I slide my fingers up her leg. Her thighs are such gorgeous curves, soft and firm at the same time.

She shifts, pulling her dress to her waist. My hands find the inside of her thighs, and I plant long, soft strokes on them. I touch her until she's moaning. Until she groans and digs her hands into my hair.

Her back arches, her chest shifting towards me like she's begging me to touch her. I lower myself and press my lips into the soft skin of her chest. She sighs, relaxing into a puddle of need.

I drag my mouth over her chest, until I reach her

nipple. She pants, digging harder into my hair like she's begging me to suck.

Like I could resist.

I trace her nipple with my tongue. It's so hard and soft, and it feels so good against my tongue. I run my tongue over it again. And again. Fast then slow. Soft then hard. I circle her nipple with my tongue until she's panting so loudly I can barely hear the rain.

"Luke," she groans. I brush my fingers over her, against her clit. She gasps, her body melting into the ground. I run my fingers over her again and again and again. And I bring my mouth to her nipples, sucking harder and harder and harder.

She arches her body into my hands, and my fingers slide inside her. She's so damn wet, and she's so damn desperate. I stoke her slowly, going deeper and deeper.

She squirms. "Fuck me. Fuck me now." She tugs at my t-shirt, pulling it over my head. Then, her hands are on my body, hard against my chest, my back, my stomach. She undoes my belt, tears at my jeans and slides them past my ass.

And then her hands are on my cock. Fuck. She wraps her hands around me and strokes me.

Warmth spreads through me, and I start to lose touch with anything except Alyssa, lying in front of me. She's so God-damn beautiful. The rain is still pouring on her, and her wet dress clings to her curves. Every part of her is perfect--her soft, round breasts, her smooth thighs, the gentle curve of her neck. And her lips. Damn, her lips are so soft and sweet and warm.

She rubs me, harder and harder. I can't wait anymore.

I shift out of my boxers and press her thighs apart, pinning her legs onto the ground.

She wraps her hands around my cock, rubbing it up

and down. I shudder. Alyssa. Damn. Alyssa. I push her dress higher, past her bellybutton and she guides my cock inside of her.

Damn. She feels amazing. So warm and wet and tight.

I press my lips into hers, kissing her hard. She responds with her tongue in my mouth. It slides over mine with urgency.

I start slowly, thrusting into her. She grabs my back, sinking her teeth into my shoulders. Then, I feel her teeth on my neck, my chest, my ears. She runs her hands down my back and settles on my ass. She pulls me towards her, and I thrust deeper inside her. We move like this for a while; slow, gentle thrusts filling us both with waves of pleasure.

She stops me, digs her hands into my hair and kisses me hard. When the kiss breaks, she stares into my eyes. It's like she can see into my fucking soul, see every single part of me.

We don't say anything. We don't have to. We both know what this means, that, this is all the apology we need.

I run my hands over her body, feeling every part of her. We kiss again, a long, slow, deep thing. Then, her hands are on my back, and she's pulling, arching into me. I thrust into her, deeper and deeper.

Mhmm. She feels so damn good. Warmth radiates through me and I start to fill with pleasure.

She groans and arches and pants and digs her nails into my back. She lifts her right leg and swings it over my shoulder. Then she does the same with the left.

I pin her to the ground. She's here. She's mine. And she's completely helpless to do anything but come.

So I thrust into her, deeper and deeper. She moans, her arms flat against the ground, her hands clutching at the grass.

"Don't stop," she groans.

I rock into her, filling her until she's almost there. Her eyes flutter closed. Her teeth sink into her lip. Her breath is ragged and shallow. And she groans. She tears up the ground.

She screams.

"Luke." She moans, louder and louder, arching deeper and deeper. Her face is flushed and warm. Her lips are red, her eyes closed.

And she comes. I can see it in her face as all her muscles relax.

It's the sexiest damn thing I've ever seen.

Her eyes open and she stares at me again. She shifts her legs off my shoulders and pulls me close.

Her mouth hovers over my ear. "Fuck me," she says. "Come inside me."

Her hands are flat on my ass. She wraps her legs around me and rocks into me.

Fuck.

I thrust into her. Again and again and again.

Pleasure overtakes me. Every part of my body is on fire. There's nothing in the world except for us.

She digs her nails into my back and I bite the soft skin of her neck.

"Fuck," I groan. The ache inside me explodes, and I come, my cock pulsing inside her.

I collapse on top of her. She wraps her arms around me, holding me tight.

"God damn," she sighs. She kisses my neck. "You better get dressed."

"Wouldn't you prefer it if I stayed naked?"

She giggles and presses her lips into mine.

Unfortunately, we have to go.

I struggle into my wet clothes, watching as she adjusts her dress.

"You want to go back to the apartment and get dry?" she asks.

I shake my head. "No. I want to go back to the apartment and get wet."

Her cheeks flush red.

"Deal."

Chapter Fifteen

ALYSSA

After we clean up and get dirty all over again, Luke tells me he's made dinner reservations.

"Somewhere nice," he says. And shakes his head. "Dammit, now, I sound like Samantha. But you will probably want to dress up."

"In something nice?"

"Now, you sound like her." He kisses my forehead and pulls me into his arms. "God, I'm so tempted to cancel the reservation, stay in, and fuck your brains out."

I gulp. "I have no objection to that."

"Too bad. You're not getting out of this." He digs through his luggage and pulls out a pair of slacks and a silk shirt. God damn, he's going to look good in that. "You'll like this place. And after dinner, I'm going to take you to... it's a surprise."

A surprise after dinner? My immediate thoughts are filled with dread, but I push past it. Luke looks at me like he knows what I'm thinking.

"It has nothing to do with eating or not eating or

talking about eating. In fact, I swear that I'm not going to talk about eating for the rest of my trip."

"I'll believe it when I hear it."

He shakes his head playfully. "Still not a fan of promises from Luke Lawrence?"

"Definitely not."

There's an hour until we need to leave, so I drag Luke to the couch. We sit together, flipping through the channels and talking about nothing in particular. It's almost like a normal day at home, like I'm not in New York with my life turned upside down.

For a minute, I can see this as a future. I can't see the big moments--the proposal, the wedding, the thirty-year anniversary. I can't imagine us with kids. I really can't imagine me with kids. After all, I can barely take care of myself.

But I can see this. I can see lying next to him, doing nothing in particular. I can feel this, how safe I am when I'm around him, how much I know everything will be okay.

He gives so much of himself to me, puts up with so much of my bullshit.

I have to do better. I have to talk to him. I have to show Luke that I'm as madly in love with him as he is with me.

But not yet.

Right now, all I need to do is relax in his arms and soak in his presence.

Right now, all I need is Luke.

———

THE RESTAURANT IS, IN FACT, SOME PLACE NICE.

Insanely nice, actually. It's in midtown, hidden between a few skyscrapers. Best of all, it's private. Really private.

Tinted windows. Drawn shades.

Our booth is in the back of the restaurant, in a quiet corner where almost no one can see us. It's still early in the evening, before the place is full of executives on dates with models, and there's almost no one here.

Just me and Luke in our own private world.

Luke orders wine. Yes wine.

"Since when do you drink wine?" I ask, surprised.

"It's a special occasion."

"Is it?"

He nods. And, is he... is he blushing?

Luke fucking Lawrence, my obscenely confident boyfriend, is blushing.

This is unheard of.

And, of course, he doesn't look adorable or endearing. He looks hot as hell with that color in his cheeks.

He looks like he's just come down from an amazing orgasm.

"What are you thinking?" he asks.

I grin. "You don't want to know."

"Now I do." He sips his wine. His hands are a little shaky. It's a slight thing, barely noticeable, but it's there.

He's nervous.

He's never nervous.

"I was thinking about the way you look when you come," I explain.

He grins.

"Well, at least you're buying me dinner before you try and get in my pants."

"I'm buying you dinner here?"

He shakes his head. "No, it's on me." He flags down the waiter and orders another glass of wine. When the hell did he start drinking wine? He looks back at me, his confidence seemingly restored. "Really, Ally, when did you become such a pervert?"

"I'm the pervert?"

"Mhmm."

"Cause I'm the one who seduced you?"

He nods, his messy hair falling over his eyes.

There's something different about him right now, and it's not just nerves. His eyes are lighting up the whole room. He's in slacks and a silk shirt. He almost always wears Egyptian cotton. He brags about how smooth it feels against his skin as he undoes his buttons, torturing me as slowly as humanly possible.

Usually, when Luke is in a suit he looks like the epitome of confidence. He looks like the guy you would want behind your bench in court--serious, self-assured, with just a hint of sex appeal.

But there's something about him today... it's almost like he's a little boy playing dress up or like a terrified teenager on his way to the prom.

He brings his gaze back to me. "Miss Summers, are you complaining?"

I shake my head.

"Because, if I recall correctly, I did deliver on my promise."

"And what was that?"

"To make you come."

I smile.

"And you love to remind me."

"I'm only trying to lay out the facts."

"Are you?"

"The truth is very important here."

"And what truth is that?"

"You were implying some sort of dissatisfaction. And I simply cannot have that. In fact, I'm not going to be happy unless you're incredibly satisfied." He runs his fingers along my arm. "Incredibly satisfied, incredibly often."

I look into his eyes.

There's lust there, but there's something else too. There's a vulnerability.

"Mr. Lawrence, don't tell me you're suddenly doubting yourself."

"No, I still have vivid memories of that night. And I'm damn certain that you came at least three times."

And now I'm the one with flushed cheeks.

Luke smiles.

"I love when you get shy," he murmurs. "There's an adorable innocence about it. An innocence I want to corrupt."

Well, fuck.

He's certainly pushed aside any nerves. Or maybe he hasn't. Maybe he's masking them with the one thing he can always be confident about.

I can't blame him. He's fucking fantastic with his hands, his mouth, his cock.

If I were him, I'd brag more than he does.

The waiter returns with another round of drinks and we order. Luke says nothing when I order the usual seared fish and vegetables. Not a peep about treating myself or recovery or any of that bullshit. There's nothing on his face either.

Maybe he's going to mind his own business from now on.

No, that's not fair. I want to bring him into this. I want to tell him how I feel. But I have to do it on my terms.

"You can say it," I prod him.

"Say what?" He takes a long sip of his wine, his lips wrapped around the edge of the glass. God, have his lips always been that gorgeous?

"Make a comment about what I've ordered. We can get

this all out of the way now, so I don't have to stew while you're watching me eat."

"No comments. I promise. You said you're doing okay. I trust you." He leans closer. "I love you so much, Ally. I don't want to do anything that would hurt you."

"Everyone hurts each other. It's inevitable."

He shakes his head. "Maybe. But I have an almost painful urge to protect you."

"Then why did you tell me to do the play?"

"I have an equally painful urge to make sure I'm not getting in your way."

"You never could."

His expression says he doesn't buy it.

"What if you stayed in LA because of me?"

"We'd have been spared this afternoon's fight."

He brings his gaze back to me. His eyes are on fire again. "Be honest. Do you wish you'd turned down the play?"

There have been a lot of awful moments, too many temptations to count, and it's terrible being so far from Luke.

But I'm still glad I'm here. I was a nervous wreck for two weeks straight, but I'm finally calming down. And I'm on fucking Broadway.

"No," I admit. "But I really wish there was a way you could be here with me without uprooting your life."

"Me too. My life is pretty empty without you in it."

My face flushes. I take a sip of tequila, but that only makes the situation worse.

"A year together and that still makes you nervous?" he asks.

I nod.

"I'm not sure if I should be flattered or concerned." He lays his hand on top of mine and looks into my eyes. "Hell, you look so damn adorable when you're blushing. I don't think it's possible for me to feel anything negative when I see that."

And now it's much, much worse.

He laughs.

"Shut your beautiful mouth," I say. "I will have none of your sass."

"Not even a little bit?"

I shake my head.

"Even if it's the only way you can get into my pants?

"Always the same trump card."

He shakes his head. His eyes lock with mine. There's something so intense about it, almost as intense as before in the park.

I swear, it's like he was looking straight through me.

I bite my lip, my cheeks no doubt even redder. He smiles and squeezes my hand. "You're amazing, Ally. I hope you never change."

"What if I become jaded and cynical in my old age?"

"I'll still love you."

"Even if I get fat and ugly?"

"You could never be ugly."

"What if I was in a disfiguring accident," I prod. "A truly horrific one."

"Doesn't matter. You're still my Alyssa, even if you're my bitter, jaded, disfigured Alyssa." He looks around the room like he's checking for something then he brings his gaze back to me. It's back, the nervousness. There's a hint of it in his eyes.

We lock eyes for a long time. It's alarming at first, but, after a few moments, there's something so comfortable about it. I study all the contours of his face--that messy hair, the big, brown eyes, the too beautiful, too skilled for words mouth. That's Luke.

Yes, he's handsome as all hell. But that isn't what I think when I look at him.

It's just him. Luke. My boyfriend. The man I love more than anything. And, even though he still gives me butterflies, still takes my breath away, there's something about looking at him that makes me feel comfortable.

"I've been doing a lot of thinking," he starts. I can tell this is important.

"When you aren't torturing me?"

He nods. "My schedule of torturing you, maintaining my amazing body, and running a one-man law firm doesn't leave much time for thinking, but I make do." He smiles. His cheeks fill with a hint of color, again. God, he really is nervous.

I let him speak.

"You're amazing, Ally. We can get the obvious out of the way first. You're the most beautiful woman I've ever seen." He pulls his hands into his lap. "And you're so damn thoughtful. You don't even realize it. I love that you would rather spend your night reading than at a party. I love that you get excited about Tennessee Williams, that you aren't afraid to correct me or tell me when I'm being an idiot. And I love how shameless you are about your lust for coffee."

My heart thuds against my chest. It's so damn sweet. Of course it is. It's Luke. But what is he getting at?

"I promise I won't get sidetracked by the part about you feeling pleasure." He smiles. "But, Ally, when you're happy, I'm so fucking happy. I can't think of a better way to spend my life."

No. There's no way... he can't be...

"Luke, I..."

"There's no one else who compares to you."

He slides out of his seat and drops to one knee.

Oh my fucking God.

He's... I can't breathe. I can't feel my limbs. The room is spinning.

Or maybe it's me.

Luke looks up at me with those achingly sincere eyes. He pulls a ring box from his pocket and holds it flat on his palm.

He pops it open.

It's a ring. A gorgeous round solitaire in a platinum setting.

I stare, focusing on the details to try to ground myself.

It's stylish, classy, timeless not trendy, subtle not hey look at me.

It's exactly the kind of thing I would pick out for myself.

"Alyssa Summers, will you marry me?"

My hand flies to my mouth. My heart is racing so quickly, and my stomach is full of butterflies. I can barely move to nod my head. I don't think. I just respond. "Yes," I nod. "Of course."

He slides the ring onto my finger. It's even more gorgeous up close. God, it's so perfect. He's so perfect. This whole thing is so damn perfect.

He stands and wraps his arms around me. I lean into him, hugging him as tightly as I can. His grip is strong around me. He would keep me up if I collapsed in his arms.

I feel his lips on my cheek. I move to meet him, and we kiss, long and deep, not caring if anyone in the restaurant is looking at us.

When we break, I am dizzy and breathless. I slide back into my seat, gripping the table for support.

He looks at me with a million-dollar grin. I expect

some witty quip, but he says nothing. He just squeezes my hand and stares into my eyes.

Luke asked me to marry him.

I should feel like the luckiest girl in the whole damn world.

———

I'M TOO NERVOUS TO EAT MUCH OF MY DINNER.

As promised, Luke doesn't make any comments about it. He sits across from me, grinning as he answers all of my obnoxious questions about how long he's been planning this. I gather that it's been a little while, a few months at least.

He probably wanted to do it in San Diego at some romantic place by the house where he grew up.

After dinner, he tries to suggest we continue sightseeing.

Yeah right. I tell our limo driver--yes, he arranged for a limo-- to take us back to the apartment, but I can't wait until we're there. Luke's nervousness hasn't completely worn off and he looks so damn sexy with flushed cheeks.

I shift towards him and press my lips into his. I expect him to resist, to insist I wait the way he always does, but he kisses me back.

He doesn't waste any time, actually. He slides his hands over my hips, groaning into my mouth. He plants kisses down my neck, soft and sweet and hungry all at the same time.

Then, he brings his lips to my ear, his breath hot and heavy. "It's been torture trying to concentrate with you in that dress," he says. "You must pick these out just for how much they'll distract me."

I nod.

His teeth sink into my earlobe. Jesus. My sex clenches, my body filling with a pleasant rush of want. I'm not sure that I can make it to the damn apartment before I get his cock in my hands.

But Luke has no intention of relinquishing control. He slides his hand under my dress, stroking me over my panties. I kiss him, hard, sucking on his tongue.

His eyes are open, and he's already lost in some world of desire. He wants me, and badly.

I press my lips into his neck, making my way to his ear. I suck on his lobe until he's groaning. "That's only a teaser," I say, pressing my hands against his slacks. He's hard. God is he hard, and I need to feel him in my hands. I need to make him come.

He digs his hands into my hair as I undo his belt and unzip his slacks. "Ally, are you sure?" he asks. "We're not exactly alone."

"That didn't stop you this afternoon," I say. I press my lips into his, sucking hard on his bottom lip as I wrap my hands around his cock.

God damn, he feels so good in my hands. I stroke him, pumping hard and deep. He shudders from my touch. His tongue slides over his lips, his eyes pressing together in ecstasy. He reaches for me, presses his fingertips against my back.'

"Alyssa," he groans. He grabs my shoulders pulling me into him, pulling us together. Our lips touch. It's electric. There's so much between us--so much want and need. I grip him harder, pumping harder. This isn't enough. I need more.

I need to suck him off.

I break our kiss and plant my lips on his ear. I suck on the lobe, pressing my tongue flat against it. Then, I move to his neck, scraping my teeth against his skin. He tastes damn good, some mix of sweat and Luke and the soap in my shower. God, he must taste that good everywhere.

He shudders as I unbutton his shirt and press my lips against his chest. He's so hard, everywhere. He feels so damn good.

I don't waste any time. I wrap my hand around his base and brush my lips against his tip. He shakes again, a moan escaping his lips.

He's mine, completely powerless to resist me.

I take him into my mouth and suck on his tip. Damn, it's been too long since I've been here. His skin tastes better than I imagined, and I love the feel of his firm cock against my tongue.

I slide my tongue around him, exploring every inch of it like it's the first time. His hands flee to my hair. He tugs gently as I lick him up and down.

I tighten my lips around his cock, sucking harder and harder. He shakes, his hands tugging hard at my hair. "God damn it, Alyssa," he groans. His voice is so deep and needy. Because of me. I'm making him feel this. I'm making his face contort and his body shake.

His hands are on my shoulders, then on the straps of my dress. He pushes it out of the way, freeing my breasts. He cups, them, rubbing his thumbs across my nipples.

My sex clenches with need. Damn, he would feel good inside of me.

But he feels damn good in my mouth. I suck hard, stroking him as take him deeper. He brings his hands between my legs and pulls my panties to my knees. He runs his hand against my clit, stroking me. Fuck. Waves of pleasure spread through me, pressurebuilding in my sex.

I slide my tongue over his tip. He groans, louder than before, and slides two fingers inside me.

Jesus fucking Christ. I almost drop. I have his cock in

my mouth, his fingers in my sex. He's filling me everywhere, and he's going to make me come with him.

I have to make him come, to feel him pulsing in my mouth.

So, I suck, harder and harder, until he's groaning and shaking, until he's fucking me with his fingers. My sex clenching, tensing with this unbearable pressure.

Fuck. I keep my lips tight around him, my tongue against him. He thrusts into my mouth, deeper and deeper. "Damn, Alyssa," he groans, and he plunges his fingers inside me, deeper and deeper.

I grip him tightly, pump him up and down as he thrusts. He's at the edge, almost there. He thrusts into me again, and I suck as hard as I can, keep him as deep as I can. He groans, his cock pulsing as he comes in my mouth.

I wait until he's finished, until I've caught all of him, and I swallow hard. He pushes me flat on my belly, spreading my legs apart, and he slides his fingers inside of me. Again and again, harder and harder.

The pressure builds and builds, my whole-body filling with pleasure. It's so much, almost too much. I'm sure I can't take it anymore. But he keeps going, and it keeps building. I groan, digging my nails into his thighs as an orgasm rips through me.

Luke pulls his hand back, helps me fix my dress and get back into my seat. He kisses me, deeply, possessively. "I'm going to get you back for that," he whispers. His lips are back on mine before I can reply.

Chapter Sixteen

LUKE

The first night back home without Alyssa is depressing.

The house feels so empty without her. The bed is so cold without her in it. I give up on sleep and spend my night on the couch with my collection of *Law and Order* DVDs.

But even while I watch, I wonder how she'd react to seeing New York flash over the screen if she were here.

That night passes and then I'm busy all week, unable to offer much more than "good luck tonight" or "I miss you." When I'm finally released from my mountain of work--well into Saturday evening--I call her.

"Hey you," she answers. It's loud behind her, like she's still at the theater.

"How was your show?"

"I killed it. No big deal."

She's confident for once. I'm glad. She'll never take my word for how damn good she is.

"You have time to talk?"

"Ellen invited me out, but I'd rather talk to you."

"You sure you're in the mood?"

"It's not a *we have to talk* kind of talk, is it?"

"We're engaged now."

"Really? I almost forgot." She nearly squeaks. "It has been days."

"Have you thought at all about a wedding?"

A small pause.

"Like I said. It's only been days."

Something about her voice sounds off.

"Are you okay?" I ask.

"Tired. Long night, lots of performances."

Tension knots in my back. "Ally... you do know you can talk to me about anything."

She swallows, hard. "I know."

I shift, moving the phone to a different hand. Is there an easier way to get her to open up? "There's no rush. Both my parents are dead, after all."

"That's awful."

"No, it's just how it is. But, what about your mom?"

"What about her?" Her voice drops completely void of even a hint of enthusiasm.

I could let it go, offer to talk about this when Alyssa has more energy.

But I won't. She's my fiancée now.

And I'm not going to bullshit her or handle her. I'm not going to pretend everything is okay the way I did with Samantha.

I'm going to tell her the damn truth.

"If you want to stay estranged from your mom, I won't force you to reconsider," I reassure her. "But if not, I'd love to have her at the wedding."

"That's not a good idea."

"Why not?"

She sighs.

"She loved Ryan. Every other question out of her mouth, when we were still talking, was why can't you see that Ryan boy cares for you? Why don't you give him a chance?"

That doesn't sound promising.

"You did listen to her eventually."

"She doesn't know what happened," Alyssa says flatly. "She'd hate me even more if she found out."

Hate is a strong word.

"Are you sure that she hates you?"

"Maybe not hate, but... You wouldn't understand." She says it with such resignation, like no one ever could or will understand the things she keeps locked up.

"I want to."

"I thought we were talking about the wedding."

Alright.

"Do you want to invite your mother?"

"No."

"Okay. If you don't want to invite her, we won't."

"You're not going to give me attitude later?"

"I've never given anyone attitude in my life."

She scoffs.

"Right..."

I smile to myself.

"What is it I wouldn't understand?"

"My mother. She's not a bad person. She worked hard to make sure we had a nice house and food on the table, but she's not there. She's an empty shell."

I frown, thinking of a younger, more vulnerable Alyssa.

"That must have been lonely."

"It was nothing," she says.

"It's not nothing."

"You know what it's like to grow up lonely."

"You can admit you hurt once," I murmur. "I'm not going to think less of you."

She takes a deep breath. "I'm not sure if I'm ready to start thinking about that."

"Okay."

"I'm sorry. I'm disappointing you. I'm such a mess."

"You're not."

"Don't lie. I am." She takes another deep breath.

"Okay. You're a mess, but you're my mess. Besides, I'm not so fucking neat either."

She chuckles, the sound a little choked.

"That's true."

"Watch it."

She laughs. Finally. "Thanks, Luke."

There's such a warmth to it. For a moment, I'm sure everything between us will be okay. I'm sure she'll be okay.

The muscles in my back relax. "I need to circle back to the original point. Have you thought about the wedding at all?"

"It's been like four days."

"I don't particularly want to plan something for five years. I want to be married. To you."

She laughs, again, but this time there's a nervousness to it. "You're so fucking cheesy."

"I can envision a hundred different weddings. We could do it at some fantastic hotel ballroom or in the park or even at city hall. Whatever you want."

"I haven't thought about it."

"Were you planning anything with Ryan?" I regret the words the minute I say them.

"I don't know. He was taking care of it." She sighs. "I'm sure he would have invited everyone he knows. And I'm sure it would have just been some ridiculous, lavish affair. And I am sure I would have hated it."

I can see it. I can see a massive wedding at an obscenely expensive hotel, the room adorned with so many flowers it sets a new definition for ostentatious. It would be the perfect excuse for Ryan to show off all his money. An even more perfect excuse for him to show off his fresh, new trophy wife. "Luke," she says. "You there?"

"I'm here."

Even if here is 3,000 miles away.

"I'll start thinking about the wedding." She says it with a sigh, like it's a burden.

"I don't care about the fucking wedding. I just want to marry you."

"Okay." She swallows hard. She's nervous. "Well, I'll think about it. And I'll think about the guest list. And, uh..."

"Take your time. You were right before. It's been less than a week."

"I want to figure this out so it's not hanging over my head."

Great.

"That came out wrong," she backtracks immediately. "It's just. I'm not a fan of planning parties. And this will pretty much be the most important party of my life."

"It doesn't have to be big. It can just be the two of us."

"Yeah." She takes a shallow breath. "I'll think about it."

"Are you sure you're okay?" I ask. There's something off.

"Fine. But it's getting late. I should head home before the subway gets all fucked up."

We say our goodbyes and I collapse at home.

I can't shake the feeling that something is wrong.

Was it a mistake to propose? I tried to talk about it beforehand, but she never wanted to talk...

So, I just fucking went for it.

And now I'm on the other side of the country.

Fuck.

Chapter Seventeen

ALYSSA

I t's a sunny day. Bright and warm and beautiful the way all summer days are. The sand is rough and hot beneath my feet, and I struggle to take another step. The beach. I must be on a beach. Obviously, I'm on a beach. The beige sand is right in front of my face. And it's so damn bright. The sun must be bouncing off it. The sun must be high in the sky.

God, it's bright. So bright I can barely see anything but the blue sky surrounding me. I squint and throw my hand up to shield my eyes. Something comes into focus. Someone standing a dozen or so feet away in a black tuxedo.

Fuck. This can't be... I bring my other hand to my forehead, shielding my eyes from the oppressive glare of the sun. It is. That's Luke, but there's something off about him. Something different. I can't put my finger on it.

He nods, smiling, or something like smiling. It's hard to tell from here. It's so damn bright. I press my eyes closed, but the sun is so hot on my face. Everything is this awful shade of yellow black.

Then it starts. That music. Jesus, not that music. It's the fucking wedding march. This can't be my damn wedding. Not here. Not like this. Not yet.

I have only two choices--run away or take a step forward. A step towards the rest of my damn life. I do. The heavy, satin fabric of my dress presses against my legs. I bring my gaze to it--it's such an oppressive, blinding white. It's some polyester terror, a tacky thing better suited for a 16-year-old debutante.

But the clothes don't make the woman.

I take another step. Squeeze my eyes shut. There's nothing else I can do. Nothing better to do. No other way to block it out.

"Alyssa." It's a whisper, a tiny quiet thing. Luke. It's Luke. I finally open my eyes, and he's right in front of me. But there's still something off about him, a coldness, a hardness, a strangeness.

I can't do this.

I open my mouth, but nothing comes out.

"We are gathered here today..." An officiant is standing before us. But, where the hell did he come from?

I nod. Fine. I'll play along. Get through this. I've gotten through plenty before.

The officiant smiles at me. He's in a suit but he's faceless. It's a blur. It's nothing. He's nothing. This is all nothing.

Then, something shifts about him. His voice comes into focus. "Who are we kidding? We're here because we're shocked these two finally made it down the aisle. Who did this whore think she was trying to kid before?"

That's Ryan's voice.

That's Ryan.

He glares at me, his eyes tiny orbs of hate. This is all wrong.

I step backwards, but my heel lands on the dress and I stumble. My ass hits the sand.

"Alyssa." Luke reaches for me, but I can't grab his hand. He's too far away. It's like the sand is stretching further and further away.

Everything shifts. The bright sun is gone, and darkness drifts in. It's pitch black. No moon. No stars. Nothing but the sand and the ocean.

I run, my feet pounding across the sand then landing on my dress.

Fuck. My hands hit the sand, and the shock reverberates through my body. It's okay. I'll pick myself up. I'll get out of here.

But there's a sound, and it's getting louder and louder. I close my eyes, willing it to go away, but it only gets louder. It's a wave, a huge wave. I cling to the sand in hopes of holding onto something, anything as the waves crash on my back.

The water is freezing cold and it's damn salty. I reach for the sand, but there's nothing but water. Freezing water.

I try and tread, but this dress is so heavy. It's dragging me down. I open my eyes and scan the horizon. There, I can see the land. There's a fire. A flashlight. Something. And Luke is standing there, looking at the water. Looking for me.

"Luke!" I scream, kicking as hard as I can. But the tide pulls at my legs. There's no way I'm getting out of this. There's nothing I can do.

It's over. There's no use in fighting. It's better to surrender.

I JERK UPRIGHT, GASPING AS I PUSH THE BLANKET OFF MY chest.

The curtains are wide open, and the sun is streaming through the window. Outside, it's all glass and blue sky. I'm still in New York City, in this apartment, alone.

But if it's this bright, my alarm will go off any second. Squinting to block out the light, I make my way to the phone. It's nearly eleven. Past my usual wake up time. I need to get moving. To fix coffee and breakfast, anything to shake off whatever was running through my mind.

Then it catches my eyes--a glint.

The ring.

Jesus, not again.

This isn't like before. It can't be like before. I was miserable before, miserable with Ryan. I knew I was trapped, giving up everything beyond mere survival.

But I'm barely managing survival now.

I bite my tongue. I can't think like that. This engagement is a good thing. I love Luke. I'm happy to be with him. I want to marry him.

It's not like before.

It can't be.

There's a message on my phone, a text from Luke:

"I love you. I can't wait to spend the rest of my life with you."

My mouth is dry. My knees are weak. I slink to the ground and pull my legs into my chest.

This can't be like before. It can't be anything like before.

———

THE REST OF THE DAY GOES MORE SMOOTHLY. I MOVE through my usual routine--coffee, breakfast, TV, gym, shower, work--pushing any doubts as far down as they will go.

I'm not the same stupid girl I was a year ago. I'm not about to let these nagging thoughts ruin what I have with Luke. He acts as if he's got all the patience in the world, but there's something in the way he sighs, in how dull his eyes seem when I dodge questions with a "can we talk about this later."

He's losing patience with me. I can feel it.

The theater is almost empty when I arrive. I'm early. Very early.

But almost isn't completely empty.

"Hey, Alyssa. You're early."

Nicholas.

I turn to him, pasting a smile on my face.

"Hi. Yeah, got done with an errand early."

He stops in front of me, his eyes sharp as they scan my face.

"Are you okay?"

I shove my hair off my face, nodding as I take a step back.

"Yeah, I'm fine."

His eyes go to my hand.

Shit.

He frowns, meeting my eyes again.

He doesn't offer a congratulations.

Apparently, I'm not actually that great an actress.

"I'm here to talk if you need me."

"I...thanks."

I nod, turning away and almost running from that conversation, from his sympathetic eyes.

Damn it.

I lock myself in my dressing room and bury myself in my Kindle. A breezy chick lit should get my mind off this. Should convince me that there's nothing to be worried about.

After all, I already have everything I could want. I have a career. I have a fiancé. I even have a great fucking shoe collection.

My life is perfect. It should feel perfect.

But my heart is pounding in my chest. My lungs are tight, refusing to expand to make way for air.

I will myself to relax. There's only an hour until my performance. Only one hour I have to get through until I'm someone else, somewhere else.

Until I'm anything except Alyssa.

I turn off my phone and collapse on the couch. My eyes drift closed. Someone will wake me up when they arrive. Knock on my door. Something to make sure I don't sleep through my damn performance.

My muscles start to relax. Nothing matters except for the next few hours. Get through this performance, go home, and fall apart in my room, alone.

Yes. Just a few minutes without consciousness to reset everything. A few minutes and I'll be okay.

Just... a... few... minutes.

"Alyssa!"

Fuck, not again.

I jerk upright, peeling my eyes open. It's okay. I'm at the theater. That must be the hair and makeup girl.

There's no more time for this. Alyssa Summers, insecure mess, needs to step aside to make room for Alyssa Summers, Broadway actor. Because there is absolutely no room for any of this in the next few hours.

No room for anything except Blanche fucking DuBois.

———

AFTER THE FINAL CURTAIN CALL, I RECEDE TO MY DRESSING room.

It's bathed in a soft yellow glow from the lights on the vanity. It's not like the dream. It's a yellow-white instead of a yellow-black, but it's unsettling all the same.

I take off my makeup, change into my street clothes, and fish my engagement ring out of my purse.

I'm leaving work. It's time to step back into my normal role.

I love Luke. I really do. There's no doubt in my damn mind that I love him.

But my skin is crawling, and my chest is heavy and I'm certain my next breath will do nothing to bring oxygen into my body.

This is good. This is great. No, it's amazing. It's everything I should want.

But I can't breathe.

There must be something wrong with me.

I'm not about to give in to whatever this is. I love Luke and I'm going to marry him and I'm not going to be afraid of a stupid fucking ring.

No, it's not a stupid ring. It's nice. It's gorgeous, actually, simple and elegant. It was his mom's ring. He gave me his mom's ring.

It's not the same ring he gave to Samantha. He gave her some shit from a chain store at the mall.

Luke wouldn't be caught dead at a chain jewelry store. Her ring was also gorgeous, but it wasn't this. It wasn't his mom's. No, he was saving this one.

He didn't realize it, but he was saving this one for me.

The tension in my lungs eases, just a little bit, just enough that I can suck in a full breath.

I slide the ring onto my finger. It's just a ring. No big deal. Not at all a big deal.

There's another knock on the door. Dammit. Everyone is around today.

"Come in," I call out. I check my hair and makeup-- good enough--and turn towards the door.

It's Ellen and Nicholas.

"Hey," Nicholas greets me with a smile.

Ellen gets straight to the point.

"You wanna go out tonight?"

Where do they get the energy? I'm ready to collapse on this stupid, ugly couch and they want to go out?

She shrieks. "Oh my God, Alyssa! When did you get engaged?"

Well, fuck. Her gaze is on the ring. This is what it was like last time. When I wore the ring, everyone wanted to see it or talk about it or offer their little commentary on it.

Nicholas keeps his eyes on my face, his eyes too knowing.

"Monday," I say. "My boyfriend was visiting."

"Congratulations are in order," he murmurs.

I nod.

"Thank you." It feels like what I should say. I deliberately look away.

"Damn. This calls for celebration shots," Ellen announces.

"I'm tired," I protest.

Ellen shakes her head. "So we'll only have one celebration shot." She picks up my purse and hands it to me. "Come on, let's go. I know a great bar. It's all theater people. They know better than to ask for an autograph."

She should have led with that. "Okay," I agree. A few drinks might help break up this awful tightness in my chest.

I follow her through the hallway, to the back entrance of the theater. Nicholas trails behind.

It's dark outside, but it's still warm. Even though she's wearing heels, Ellen walks fast. She has the no-nonsense, take no shit, take no prisoners New York vibe. I hate to admit it, but I'm madly jealous. One day, I'll learn not to take shit or prisoners.

"Are you always nervous after a performance?" she asks.

I bite my lip. I'm not hiding it well.

"Just tired usually," I say.

"It takes some getting used to. Coming down from that high of performing in front of a live audience. It's a rush like no other," Nicholas offers.

Ellen turns a corner, ducking into a quiet side street. "Fuck. If I was engaged, I'd be a nervous wreck. I can't imagine any scenario where that doesn't end with me stuck at home with some brat and him fucking his secretary behind my back."

"Good pep talk," Nicholas comments.

"So, you're a romantic," I say. That should be enough to convince her I'm totally doubt free.

I don't know about Nicholas.

"What I need is someone like Nicholas. Some pretentious tool with no interest in settling down. Who will happily be a theater actor forever." She says it with a grandness, like she's preforming Shakespeare.

"Thanks," Nicholas says dryly. "I'm flattered."

"You should be." She drops back to her normal voice. "Guys are drawn to my 'delightful spirit.' They love dating an artsy theater girl until they realize it means I'm busy all night, kissing other guys on stage. Then, they want to civilize me. Turn me into a good future housewife."

My chest tightens again. Luke has always been upfront about supporting my acting career, but things could change. We never talk much about the future. He must have expectations. He must...

I shake my head. That's ridiculous. He's obsessed with not getting in my way. And after how his father treated his mother... There's no way he expects to civilize me into a good future housewife.

Ellen points to an unmarked black door. She pushes it open and steps inside. I follow her, stepping into a dark dive bar.

It's quiet. A dozen people maybe and soft rock playing on the stereo. There are magenta lights, but it's otherwise plain--black floor, black booths, black stools.

Ellen waves to the bartender--a cute guy who barely looks old enough to drink. She turns back to me. "What's your poison?"

"Tequila."

"Nice." She smiles, and leans over the bar, pressing her arms together to give the bartender a great view of her cleavage. "Two shots of tequila."

"Both for you?" he asks. His gaze drifts to her chest, just for a second.

She laughs. "Very funny."

The bartender pours the shots and passes them to Ellen. She hands one to me. "To what I'm sure will be an amazing future."

I slam the shot back. Damn. What a waste of good tequila. My face burns, my head already swimming.

Ellen smiles-- that a girl-- and takes her shot. She shakes her head, slams her glass on the bar, and motions to the bartender. Two more.

Nicholas orders a beer, shaking his head at Ellen.

She turns back to me. "You think I can get him to go home with me?"

"Why go all the way home when there's a perfectly good back room available?"

Ellen smirks. "Damn, I like the way you think." She turns back, grabs the shots, and points to a booth in the corner.

We follow her to the booth, settling onto the plush black bench seat.

She looks at me with curiosity, like she's getting ready to return to the subject of my relationship status.

I'll deflect her. "You ever fuck in public?"

"Only a dozen different empty theaters, rooftops, dressing rooms. Never somewhere like this or when people were around." She sips her shot, her face puckering. "Why? You need to brag about some crazy story with your future husband?"

I laugh weakly. It's pathetic. "Nothing like that."

"Hmm. If I didn't know better, I'd say you're fishing for

me to ask about it." She leans towards me. "So, tell me, Alyssa, what is it you want to confess about this future husband of yours?"

"Nothing."

"I don't buy it. Something is up."

"He's there. I'm here. It's hard." I take a long sip of my tequila. It's crisp, clean. The kind of thing I'd drink with Luke.

"Is that it?"

I nod. "Totally. That's totally it. I love him. He loves me. We're going to be very happy." Jesus, even I don't believe me. But that is the truth. I do love him. He does love me. There's no reason why we wouldn't be happy.

"That sounds awful." Ellen laughs and slams her shot back. "Sorry. That was super rude. I'm sure he, uh, like Star Wars... Luke, right?"

"Like Star Wars."

"Is Luke like Star Wars great? The kind of guy you can see yourself waking up with every day for the rest of your life? Not that I could ever envision anything like that."

"I think you've interrogated her enough on this subject," Nicholas interjects, watching me.

Luke is great. And I can see myself waking up next to him, wrapping my arms around him to try and keep him in the bed. He won't leave me home, all by myself, while he's fucking his secretary.

"Earth to Alyssa..."

"He's great. He's really great. And he's hot as all hell too."

"That counts for a lot." Ellen laughs. "I'll go get some more shots for us." She says, getting up.

Leaving me alone with Nicholas.

"You should talk to Luke if you're feeling this conflicted," he says when Ellen's out of ear shot.

"I'm not conflicted."

"And I'm not an idiot." I look over at him. "I've never seen you look more anxious, more worried. Not even your first night on stage."

I look down at the table.

I don't like knowing he can see that.

"I... there's just a lot happening in my life right now. I'll be fine."

Luckily, Ellen arrives with fresh shots right then.

"Down the hatch!"

I slam another one.

We'll need more of these. A lot more.

Enough to drown the thoughts that keep trying to surface.

Chapter Eighteen

LUKE

"I'm scared."

It's two little words. Two tiny words.

Even if the initial shock is a kick to the throat, they're a good sign.

Alyssa is talking to me.

It's something.

I check the time. Just after seven.

She sent this hours ago, around one a.m. here. It's too early to call her. Too early for work.

There's only one thing that will help me deal until I can talk to her.

Running until my legs are numb.

I change into my shorts and slather on sunscreen. It smells like her when she's at the pool or the beach. She's always on my case about wearing fucking sunscreen.

It's warm outside. The early morning light casts a white glow over everything. There's a softness to it, a certain lack of vibrancy.

She's trying to talk to me. It's not exactly a love poem, but it's something.

———

I stay busy at work.

There is so much piling up. I have too many clients, and several of them are difficult.

Mrs. Waters has been in the throes of her divorce for almost a year. She rejects every one of her husband's very reasonable settlement offers, insisting she deserves more.

I have a conference or a meeting or a court date with Mrs. Waters every week for the next two months. But if I can convince her to settle, I have a free week at the end of next month.

I want that fucking week so I'll finally be able to visit Alyssa.

It's not the safest play. Mrs. Waters is keen to hold on until the end. She's either getting what she wants from her husband or she's getting her ass handed to her in court. In fact, she had some choice words last time I tried to talk her into accepting her husband's offer.

But I'll just have to convince her this is the best offer she's going to get.

It *is* the best offer she's going to get.

I look at flights. It's a popular week to go to New York, dangerously close to the end of fall, the last chance for anyone to see leaves changing colors.

Fuck it.

I have to be in New York with Alyssa. Mrs. Waters is going to have to come around. It's in her best interests.

I'll have to dial up the charm.

I book a flight to New York and a trip for the two of us to Hawaii as soon as her play wraps. I email the details to Alyssa.

She replies back with a smiley face and a promise to wear her skimpiest bikini.

If all goes well, she won't spend a lot of time dressed even that much.

Or little.

I make preparations for the week.

I want it to be perfect. Dinner at the finest restaurants, moonlight walks, trysts by a fireplace.

This is my best chance to erase all of Alyssa's doubts. I'm going to make the most of it.

It's late when I finish. So late Alyssa must be done for the night. It may not seem like much, but "I'm scared" is practically a soul bearing confession for her.

I put my phone on speaker so I can undress while I call her. I have a change of clothes somewhere around here.

"Hey," she answers. Her voice is sweet but tired.

"Hey yourself." I remove my tie and undo the rest of the buttons of my shirt.

"I, um... I'm sorry I sent such a lame freaking text. I probably should have offered a little more."

"It was unsettling. But I'm glad you're talking to me about it."

"I just got off the subway. Can I call you back when I'm in the apartment?"

"Sure," I agree. "But, I am in the middle of taking off my clothes."

"Oh." I grin as her voice perks up. "You're still at work?"

"Unfortunately."

"You've been working late a lot."

"I won't make it a habit."

She takes a deep breath, exhaling slowly. "So, what are you still wearing?"

"My boxers."

If she were here, she'd be staring at me with raw desire.

And I could press her against the wall and rip off her clothes.

Fuck. This distance is killing me.

She takes a nervous breath. "I'll call you back in five minutes. Don't even consider starting without me."

"Starting what?"

"Mr. Lawrence, I know you aren't that naive."

Alyssa is finally trying to talk to me. I shouldn't ruin that with sex, but my body is not cooperating.

I can see her in that apartment, slipping her dress off her shoulders, sliding her fingers over her curvy thighs. I can see her eyes pressing closed, her teeth sinking into her lips, her back arching. She's moaning, squirming on the bed, digging her toes into the sheets.

I tighten my fists. No. Not yet. I won't let my body get the best of me, no matter how damn good it would feel to come with her.

It's not happening until we finish this conversation.

My phone rings.

I pick up, about to say hey, when she speaks. "Are you alone?"

I could lie, tell her my assistant is here, that I'm not ready yet. But my body won't allow such a thing. It needs some possibility of this ending with her moaning in my ear.

"Yes."

She takes a shallow breath. "And you're... God, this is still weird."

"Ally, maybe we should talk first."

It pops out almost without thought.

A startled pause at the other end.

"Okay."

"You're scared," I start.

"I—yes."

My heart sinks. But I need to hear what's in her head.

She takes another deep breath. "This is so much harder when you're not here."

"Pretend I am."

"It's not the same. It never is."

She's right. It's not the same. "Go to the bedroom and wrap your arms around a pillow like you're hugging me."

"That's ridiculous."

"Less ridiculous than what you'll be doing later."

A tiny sigh escapes her lips. Damn. I bet she's flushed and nervous, that adorable blush across her cheeks.

"Don't give me ideas," she warns. There are some noises from the phone, movement or something. Maybe she's actually hugging that pillow. "Alright—here it goes," she mutters. "You get so excited about these things. About an engagement and a wedding. It feels like I'd crush you if I told you things aren't perfect."

"I need to know how you feel, Ally. Keeping it to your-self isn't doing me any favors."

"Okay." She lets out a tiny sigh. "The thing is... I'm not sure if I'm ready."

My muscles tighten.

She's not sure if she's ready.

Part of me was hoping a proposal would help her move forward with me, help her envision a future for us.

Surprise fucking surprise—it didn't.

Hell, I should have expected this.

But that does nothing to make me hate it less, and it certainly doesn't help the tension building in my neck.

"Okay," I say carefully.

She makes an impatient noise.

"Luke, I know it's not okay."

"If this is too fast for you, I'll slow down. We don't have to set a date. We don't have to plan anything. You'll be ready eventually."

There's a long moment of silence. "What if I'm not?"

Fuck.

"How did you feel when I proposed? Right in that moment?"

"Excited."

There's a hint of fear in her voice. She's still trying not to disappoint me.

"You've got to stop this, Ally. Stop being afraid of hurting me. Sure, I don't like that you're terrified. But I want to know, so we can work through it together."

"It's not that easy." Her tone is sharp, now. Annoyed.

"You're right. It's not easy. But we can't just avoid it because it's hard."

She sighs.

The silence goes on for long enough that I start to wonder if she'll stop there.

"I'm terrified," she finally admits. "Terrified I'll disappear again. Because, once again, I'm not doing all that well without you."

I start to protest--she's living by herself while working in an incredibly demanding field--but that's exactly the type of thing that makes her recoil.

"Why do you feel like that?" I ask instead.

"It's getting harder for me to hold onto everything. I'm tempted to drown out my thoughts any way I know how."

"What kinds of thoughts?"

She exhales into the phone. "Thoughts that I'll fail, ruin what we have, nosedive in my career. Something awful. Or that you..."

"You can tell me."

"Okay." She sucks the air back into her lungs. "That

you'll keep wanting more from me... and I'll keep failing to deliver."

My stomach clenches. It's a fair assessment. However much she gives me, I want more, and I'm not shy about making my feelings known.

She takes another breath. "Or worse. That you'll change. You'll get tired of supporting my career, and start encouraging me to stay home, to not take gigs, to close myself off from the world again. And I'll do it, because it's easy and familiar. You'll start to work all the time, until it's the only thing you care about. And our weekends together will become you at the office and me on the couch, hugging my Kindle, wondering how we fucked things up this badly."

Shit. Our combined baggage is complimentary in the worst way.

"I'm afraid of the same things," I admit.

"We're far apart. We're both working too much. But those are just excuses..." She trails off, her voice getting lower and lower.

We're quiet for a moment, nothing in the room except the sound of our breaths.

I think this through, not dismissing what she said but working through it.

"How about I promise to try and keep you on level ground and you promise to try and keep me from turning into my father?" I offer.

"I... okay," she murmurs, some life returning to her voice.

"I'm taking a week off at the end of next month. I'm going to spend it in New York with you."

"But I'll be working the whole time," she protests.

"What is that--three hours a day?"

She laughs, the release of tension so damn necessary.

"Shut up. Asshole."

"Is it more like four hours?"

"I got the point." She laughs, again, the anxiety melting from her voice. "I will be free most of the morning and day to hang out with you."

My muscles relax as I exhale. This is going to be okay.

"I'll stay out of your hair when you're working," I promise. "But, when you're not, you're mine. I'm going to make your days so fucking great you won't be able to stand it."

"What kind of things will you do?" Her voice is soft.

Sultry.

My body wakes up again. I never did make it all the way out of my clothes. "Maybe I can give you a preview."

"Do you, um." She lets out a nervous laugh. "Do you want to try Skype again?"

Chapter Nineteen

ALYSSA

"That could be arranged."

Luke's voice is playful, but there's a heaviness to it. Exhaustion maybe. He's not great at hiding his impatience over my inability to feel ready, whatever that means.

There's not a good way to phrase it, to say, don't fucking do this just because you think it's the only thing I want from you. There's not a good way to tell your boyfriend, fiancé actually, that you suspect he is only giving into your requests for sex to placate you.

I rub at my eyes. I hate being in my head at a time like this, when the only thing coursing through my brain should be how much I want to get Luke's clothes off.

Sure, he's not really here. The best I can hope for is his voice in my ears and his body on my computer monitor.

"Ally?"

"Sorry. I was just thinking..." About how fucking crushed I'll be if we don't last.

Fuck. A tear rolls down my cheek. It stings, salty and hot. I can't cry. Not now. Not after we had one of those *I can be patient, I love you, I don't mind putting up with all your bull-shit* conversations.

"I'm sure asking if you want to talk will only make things worse." There's no annoyance in his voice.

It's still playful. He's joking now.

"Maybe I should go," I say.

"Maybe you should humor me and tell me what you were 'just thinking.'"

I press the phone against my ear, sliding my fingers over its glass back. "You won't like it."

"You aren't the expert on everything I like. There are plenty of things I like that you know nothing about."

Another tear rolls down my cheek. I try and blink it away, but it only makes everything around me blurry, like some kind of Instagram filter from hell.

Damn it. Not now.

"Ally."

"It's nothing." I wipe tears from my cheeks, wiping my hand against the sheets to dry it.

"Talk to me."

"I can't."

He sighs, low and heavy. "You were talking a few minutes ago."

"I'm going to go." I slide my fingers over the edges of the phone. It's so slick and smooth. It repels anything that tries to stick to the surface.

"And cry in your room by yourself?"

"I'll be fine."

He sighs, again. "Don't do this. Don't shut me out."

"I'm not doing anything. I'm fine. Tired, but fine."

"You're crying."

"I'm well aware of that." I blink back another tear, breathing deep to calm my stupid fucking diaphragm.

Tears, I can hide. But I can't do anything about these stupid sobs.

There's a long moment of silence. He takes a deep breath and exhales slowly.

"We were talking," he says.

There's no fight in his voice. He's losing patience and I can't blame him.

The quiet surrounds me. There's nothing outside--no horns, no pedestrians, no wind.

"Ally..." It's soft, like he's stroking my hair, like he's whispering in my ear.

I move to the window and press my palms against it. The glass is cold and sleek, but I almost believe I'm touching the night outside.

I almost believe I'm not in a prison of my own design.

"Don't give up on me," I say. It's so weak, so quiet. A pathetic plea when it should be a demand.

"I don't want to." But there's a hesitation to it.

It's not I won't. It's I don't want to.

So he might. He knows he might.

"But," he continues. "I'm not going to be able to do this if you keep locking me out."

He's asking for something I can't deliver. This won't end well. It will end in flames and tears.

But not yet. Not now. I have to push this aside, some-where where it won't eat at me again. I was doing okay with talking before. I can do it again.

"I understand," I respond quietly. "But I really am tired."

He doesn't want the truth. He'll freak out. It's better to keep this to myself, so at least he'll be around.

"Ally."

"I'll talk to you later, okay?"

He hesitates. "I don't want to give up on you."

But, if I keep this up, he will.

"Goodnight." I hang up the phone before he has the chance to reply. Before he has the chance to confirm my suspicions that he can't put up with me much longer.

———

A DAY PASSES WITHOUT ANY WORD FROM LUKE.

We don't text or call or email. I sleep in late and spend forever on the couch nursing yet another cup of coffee. I skip my usual oatmeal. As far as I can tell, everyone is against me eating it anyway. I may as well eat nothing.

When I get a similar urge to skip lunch, I call Angela.

I'm not letting myself backslide. Not after I worked so hard on my recovery.

Not even if things aren't going well with Luke.

"Hi Alyssa," she greets me. "How are things going?"

"Not great," I admit, taking a deep breath.

The conversation isn't long, but it grounds me.

I eat my skipped bowl of oatmeal for lunch.

But that doesn't mean everything is fixed.

My Kindle becomes my enemy instead of my best friend. The once-comfortable breezy chick lit mocks me. I can only read *War and Peace* for so long before I'm convinced life is a bleak shit hole, and I can't stomach these sassy quests for satisfaction.

Eventually, I go to the gym, shower, and take a silent subway ride to the theater. The only break from my numbness is performing on stage. It's the only place where I can feel things without imploding.

Nicholas invites me out for a drink.

He asks about Luke and I try to distract him by changing the subject.

It doesn't work.

"Look, you're definitely off," he says bluntly. "And it doesn't take a genius to figure out it probably has something to do with Luke."

I sigh, looking down at the shiny surface of the bar.

I would never talk to him about Luke under normal conditions. I like my privacy and I really don't like feeling vulnerable.

But I am vulnerable right now. And I feel like everything is just bubbling up inside me. Maybe it would be good to talk about it.

"I... I don't know if I'm ready to be married," I admit, still not looking at him.

"Okay," he says slowly. "Not ready because of Luke? Or because of the timing? Or something else?"

"I... I don't know," I admit. "I love Luke. And I want to be with him. But he's moving so fast and... " And there's so much wrong with me, so much he has to put up with.

And I feel... trapped. Though even that doesn't fully encompass the weird combination of emotions fighting inside me.

I look up when Nicholas's hand covers the back of my own.

He gives me a sympathetic look.

"I know there's probably stuff going on that I don't know about. But... Alyssa, you don't have to be in a relationship at all if you don't want to be. Trust me—there are plenty of guys out there who'd be perfectly content with something a lot less... formal than marriage."

I break eye contact, feeling a little uncomfortable at the intimacy of the moment.

I pull my hand away.

"Thanks for listening," I say into my drink. "I just don't want to think about it right now."

"Okay."

The pause that follows is a little awkward, but we slowly shift the conversation to more shallow topics.

I am careful not to overindulge. Two or three drinks max. But it's enough to unlock all the thoughts I'm trying to drown.

Luke isn't here, and it's not just the distance. It's so much more than that.

It's not like him to go cold.

He must be hurt. Of course he's hurt. Most people would be running for the hills in this situation. I should jump for joy that he's only hurt.

The weekend comes and goes, and I start to hear a few peeps from Luke. A "hey" here or an "I miss you" there. We keep things light and easy, no mentions of trust or communication or, God forbid, whether or not I'm eating.

We talk on the phone, but it's about nothing. About TV or work or the weather.

He's holding back. It's not like I blame him. He's entitled to space if needs to lick his wounds.

But he won't admit he's upset. He won't admit I'm disappointing him.

One week turns into two. Then three. Then four.

I struggle with eating, but I use all the techniques I've learned to cope. I call Angela, talk to my therapist.

I keep it together.

I know how devastated Luke would be if he found out I wasn't eating. But that's not why I do it.

I do it for me.

I don't want to let myself down again.

Then, as if all that's happening isn't enough, Luke emails me that he's delaying his trip.

Hey Ally,

I'm so sorry, but I have to move this trip. Remember me talking about Mrs. Waters? Well, she won't be talked into settling (even though a judge is only going to give her half the alimony her husband is offering. I swear. She's ridiculous). And, ethical obligation, all that bullshit. I can't pawn her off on someone else when it's just me here.

I'm taking most of a month off at the end of your run. I'll spend two weeks with you in New York. Then, we can go wherever you want. Somewhere warm and gorgeous where there's a ton to see (but we'll stay in the hotel room anyway).

I love you, Ally. I'm so sorry about this. I promise it has nothing to do with us. It's just work butting into my life the way it tends to.

I can't wait to see you. It will be here before you know it.

Love,

Luke

A FUCKING EMAIL. HE TELLS ME THIS IN A FUCKING EMAIL. Yes, the email is time-stamped at a very unreasonably late hour. And, sure, I would have hated it if he'd called me at six A.M. (what the hell was he doing up at three?), but it's not like he found out about his client's bullshit sometime after midnight.

He could have called.

Sure, he promises it has nothing to do with me. But he's always promising something.

It's not that far away. It's only an extra month. Only one more month of everything falling apart.

And then it will just be us again, back together again, with absolutely no excuse for why things aren't working the way they should.

With no excuse for why I'm not gung-ho about planning some damn wedding.

He tries harder, calling me after my performance to wish me good night, offering to come for a day and a half. Talking to me, offering more of himself.

But I don't want him to rush here and back—I know how much work he has to do.

I offer to fly in for a day, but he says the same to me. That it'll be too much for me and I should conserve my energy.

Which leaves us right where we already are.

On opposite coasts.

It's no good.

But there's no help for it.

Chapter Twenty

LUKE

Time passes quickly. I'm busy. Alyssa is busy. We barely have room for our usual phone calls.

There's a nagging voice in my mind. Telling me I didn't try hard enough to convince Mrs. Waters, that I could have convinced her to settle if I'd cared more, that, deep down, I wanted to cancel the trip.

But that's ridiculous.

I spend the flight to New York thinking about how I'm going to make this up to her.

THERE'S A PLEASANTNESS TO THE COLDNESS OF NEW YORK City in the fall. It seeps in from the gray streets, to the front of every building.

Everywhere I go is either freezing from the cold outside or sweltering from a heater. There's no just right, no place where it's comfortable to sit without a coat.

I reach the theater early, not wanting to risk missing the show.

My phone buzzes with an incoming message almost immediately.

It's Alyssa.

Smiling, I open it up.

Luke—Mom just texted me she's coming to the show. I can't deal with her right now—I need my head in the game!

Her mother?

Oh no.

Shit. Why the hell would she just show up like this, surprise her daughter while she's working, while she needs to concentrate.

I type back a quick message.

Don't worry. I'll take care of this. Is she already here?

She writes back immediately.

Thank you!!! I doubt she'd be this early. But let me send you a picture so you'll recognize her.

She sends me some hearts followed by a picture of a middle-aged woman.

I memorize it, looking around to make sure she really isn't here yet.

I don't see her.

I PACE AROUND THE THEATER'S LOBBY WITH MY HANDS IN my pockets. I'm sure I look crazed. A man in a suit pacing around like he's waiting for an execution. But I have to do something to keep my anger in check.

I check the clock. She's late. It's not like I expected Alyssa's mother to show up early, but she can't show up late. She won't be let into the play.

Alyssa has never had any particularly kind words about her mother, but I can't believe that her mother would care so little about the play. The least she could do is get here on time if she does indeed want to see Alyssa in her element.

It's twenty minutes until curtain when Barbara arrives.

She pushes the door open with a weak grip. She looks like her picture. Mid 40s, short, with her ash brown hair pulled into a loose bun.

There's a weariness about her. Like she's not fully here almost.

Alyssa has never been shy about pointing out her mother's near alcoholism.

But I'd hope she'd show up sober for this.

She spots me, a hint of recognition on her face. Alyssa must have sent her a picture of me too.

I wave her over and she nods like she finally gets it.

We shake. Her grip is weak. Her attention is somewhere else.

I force a smile. "I'm Luke, Ms. Summers. It's nice to meet you."

She nods. "It's nice to meet you." She looks me over, just a glance, the kind I'd expect from a mother assessing her daughter's boyfriend for potential.

"Have you heard much about Alyssa's play?"

She shakes her head. "I've never been one for theater." Her gaze turns towards the bar.

"Haven't seen anything since Alyssa was in high school?"

She offers a weak smile. I'll take that as a no. So she couldn't be bothered to care much about Alyssa then either.

Still, I smile. "She's great in it. You're lucky. Your daughter is very talented."

She nods and her eyes turn back to the bar. There's a need to her expression, like she'd kill for a drink.

She seems sober enough. But who knows?

"Would you care for a drink?"

Should I agree?

Then again, I'm not her keeper. I can't stop her from doing what she wants to.

I motion to the bar. "After you."

Her eyes light up, but she tries to play it off. "Just to pass the time."

Of course.

I offer to help her out of her coat, but she shakes her head. We move to the bar, making small talk about the weather while we wait. She's trying to have a conversation. That counts for something.

Barbara orders a glass of white wine. She watches the bartender pour like she's watching a work of art. Her tongue slides over her lips. Her pupils dilate.

"How was the trip?" I ask.

Her eyes stay on the wine. "It was a long drive, but it was nice."

The bartender hands over our drinks and I pay. I consider warning Barbara that we can't bring our drinks into the theater, but I doubt she's going to have a drop left in her glass come curtain.

Barbara downs half her glass in one sip. She offers another smile, weaker than the last one. "I didn't know Alyssa was seeing someone."

"You two are in touch?"

She shakes her head. "No. It's been a while."

I bite my tongue. "How long has it been?"

She shrugs. "She's a very independent girl."

There isn't a hint of sadness or regret in her voice. She can barely bring herself to care that she isn't in touch with her only daughter.

But she's here. That has to count for something.

"I'm sure she made efforts," I venture.

"A few years after she moved to L.A., but we got into a fight and she made it clear she didn't want to speak to me anymore."

Yet she's here now.

"What happened?"

Barbara finishes her glass. "That's a family matter. Excuse me." She moves to the bar, waits in line, and orders another glass of wine.

It's ten minutes to curtain now, but I'm still certain she'll finish in time.

When Barbara returns, I offer her my most charming smile. She and Alyssa may not have the greatest relationship, but she must want to reconnect.

"Alyssa told me that you work in real estate."

"Yes."

This is going to be more difficult than I hoped. "I'd love to hear about it."

There's a tiny hint of life on her face. It may just be the second glass of wine, but I'm trying to stay optimistic.

We slip into a conversation about her job. She works as an office manager for a real estate company. Long hours, lots of weekends, but it pays well enough.

The P.A. system turns on and a voice directs us to take our seats. I lead Barbara inside. We have a spot in the fourth row—Alyssa must have arranged it. But this is not of much interest to Barbara.

She sits and plays a game on her phone. Conversation over.

I take a deep breath, but my clenched muscles refuse to relax.

The theater starts to fill, and Barbara reluctantly puts away her phone. I rack my brain for something to encourage her. She did want to come. She must be proud of Alyssa. There must be something there.

"Your daughter really is amazing," I try.

She shrugs.

Fine, she's shrugging now, but she's not going to manage to keep that up. No one could watch Alyssa perform and come away from it apathetic.

The lights go down, and the play begins. Stanley joins his friend Mitch and calls up to the apartment above.

Barbara is already in another world, leaning back in her chair, staring at her fingernails like they are the most fascinating thing she's ever seen.

It doesn't get any better.

The whole damn play, Barbara can't even muster the energy to fake interest. Even when Alyssa is on stage. Even in the last scene, where Alyssa's character is carted off to a mental institution.

Even during the final bow.

The lights go on and I look to Barbara for some kind of reaction.

There's nothing on her face. Not excitement or pride or even a hint of happiness.

Nothing.

I pull out my phone and text Alyssa. "You were great. Meet me at the restaurant across the street in twenty minutes? I know you need to get dressed."

I lead Barbara toward the lounge. She looks at the closed bar longingly.

I'm tempted to spill that we're going someplace with alcohol, but I keep it to myself.

———

THE DOOR SWINGS OPEN AND ALYSSA STEPS INTO THE restaurant.

She scans the restaurant. Her eyes meet mine. For that

split second, my tense back relaxes and the weight on my chest lifts. She still loves me. She still wants this.

Then, her gaze moves over, towards her mother, and the short burst of excitement drops off her face.

"Mom."

Barbara stands to greet Alyssa. They stare at each other for a moment. Finally, Alyssa offers her hand and they shake.

Alyssa turns to me, her face tense.

I don't say anything, just pull her into a tight hug.

She squeezes me, lingering for a moment before pulling back.

She takes a seat next to me, pressing her legs against mine. Our eyes connect again, but I can't place her expression.

I turn back to Barbara. "Wasn't Alyssa wonderful?"

"Oh, yes." Barbara nods and sips her drink.

This is her fourth glass of wine.

"How was your trip, Mom?" Alyssa asks. She turns her gaze to her menu, somehow lost in the description of a salad entree.

"Fine," Barbara responds.

"And you enjoyed the play?"

"You know I'm not a theater person, Alyssa."

Then why the hell did she even come?

"We don't need to have this conversation," Alyssa mutters. She buries her head further in her menu. Presses her fingertips flat against the pages.

There's a long silence. Apparently, these two have absolutely nothing to say to each other.

It's broken by a grinning server. "Oh my God, you're Alyssa Summers, aren't you?"

Alyssa looks up from the menu, clearly exhausted. "Yeah."

"I love your show. It's so funny. My roommate and I watch it together every week!"

That gets Alyssa to smile. It's a real smile, and it brightens the whole damn room. "Thank you. That's very kind of you to say."

The server squeals, clearly beside herself with excitement. "Sorry. I shouldn't ask for an autograph."

Alyssa laughs. Under the table, she squeezes my hand. Her fingers are so soft and warm.

"I'll see what I can do," Alyssa says. "But, until then, how about tequila on the rocks? A double. And a wedge of lime if it's not too much trouble."

"No, not at all." She almost jumps up and down as she looks at me. She clearly wants to say something, but she doesn't. "Are you guys ready to order your food as well?"

"Mom? Do you want to go first?"

The server nearly drops her notepad, but she manages to keep it together long enough to write down all our orders and collect our menus. More drinks all around, especially for Mom.

Alyssa turns to me, squeezing my hand tighter. "You think she'll freak if I offer to leave tickets and a signed playbill at will call?"

"She might faint."

Alyssa smiles. "I'm going to say she's barely eighteen. God damn, I would have been just as excited to see... whoever the me equivalent was."

Barbara clears her throat. "I hope that young lady is in school."

Alyssa doesn't reply. I guess she knows better.

"She has a long time to figure out what she wants," I say. I run my fingers over Alyssa's hand to feel for her engagement ring. It's there. More of that weight lifts off my chest. Everything will be okay.

"Well, I hope she's using contraception."

"Mom!"

"She's not going to figure out what she wants if she gets knocked up."

Alyssa turns her attention to her napkin.

"You should warn her," I urge. "In case she doesn't realize the dangers of unprotected sex."

Alyssa stifles a laugh and squeezes my hand tighter.

The silence lasts until our server returns with drinks. Thank God. They could not be here soon enough.

I raise my drink to offer a toast. "To reunions."

They repeat it weakly and we take long sips of our respective drinks. I wink at Alyssa as I slip my lips around the straw.

She shakes her head. Apparently, my charm isn't working.

I lean towards her, much closer than is socially acceptable in a nice place like this. And I press my lips against hers, soaking in the taste of her lips, her Chapstick, her tequila.

"I missed you," I whisper so softly that only she can hear it.

She nods, a look in her eyes that says she missed me too. "I'm sorry she's here." It's a whisper, even softer than mine.

"It's not your fault. Maybe a little time alone will help."

I squeeze her hand before I get up.

She turns to her mother, her lips pressed into a thin line.

The bathroom is around a nearby corner and down a long hallway. Damn wine went straight through me. I check my phone. Sometimes, in these kinds of circumstance, Alyssa will send a stealth text. "Get me the hell out of here" or "I'm faking an emergency in twenty minutes."

Today, there's nothing. I roll my shoulders back. Maybe it's a good thing.

I'm in the hallway, about to round the corner, when I hear Alyssa.

"Mom, you're being ridiculous."

"What did you think that boy was after? He was so sweet to you--always driving you home, taking you to dances. Didn't he buy your dresses?"

"Because his family has money and ours doesn't."

"You knew he was in love with you," Barbara insists.

"If he was in love with me, he would have said so. Ryan was never shy like that."

"He's good looking. Don't you think?"

"He had his chance," Alyssa counters. "I'd rather not rehash this. It's already on TMZ."

"You're not a rock, sweetie. You need a rock. Someone dependable. Like Ryan."

Alyssa groans. "I'm with Luke. And you have no right to tell me how to live my life. Not when you haven't spoken to me in three years."

"Was it a sexual problem?"

"Mom! No. He was fine, but he was only fine."

"You know, your father was great in bed. Best sex of my life. Do you see where that got me?"

"Yes, if only you'd never decided to have a child. Maybe he'd still be around, and you wouldn't have to deal with me."

Well, fuck.

I double time it back.

Alyssa needs reinforcements.

Chapter Twenty-One

ALYSSA

L uke steps around the corner, a pleasant expression on his face.

Fuck. If he heard that...

I dig my nails into my wrist. It's fine.

Deep breath. It's not that bad. Boyfriends meet mothers, even estranged, clueless mothers who are trapped in the past.

It's not like Luke isn't aware Ryan is the only person who ever cared about me. Before him at least.

Mom stops her bullshit suggestions and returns to her wine, drinking it like it's my supposedly so great at sex father. That's not a detail I need.

She looks Luke over like he's a bad boy from the wrong side of the tracks, a greaser with a motorcycle and a leather jacket. It would be hilarious if it wasn't so ridiculous. Luke is a lawyer.

He's even wearing a suit, his tattoos completely covered. His hair is neat. I'm sure he's been polite and charming. He always is.

Mom shakes her head. She disapproves.

Acid churns in my stomach. I shouldn't care if she disapproves. She's been out of my life forever now, and I have no intention of bringing her back into it.

Luke offers his hand and I take it. It's such a little thing, but it's so much, too much all at once. I'm glad I'm sitting, because there's no way I could stand.

I miss him, I love him, I'm irritated with him.

Mostly, I just want to drag him to the bathroom, rip off his clothes, and lick every inch of his perfect body until he's screaming so loudly the whole damn restaurant can hear it.

It's been so long since he's been next to me—three months now—and we haven't had a hint of foreplay since my last meltdown. No pictures, no Skype, not even a few dirty texts.

"Mom wants to know how you met Ryan," I throw out. That ought to keep them busy for a while. Hopefully long enough that I can polish off my double.

Luke smirks. So, he heard some of that conversation.

But he plays along. "It's not a very interesting story. He wanted to form a law firm. I was the only other family practice lawyer he knew. The only competent one at least. So, magic happened."

Mom snickers.

She's had more than these two drinks. It figures. I never blamed her when I was a kid--she worked hard and worked late and hey, there was always food in the fridge--but enough is enough.

"I'm sure you're more interested in how I ended up with Alyssa."

"It's none of my business," she says primly.

At least she's trying to be polite. It must be the second glass of wine. When she's sober, she's mean. Or she was.

It has been forever since we've spoken.

Luke squeezes my hand as he flashes my mother a million-dollar smile. "It's not complicated. You see, your daughter is irresistible."

"She gets the point." I don't need him going over the lurid detail of our first few encounters.

Mom may be glad to tell me that my father was great in bed, but I don't particularly want to tell her that my fiancé is a fucking sex God. Even if it's the only thing that would derail this conversation long enough for me to slip out the back entrance.

"Ryan cared for you." She's so fucking stubborn.

"Ryan is a fucking asshole."

She gasps, deliberately exaggerating the gesture.

"How can you say that, Alyssa? He was always so sweet to you!"

"When we were both teenagers," I point out, beyond exasperated. The acid churns in my throat. Fucking recovered bulimia acid reflux bullshit. "And sometimes even when he was in law school. But he wasn't like that later. Not after my..." I bite my tongue. I've never told her about my eating disorder, and I'm not about to start now. "Not after he started working. It was all about him, his career, what he wanted."

Mom shakes her head like there's no way this could be true. "He would have taken care of you."

"Yeah, well, I don't need that kind of taking care of."

"Do you really think you can be an actress forever?"

I bite my tongue to keep from screaming. This isn't surprising. She's been checked out for a long time.

"Yes, well. Luke has a lot more money than Ryan does."

That shuts her up. I look over at Luke.

He grins, that shark grin I'm sure he wears while winning in court.

He's clearly not worried whether or not Mom likes him.

"A lot more," I add. "Probably ten times as much."

I look at Luke to confirm my hypothesis. I've seen his bank statement before, but we never really talk numbers.

He shrugs…

"Ryan thinks he's a good businessman. But he doesn't know shit about investing."

I turn towards my mother. She's just sitting there, barely taking all this in.

Hell, if I'm in, I might as well go all in.

"Since you're so comfortable telling me about my absent father's sexual prowess, I may as well return the favor," I say. "Luke is much better than Ryan was."

My mother shakes her head. She's already made herself clear--sex is really no motivation for a relationship in her eyes.

She's already convinced I should still be with Ryan. Nothing will change her mind, but…

I turn towards her. "Ryan wasn't exactly… giving. Luke, on the other hand…"

"I aim to please," Luke murmurs with a smirk.

I fold my arms. I'm done doing what other people want.

"And he's bigger too," I say.

It barely registers with my mother, but Luke laughs his ass off. God, I'm not going to live that one down.

"You've made your point." Mom taps the table. Her only move after she's finished her drink.

I suck the last drop of tequila from my drink then move on to Luke's. It's sweet and salty and it tastes like his lips.

"If you want to talk about something besides what a mess my life is, we can continue this conversation. Otherwise-" I fish my wallet out of my purse and take out three, hundred-dollar bills. "Here's cab fare back to Massachusetts."

I throw the money in her face. She frowns. "You're making a scene."

"That's my money, you know. Money, I earned from acting. And, guess what--my fucking show is coming back for another season, and I'll make even more money. More than Ryan does even."

She just shakes her head. There's no reason to bother. She's not here, not really. She doesn't have it in her to understand me.

I push myself out of my seat.

I step back, and suck in a deep breath. My heart is pounding against my chest.

Luke stands up and wraps his arm around my waist. It's possessive, a clear indication that we're together. "Are you sure you want to go?" he asks quietly.

I nod. "I'll pay the check first. With the money I earned acting."

I glare at my mother again, but she's too fucking drunk to even care.

"Did you even watch the play?" I ask.

She shrugs like it's nothing.

"I don't know why you even came."

I shake my head, hurt and mad that she still has the power to wound me.

Our server is in the corner, watching with her jaw hanging open. I move towards her and hand her two more hundred-dollar bills.

"Keep the change."

"But, Miss Summers. That's so generous."

I turn to leave but stop. "Wait. What's your name?"

"Daria Sanders."

"What's your night off?"

"Tuesday."

"I'll leave tickets for you at will call for next Tuesday. Don't miss it, okay? We're going into our last week."

She gasps, her hand going to her mouth. "That's so— thank you! Should I write my name down?"

"Okay." I nod, and lean in towards her. "Could you just keep this all to yourself?"

"Of course!" Her eyes go to my engagement ring and she gasps again. "Is he really as good as you were saying?"

I can hear people go quiet around us.

So the whole restaurant heard that.

"Yes," I say, loudly enough that he'll hear. "He can be an idiot, but he's fucking amazing in bed." I lean in closer. "Or in the shower or the car or the park or a movie theater."

I'm pretty sure she's about to faint, but she manages to hold steady as she hands me a slip of paper with her name, number, email, and--that must be a Twitter handle.

"Can you make sure my mom gets into a cab?"

She nods. "Of course. And, I have to say--you handled that very well. I would not have stood up to the pressure if it was my mom."

I smile.

"Thanks. I'll see you next week." I turn to leave.

Luke offers his hand and I hold on for dear life as we walk out of the dinner from hell.

At least it's over.

I STEW ON THE RIDE BACK TO THE APARTMENT.

For once, Luke knows better than to ask what's wrong. It's painfully obvious.

That was a bullshit ambush.

The cab pulls up to the apartment building and I'm out the door before Luke can swipe his credit card through the machine.

"Ally, wait," he calls out from the cab.

I keep walking like I can't hear him. He'll be in the lobby soon enough, in the same tiny elevator.

My knees go weak. Being in an elevator alone with Luke would be hot as hell under other circumstances.

I look back towards the cab. He's already out, on the pavement, making his way to the building.

Even in his suit, he looks stronger. Like he's spent the last three months at the gym, somehow improving his already perfect physique.

I press the elevator button. Faster. Come faster.

The doors of the elevator slide open and I step inside, making no attempts to hold or close the doors.

It's not like he'll reward my efforts by pressing me against the mirrored walls and ripping off my clothes.

Luke steps inside the elevator. His eyes find mine. His expression is intense. Like he's angry.

But I've never seen him angry. Not really.

The doors slide shut behind him, but he doesn't turn to press the button for our floor. He takes another step towards me, his eyes still on mine.

I press my back into the mirrored wall. "I don't want her at the wedding."

He shakes his head. "Fine. But this is the first time

you've even spoken about the wedding without me bringing it up."

"So?" Even through my coat, the wall is hard behind me. Cold.

Luke moves closer. His crotch connects with mine. Then his chest. Then his fingers are on my neck. My chin. My cheek.

"You're killing me with this."

"I know." I shrink back, but I have no room to move, to do anything but feel him pressed against me.

He shifts his hips, pressing me against the wall. I shudder, wrapping my arms around his waist so I won't fall.

"Luke..." My voice is soft, almost helpless. I close my eyes. Maybe I can forget everything but how his body feels against mine.

"I'm sorry she ambushed you," he murmurs.

I blink my eyes open. He's still staring at me like I'm the most interesting thing he's ever seen. My stomach flip flops.

I dig my fingers into the hard fabric of his blazer, until I can nearly feel the warmth of his skin underneath it. "You've barely talked to me since last time you were here." My voice is a whisper.

"You've barely talked to me since the last time I was here." It's not an accusation, just a simple statement of facts.

I sink my teeth into my lip. My legs are so shaky. I have to squeeze him tighter just to stand. "But that's not like you."

He brushes his lips against my cheek. "I'm sorry."

My heart races. There's nothing I can say. Nothing that can make it easier to admit I nearly gave up on us.

"You should push the button eventually."

"But the second I let you go, you're going to move away from me. Probably for a while."

I shake my head, but I can't bring myself to deny it. "You're the one... You pulled away from me." I reach for something to grab onto, something that will help me stand, but there's nothing in this whole stupid elevator. Nothing but him.

"I know." He shifts back, releasing me, but his eyes stay glued to mine.

I stumble to catch my balance, trying to hold onto the slick mirrored walls.

"Did you stop... loving me?" I ask, almost afraid to voice the question.

"Of course not."

"Lose your patience?" I close my eyes like that will somehow lessen the impact of a yes.

Damn it. Just hit the fucking button. End this conversation before it steers us off a cliff.

"Maybe."

Luke presses the button for our floor and the elevator starts to rise. He turns back to me, his eyes passing over me. It's not sexual. It's more like he's a doctor checking to make sure I have no obvious signs of illness.

The elevator dings and the doors slide open.

I step into the hallway, power walk to the door, and shove my key into the lock. Luke is right behind me, his hands on my arms, his breath on my neck.

Dammit. How can he make me feel so mixed up? So angry and hurt and turned on all at once?

"Alyssa. Can we talk about this?"

"You had plenty of chances to talk to me in the last few months."

I push the door open and walk inside. He follows me. I make no effort to stop him.

"Alyssa." It's a demand.

"Later."

I go into the bedroom, shut the door behind me, and crawl into bed.

It's only after I pull the covers over my head that I feel like I can breathe.

I'm fucking this up so badly. But I have no clue how to stop.

Chapter Twenty-Two

LUKE

I sit on the couch and suck the last bit of tequila--the only alcohol in the apartment, of course--from my glass and place it in the sink.

Alyssa doesn't want to talk. Fine. But that isn't going to keep me from being near her, not when my body is screaming for proximity.

I turn the handle to the bedroom door. It creaks, filling the living room with a gorgeous midnight blue light.

Damn. The view in this room is better than I remembered. The windows are huge, letting in an expanse of skyline.

Alyssa is lying on the bed, comforter wrapped around every part of her body but her head. She murmurs something I can't make out.

It's closer to an invitation than to an objection.

I close the door behind me and slip my jacket off my shoulders.

She rolls over, pulling the comforter tighter around her body. Her eyes pass over me. "This isn't much later."

I loosen my tie and undo my top two buttons. Her eyes go to the exposed skin, her teeth sinking into her bottom lip. But she snaps out of it, shaking her head.

"I'm not here to talk."

Her gaze goes straight to my chest. She swallows. "What are you here to do?"

I pull my tie off, letting it fall to the floor.

Her eyes are glued to me, like I'm performing in a private show just for her. Maybe I am. I undo the rest of my buttons and shrug my shirt off my shoulders.

It slides down my arms, falling to the floor behind me.

"I'm here for your viewing pleasure." I raise my eyebrows and throw her a cheeky wink.

She tries to stifle a laugh, but she fails. Her lips curve into the tiniest smile. For a split second, her eyes are bright. Happy. Then it's gone, and she's back to her distant expression.

I unbuckle my belt, pull it from its loops, and drop it on the floor. Alyssa sighs, her tongue sliding over her lips.

It has been a long time.

I unbutton my slacks and slide them down my thighs. Her eyes go wide, but she shakes her head to try and hide her interest.

"I'm not." She takes a deep breath. "We shouldn't... Right now. Luke, I..."

"I'm only getting comfortable." I sit on the bed, a few feet from her, and pull off my dress socks.

She scans my body again, taking in every inch of it. Every inch she can while I'm in my boxers.

I lift the comforter to climb in with her. "Do you mind?"

"No."

I climb in with her. It's damn warm, all from the heat of her body, and she's so close. Only inches away.

I bring my body behind hers, pressing my chest against her back, my crotch against her ass. She groans, lightly, and tilts her head back to meet mine. There's something so familiar about the way she smells. Something that feels like home.

The tension in my neck relaxes. Her thoughts might be a million miles away, but she's not. She's here. She's close enough to touch.

I slide my arm around her waist, pulling her closer. She sighs, melting into me.

I hold her for a while, listening to her breath, her heart-beat. The room is quiet, no sounds except for us. Nothing in the world matters except for us.

She arches her back, bringing her neck to my lips. She's so soft, so warm, so sweet.

I suck against her neck, scraping my teeth against her skin. She moans, putty in my hands.

"Luke..." Her voice is barely a whisper, but it's so strained and desperate. There's no doubt to her intention.

I slide my hand over the thick wool skirt covering her hips. Then it's on her tights. They're soft, and thin enough that she starts to shake from my touch.

Damn. I almost forgot how good it feels to touch her, to watch her light up with pleasure.

I plant another kiss on her neck and drag my fingertips over her thighs.

She purrs, arching her back and rubbing her ass against me.

I bring my mouth to her ear. "Are you sure?"

She nods and turns to face me. Our eyes meet, just for a moment. She's sure.

Her eyes flutter closed and she presses her lips against mine. Everything we've felt during these awful three months pours out between us.

Her kiss is hungry, desperate, needy.

She shifts back into position, her neck against my lips, her ass pressed against my cock.

Pleasure pools inside me. I need to get her clothes off, to get my hands on her skin.

I find the top of her tights and slide them off her ass. She purrs, throwing her head back so her neck is at my mouth. I sink my teeth into her skin.

She shakes.

My body takes over.

I sigh, kissing her neck as I slide my hands over her thighs.

I pull her tights to her feet. Her legs are smooth, curvy, perfect.

I run my fingertips from her ankle to the inside of her knee. Then, slowly, I trace zig zags up her thighs.

She moans, rubbing me with her ass. I kiss her neck again, and I stroke her inner thighs until she's shaking. She wraps her fingers around my wrist.

I follow her lead. She brings my hand under her blouse, dragging my fingers across the soft skin of her stomach.

Jesus.

I bring my hand to her chest, cupping her breasts over her bra. She groans, lifting her skirt so there's nothing in between us but my boxers and her black panties.

She arches into me again, sliding her cunt over my cock.

I run my fingers over the edge of her bra as I bring my mouth to her ear. "Take off your top."

She pulls her blouse over her head, revealing every inch of her gorgeous skin. There's a lacy bra curled over her lush breasts. I need to rip it off, to rub her while I fuck her.

That's it. No more waiting.

I unhook her bra and slide it off her shoulders. She gasps as I take her breasts into my hands, kneading them slowly.

She purrs at my touch, melting into me, digging her nails into my thigh. I trace her nipple with my finger, over and over, until she's shaking.

She arches into me again, her panties meeting my boxers.

"Now the panties," I order.

Her eyes meet mine as she brings her hands to her hips and slides her panties off.

Then her hand is on mine, and she's bringing it between her legs. She's wet. She's so fucking wet.

I stroke her clit, slowly, over and over. She groans, throwing her head back, pressing her neck against mine.

She rolls over, turning towards me. Her eyes flutter open, and she stares into mine. Then, they're closed, and her lips are on mine. She kisses me, hard, her tongue swirling around mine.

It's all the invitation I need.

I grab her, turning her back to her side. She arches her back, panting.

She's wet, desperate, needy.

Fuck.

I slide my boxers off and position myself behind her. Her body is pressed against mine. She's so soft, so fucking sexy. I run my hands over the smooth skin of her thighs, reveling in her soft groans.

It's been too fucking long.

She shifts, rubbing her sex against my cock. Pleasure shoots through my body, and I grab her hips and slide inside her.

Alyssa gasps, reaching back and digging her nails into my thigh.

I shudder. It's been too long.

With my hands on her hips, I thrust into her. She's so wet, so warm, so fucking tight. Pleasure surges through my body. I need her to feel this too, to feel so good she could die.

I run my fingertips over her thighs, working my way to her clit. She groans and lifts her legs to give me better access. I stroke her. Again and again. Harder and harder.

Pleasure starts to overtake me, but I can't finish yet. Not until she's...

I pull out and press her onto her back, push her legs apart. She groans, shaking, her nails digging into the sheets.

I press my lips against her knee. Then her inner thigh. A little higher. A little closer.

Then, I bring my mouth to her. I suck on her lips, as soft as I can. She purrs and her hands find my hair. I suck a little harder. A little harder. A little harder.

I follow with my tongue, licking her from top to bottom. Again and again. She takes heavy breaths, rocking her crotch into my face.

She tastes so good, smells so good. I slide my tongue over her clit, as softly as I can.

She screams, tugging at my hair. "Don't stop."

Like hell.

I run my tongue over her again and again. Her legs press against my ears. Her back arches. Her hands tug at my hair, but I don't stop. I lick her, tasting her as her groans get louder and louder. Until they're screams that could wake the neighbors three floors away.

She arches one more time. Her nails dig into my shoulders--a sharp pain I wouldn't part with for anything. I lick her again, and again, and she comes, screaming one last time.

She collapses on the bed, taking only a moment to catch her breath. Then she pulls me back on top of her, parting her legs.

She wraps her hand around my cock and guides me insider her. Damn, she's so much wetter now. And she's panting, squirming, moaning.

Her hands are on my ass, pulling me deeper as I thrust into her. The ache inside me builds. She's so wet, so warm, so tight around me.

She moans, her head thrown back, her nails sharp against my skin. I drag my lips against her neck, her collarbone, her chest. Her nipples are hard, and she's panting and digging her nails into my ass.

I bring my mouth to her nipples and suck gently. I'm so hard, and it feels so damn good inside her.

Alyssa wraps her arms and legs around me, pulling me closer. I thrust into her. The ache inside me builds and builds. It's almost too much to take.

I bring my lips to hers and plunge my tongue deep in her mouth. She kisses back, desperate and needy.

I can barely take it. I press my body against hers. Thrust into her one last time.

And that's it.

I groan, releasing everything inside her.

I don't know if I've ever come that hard. I feel weak afterwards, my body trembling.

Alyssa collapses on the bed and I collapse next to her, returning to our earlier position--her back against my chest, my arms around her waist.

We lie like that for a long time.

She pulls my arm tighter around her. "I shouldn't have freaked out like that."

I press my lips into her neck and melt back into her. She takes deep breaths, her chest rising and falling with them.

"I wish I could say she hasn't always been like that, but..." It's barely more than a whisper, and there's so much pain in it. "You probably think it's pathetic."

"You're kidding, right?"

She shakes her head. Damn. How can she be so hard on herself?

"Then tell me. How is it pathetic?" I ask.

She takes another deep breath. I run my fingers through her hair, brushing it away from her face.

She turns, her gaze moving to the ceiling. "When Mom got home from work, she wasn't really there. For a while, when I was a kid, we'd eat dinner together. TV dinners usually, or maybe pizza delivery. But it was always in front of the TV. It's not the most tragic thing, not the hardest. But it was the only time we ever spent together."

I press my fingers against her palm. She leans into my shoulder, wrapping her fingers around my hand.

"I knew better than to ask her for any favors. If I needed school supplies, I'd walk to the store with the cash she kept in the dresser. It wasn't so bad. I always liked the aisles of notebooks and pens. I had so many damn pens." She takes a deep breath, her gaze moving over the room.

She's had to do everything on her own for so long.

Alyssa turns towards me, her eyes connecting with mine. "This story presents one of your least favorite people in a favorable light."

"My father?"

"That would make *perfect* sense." She rolls her eyes. "No, it's Ryan. Of course."

"He was your best friend."

She nods. Her fingers skim my cheek. It's so soft and warm. She's here. She's mine.

"Mom promised to drive me to the Homecoming dance. I had no way of getting to school that late. Walking at night was questionable, and it way too cold in November to do it in a dress and heels."

I see where this is going.

"I didn't even ask her. She promised. She said she wanted to see me dressed up. To see me blossom into a woman. I should have known better when she broke her promise to take me shopping for a dress. She woke up late, hungover, and started drinking early."

I squeeze her fingers, soaking in the sweetness of her touch.

"That night, I put on my dress and makeup. I did my hair. She was going to take pictures. But, when I came downstairs, she was already drunk. She'd been home an hour and she was already drunk. She forgot what day it was. Asked where the hell I thought I was going dressed like a slut."

I brush her hair from her eyes, trying to control my anger.

That excuse for a woman should never have been a parent.

"She told me to change. I accused her of being drunk. Locked myself in my room, crying my eyes out. It was half an hour into the dance when he called me."

I keep my face neutral.

Sure, Ryan is a fucking prick. But he was there for Alyssa when she needed him.

"He sounds like a polite young man."

"He was," she confirms. "He knew I was excited about

the dance and he wanted to make sure I was okay. To make sure nothing had happened."

I bite my tongue, jealousy trying to fight its way in.

So teenage Ryan was sweet to teenage Alyssa. It doesn't matter. He's not here now.

"I told him I wasn't in the mood anymore, and he asked if I'd like some company. I think I whispered "yes," because he came all the way to my house, and he sat with me in my room for hours, while my mom was passed out on the couch. He didn't make a big deal of it. Other guys, they would have tried to fuck me. To at least get my top off. Other guys had before..."

She looks at me with concern. I must not be hiding how awful this is.

"I can stop," she offers.

"It's fine."

"The story doesn't end with me having sex with Ryan. I promise."

My muscles relax, ever so slightly. She laughs.

So, I'm obvious. You could try to sue me, but I'd win.

"You're awful," she says.

"I don't like thinking of you hurting. Especially not some creep taking advantage of it."

"You mean the kind of creep who seduces an engaged woman after she gets into a huge fight with her fiancé?"

I nod. "Exactly that kind of creep."

She leans into me, wrapping her arms around me. We just breathe together for a moment, nothing in the world except the two of us.

"He spent the whole night with me. We watched TV for a while, but we eventually fell asleep on my bed. Completely clothed." She looks out the window. "He's the only guy who was ever nice to me without expecting to get something out of it."

I run my hands through her hair. "I'm sorry you had to deal with that."

"It was nothing."

"It was a lot."

She shakes her head again, but she doesn't verbalize her objection.

"So... did you mean that thing you said to your mother?"

"Which thing?"

Isn't it obvious?

"About my cock being bigger than Ryan's?"

She laughs. "You really want to know?"

"I already know I'm better than he is."

She shakes her head. "No, the knowledge will either crush you or go to your head. You can't be trusted."

I run my fingers over her chin and tilt her head towards me, until we're eye to eye. She holds my gaze for a moment, but she breaks into a fit of giggles, her eyes squeezing closed.

"I'll never tell."

I run my fingers over her bare stomach. "You've never told me if you're ticklish."

"Don't even think about it."

I slide my fingers over her skin. "I'm thinking about it."

She presses her palms against my shoulders, pushing me flat on the bed. "Your ego is big enough already."

"So, I *am* bigger," I say, satisfied.

"I've said too much," she laughs, shifting back onto the bed.

"How much bigger would you say?"

I push the covers off her and look into her clear, blue eyes. She's happy. I'm going to keep her like this.

She makes a show of estimating, tilting her head to the side.

"Maybe... twenty percent."

"Oh yeah?"

"Shut up, Luke." But she's grinning as she says it.

I wrap my arms around her, holding her tightly.

We're together again. We can make it through anything, even the horrible wall of distance that's grown between us.

Chapter Twenty-Three

ALYSSA

My last performance is completely overwhelming.

Part of me is begging to move on to anything new. I've recited the same lines, ten times a week, for six months now. It's about time get the hell out.

But another part of me is terrified to say goodbye. As long as I'm here, I get to reset every day. Blanche isn't sentenced to a terrible life in a cruel mental asylum. She gets to start fresh.

I know the lines so well, know every emotional beat, every little bit of nuance. I take my last chance to lose myself in my character, to really disappear.

I don't snap out of it until I'm bowing on stage, my hand glued firmly to Ellen's. The stage lights shine in my eyes so brightly I can barely make out anything. And the applause is so loud, I can't even hear myself breathe.

It's over. The last of this is over. In the blink of an eye, I'll be back to normal life. Back at the house, in Santa Monica, with Luke.

Exactly what I've wanted for the last few months

Ellen whispers in my ear on the way off the stage. "You're coming out for shots tonight, right?"

I nod. This is my last chance to see Ellen, my last night in New York. I'm not going to spend it wondering what everything means.

I collapse in my dressing room and text Luke the address of the bar. "Meet me there, okay?" He'd prefer to come here. Hell, he'd probably talk me into giving this couch a proper goodbye.

But I need to soak all this in on my own.

I linger in the room, taking in its quaint charm. Two of the bulbs on the vanity are burnt out and I never bothered to replace them. The once beige carpet is stained in half a dozen places. There's a hole in the red, velvet couch. Hell, it's practically ripped to shreds.

It's banged up and uncared for, but it's still perfect.

It was still mine.

I catch my reflection in the mirror. Half my makeup is still on my face. I'm only halfway back to Alyssa, halfway back to my life.

Whatever that means.

I wet a towel with warm water and wash up. When I pull the towel away, it's smeared with some strange mix of black, beige, brown, purple even.

There's no more Blanche, no more pretexts, nothing left except me.

There are about three months between me and shooting the next season of Model Citizen. Three months with nothing to fill my time. Three months where my life will be waiting for Luke.

I shrug my shoulders in a futile attempt to ease my tight muscles. Three months will be great. I need a break. To stop fighting so damn much.

I lay on the couch. This is the last time I'll sink into its soft cushions, the last time I'll stare at the peeling paint on the ceiling.

My hands start shaking. After this, the only thing in my life that matters is Luke.

Unless he's already tired of me.

I press my eyes closed, willing the thoughts away. This is my last night in New York and I'm not going to spend it moping.

There's a knock on the door. Ellen, I'm sure. No doubt desperate to drink herself stupid, to go home with the cute bartender (though Nicholas would work in a pinch).

I push off the couch and open the door, but it's not Ellen.

It's Nicholas.

"I hope this isn't an imposition," he says.

I shake my head, a little confused why he's here.

While I'm half-dressed. Fuck. I pull my robe tighter, cinching its sash.

"No, of course not. Are you not going to the bar with us?"

"I am." He looks past me into the room. "Do you mind if I come in?"

"Okay."

I step back and he enters the room. Somehow, he looks taller, larger, more sure of himself in the smaller confines.

He closes the door behind himself, making the space feel even more intimate.

I take a step back, trying to create more space.

"I just wanted to speak to you in a nice quiet place before we go to the bar," he explains with a slight smile.

I smile back.

"Yeah, I guess it isn't really an environment conducive to conversation."

"Exactly." He looks around the small room. "Now that your run is over—how did you like it?"

I relax a little.

"I'm really glad I was able to do it. It was... scary, tiring, exhilarating, insane. And I'd do it all again."

I realize the truth in that as it pours out of me.

Yes, my relationship with Luke suffered. But, if I put that aside, as far as a career milestone goes... I can't think of anything better.

"Sounds like the bug's bitten you," Nicholas chuckles, his eyes gleaming with the knowledge of how I feel.

I nod.

"Yeah. But I don't know if I could do it full time. It took a lot out of me," I admit.

"It isn't for the faint of heart," he agrees, taking a step closer. "I'm sure your fiancé didn't love it."

"Uh... yes, I guess not," I say, uncomfortable with the comment.

Nicholas doesn't need to know every detail of my personal life. Maybe I gave him the wrong impression when I couldn't hide how I was feeling.

"This life is hard on significant others," he murmurs. "Especially those who aren't in the business."

"Sure," I agree, resisting the urge to step to the side.

I don't want to overreact.

"Don't let anyone hold you back," he says, his eyes locked on my own. "You were amazing in the show. A couple shows in, I would never have known it was your first time."

"That's really flattering." Did he inch closer or am I just imagining things? "You know, I think I better get ready to go. I don't want to keep Luke waiting."

I throw Luke's name in deliberately. Just in case I'm not overreacting.

Nicholas searches my face as he nods slowly.

"Sure. Anyway, I just wanted to touch base and let you know that I'd love to keep in touch. Call me if you need anything."

"Thank you," I murmur, stepping towards him, assuming he'd step back towards the door in reaction.

But he doesn't.

Instead, he takes it as invitation to pull me into a hug.

I pat his back a little awkwardly.

"You're still with the fiancé?" he asks, pulling back slightly, his hands still on my upper arms.

"Yes." I keep the answer short and firm.

He smiles slightly.

"Alright." He leans down and kisses me. It's on the cheek, but maybe it lingers just a touch too long? "I hope you make the right decision."

"Well, thank you for that," I say, the sarcasm not even thinly veiled.

Who does he think he is?

"I'll leave you be." He moves back, just a little, his eyes intent on my face. "You're one of the hardest people to read, you know that? We've spent so much time together, but I still feel like I haven't even scratched the surface with you." He shakes his head. "But I really do hope things work out for you and Luke. He may not deserve it, but you do."

"I appreciate your concern, but things are great. We're going to Hawaii. And we're engaged."

He nods. "I hope that works out."

I bite my tongue again. Whatever his intentions are, I'm not going to give him the satisfaction of showing doubt again.

"It will," I say. "Because we're honest with each other. And we love each other."

He looks at me with a hint of... sadness? But that can't be right. We're just friends. Mostly due to circumstances. Right? "I really do hope he makes you happy."

"We're very happy," I insist.

I almost believe it.

Chapter Twenty-Four

LUKE

I spend fifteen minutes listening to Ellen talk about the various patrons at the bar.

She mentions something about Alyssa needing time to pack up, since she's leaving New York tomorrow. It's not entirely believable, but I trust her enough not to question her motives.

When Alyssa arrives, she's wearing an almost... guilty look. She greets me with a hug, squeezing me much tighter than she usually does. There's something strange about it, but it's still sweet and warm.

I frown when Nicholas come in not long after, joining us at the table.

Why was he late too?

Ellen clears her throat, turning her gaze to Alyssa. "Won't you two get enough of that tonight? Geez."

"You're just jealous," Alyssa shoots back, clearly used to Ellen's harsher personality.

"We'll see who goes home with the hotter guy," Ellen returns. She looks to the guy behind the bar, a 20-something in a tight T-shirt.

She's been staring at him all night.

"Unless you and Luke somehow convince me I'm open to a threesome, I'm going home with the hotter guy."

"A threesome with another girl? No way."

Nicholas rolls his eyes. "Can either of you talk about something besides sex for 45 seconds?"

Ellen looks straight at Nicholas, copying and exaggerating his eye roll, mocking him. "I'm finding my truth, and my truth is all about cocks."

"Philistine."

"Pretentious asshat," Ellen mutters. She sticks her tongue out and flips Nicholas off.

"Play nice you guys. This is my last night here," Alyssa interjects.

"For you dear, I'll consider it." Ellen makes eye contact with Alyssa. "That's a major show of friendship--that I'll be nice to Nicholas to make you happy."

Nicholas shakes his head, but he doesn't seem bothered. They must do a lot of this kind of thing.

Ellen scoots out of her seat. "I'll get the next round. Tequila shots are on me!"

She pushes out of her the booth without waiting for a reaction. We don't have a choice in the matter. It's tequila shots or bust.

Alyssa scoots closer to me. She turns towards me and presses her lips against mine.

The rush of contact sends a shiver down my spine, but there's something off about it.

"Are you okay?" I ask.

She nods, offering a weak smile. "There's a lot to think about." She turns to Nicholas. "How do you do this all the time?"

Her tone feels almost a little... forced?

He shrugs, his expression unreadable. "You get used to it."

Ellen returns with the shots and hands one to each of us. "To... getting totally wasted."

Alyssa laughs, but she slams back her shot quickly. There's a certain joy to it, but there's also a desperation.

Ellen slams her shot, coughing. She shakes her head and jumps up and down. "You two-" She points to me and Nicholas. "This is a party. And a party calls for shots."

I bring my glass to my lips, tasting the first hint of tequila. I've never really been one for shots, but what the hell? I tilt my head and swallow it in one gulp.

Alyssa leans into me, wrapping her arms around me. I turn to her, searching for meaning in her expression, but I can't make anything of it.

"Hey, you two- enough. This is a party. Stop looking so cuddly and adorable."

"Damn, Ellen. You really are jealous," Nicholas accuses.

Ellen huffs.

"Fine. Be adorable. What do I care? It's not like this is Alyssa's last night in the city with us."

"If you want a chance to be adorable, you should probably try a second date," he adds, clearly not interested in going easy on her.

"I get everything I need on the first." She sticks her tongue out.

Nicholas shakes his head. "Then why are you jealous?"

Ellen narrows her eyes. "Oh, go find some 18-year-old college student who will want to hear all about your truth on stage."

It doesn't faze him at all.

"You could be serious about the craft."

"I am damn serious! I'm just not a pretentious fool."

Ellen steps towards the bar. "You guys want to be difficult, fine. But I'm going to get another drink. And I'm going to have fun. You can sit here and talk about truth and cuddle and whatever. I don't give a shit." She marches to the bar.

Nicholas turns to us. "She's always like this."

Seems to me he enjoys making it worse. But I don't say it.

"You guys really work together that often?" Alyssa asks.

Nicholas sighs. "Unfortunately." He slides out of the bar and offers his hand for Alyssa to shake. "It was nice working with you."

She hesitates for a second before taking his hand. "I was worried you'd hate me."

"Everyone worries about that." He holds her hand and her eyes for a beat longer than necessary before releasing, letting go and waving goodbye. "I'm sure I'll see you again sometime. Call me if Ellen gets too drunk. I'll take her home."

"Sure," Alyssa agrees. She watches Nicholas leave. "We can get out of here. Go back to the apartment for one last time."

"Are you sure that's what you want?"

She turns to me.

"We don't have to analyze every little thing to death." She pulls away from me fighting a sigh. "Okay. Forget it. I'll have another drink. We'll entertain Ellen."

"We're going to spend the next week together," I say. "I just don't want you to regret leaving early."

She nods, squeezing my hand.

"I know."

"Then, we'll back in Los Angeles. Back to our normal lives."

"I know that too." She pushes out of the booth, smoothing her skirt and her blouse. "It's fine. Really."

"What's up, Ally? There's something weird about you."

She shrugs, but there's nothing aloof about it. Something is up. Something is up and, as usual, she won't talk about it.

"Nothing is up," she insists. "I'd just rather be in bed with you than be at this party."

I don't know if I buy that.

And what was that weird energy between her and Nicholas?

"Is that all it is?"

She shakes her head. "Forget it. I'm sure we'll be too drunk by the time we leave anyway."

Alyssa offers a smile, but it's a consolation prize, a whatever you say. She joins Ellen at the bar. They joke about something, laughing and whispering in each other's ears.

I take a deep breath and exhale slowly.

This is a huge life change for Alyssa. It's possible that what I'm picking up on is simply stress.

I hope it is.

————

THE NIGHT GOES QUICKLY. ALYSSA AND ELLEN SWAP stories all night, teasing each other and professing their undying friendship. By the time we leave the bar, everyone is too drunk for sense but sober enough to get home okay.

It's dark outside, and a cold wind whips around us. The temperature is somewhere around freezing, but it doesn't faze Alyssa. She grinds her body into mine, slipping her arms under my coat, then under my shirt.

My skin burns from her touch and my body fights to take over. To convince my brain to take her into the alley, press her against the wall, and fuck her until she's screaming.

She's so desperate. She'd come in minutes.

She kisses me hungrily, her tongue sliding into my mouth as her nails dig into my skin. Mhmm. I pull her closer and slide my hands under her skirt. Damn. The fabric of her tights is thin, and it would feel so damn good to peel it off.

We were apart for so long. We have so much time to make up for.

She runs her fingertips over my stomach. It would feel so good to touch her, to have her touch me, but it's a bad idea.

Something is wrong. Sex is only going to distract her from her feelings.

When we break, she looks up into my eyes expectantly. "It's our last night in New York..." Her voice is low, seductive.

"You're drunk."

"Not that drunk." She leans closer, sliding her hands under my shirt again, sliding her fingertips over my skin.

My heart races, my blood fleeing my brain.

Will making Alyssa come really make matters worse? That doesn't seem right.

I grab her ass, pressing my crotch into hers. She sighs and leans into me. Her lips are on my lips. Her tongue is in my mouth. Her hands are on my chest, my whole damn body burning with want.

I need to be inside her now.

But I wrench myself back, breathing hard. If this goes any further, I won't be able to stop myself.

"Can we talk?" I ask, my heart pounding.

She shakes her head. "I'm not really in the mood for conversation." Her voice is harsh, but she tries to shrug it off. "I suppose we should grab a cab, get our stuff, and get ready for our flight."

Fine. I can bide my time.

I nod.

"Okay," she says, folding her arms, trying not to look annoyed.

"Did something happen?" I ask. "You're not acting like yourself."

She doesn't look at me as she mutters an answer.

"Yeah. My life was turned upside down for six months." She takes a step towards the street, throwing her arm out to hail a cab.

Chapter Twenty-Five

ALYSSA

I spend most of the flight sleeping off my massive hangover. Ellen wasn't kidding about drinking until we drop.

Luke is sweet, fixing my blanket, offering me water or club soda or saltines. He makes nothing of me not eating. Either he believes it's nausea of he's learned I can take care of myself.

Under the cover of the blanket, I slide my fingers over my engagement ring. But the feel of the smooth platinum and the hard diamond does nothing to illuminate my situation.

Luke is next to me. If I manage to peel my eyes open to let in the horribly bright lights--God forbid--I'll see him, sitting next to me, reading some paperback piece of pulp fiction, half his attention on me.

He loves me. I don't doubt that.

But... I know I'm not the easiest person to be with.

I'm beyond guarded. And the fact that Luke kept a deliberate distance shows he's just a person.

Most people aren't strong enough to put up with my bullshit.

I pull the blanket tighter, willing the pounding in my head to go away.

Ryan wanted me, but he doesn't know the first thing about love. He treated me like a damn pet. If he really loved me, if he really knew anything...

The plane hits a pocket of turbulence and I jerk out of my chair, the seatbelt pulling against my pelvis. Ow.

Luke leans in towards me, his arm around my shoulders. "You okay?"

I nod, but I keep my eyes pressed closed, my body turned towards the window.

"How's the headache?" he asks softly.

I groan. "I'm never drinking again."

He wraps his arms tighter around me, laughing a deep, hearty laugh. "I'll hold you to that."

"Maybe not never again."

I blink my eyes open--damn, it's bright--and look back to Luke. His attention is fully on me, a smile playing with the corners of his lips.

He leans in closer, until I can feel the heat of his body, smell his breath.

"If you make it to the hotel, I have a surefire hangover cure."

"And you tell me now?" I lean closer, soaking in the warmth of his body.

"Mhmm. And you'll definitely like it."

My head fills with all sorts of wonderful ideas, pushing out any memories of last night.

I press my lips against Luke's. They taste like Earl Grey tea and honey, and they're so soft and warm. This is all that matters.

———

My hangover shrinks into a dull ache bouncing around my head, but I'm still not at 100 percent. It's late afternoon here, and the sun is high and bright. It bounces off the floor, filling the whole lobby with light.

The space is open. Hell, it's practically a courtyard. The warm, humid air sticks to my skin, and it's damn sweet. Some wonderful mix of salt and tropical fruit.

I sit in a cushy leather chair while Luke takes care of the check-in business. The ocean is only a few hundred feet away and it's a perfect, crystal blue. Everything is decorated in bright colors. The chairs are teal and orange. The desks are a vibrant gold.

Luke sits next to me. He runs his hands along my cheek. His touch is delicate, and there's such a sweetness to it. All I want to do is close my eyes and melt into him.

"You ready to see our room?" he asks.

I nod. He takes my hands and pulls me out of the chair. I stumble, ever so slightly, landing in his arms.

Fuck it. I press my eyes closed and soak in the feeling of his body around mine. This is perfect. This is everything.

I pull back, steadying myself and taking his hand. He leads me to the elevator. There's already a car on this floor, and it's only ours. I step inside, leaning against the railing for support.

His hand is still on mine. "Our room is called a royal suite."

"What does that mean?"

He smiles. "It means it's amazing."

The elevator stops on our floor. Luke squeezes my hand and leads me down the hallway.

"Fuck, that window is really bright," he warns.

It is horrifyingly bright. I squeeze my eyes closed. Anything to keep from reactivating my hangover.

He laughs and helps me to the room.

"You can open your eyes now."

I do.

The room *is* amazing. The furniture is a mix of bright and calm blues, but with the curtains drawn, the room is dim enough to bear.

Luke lays me on the bed and brings me a cup of water. He laughs as I squint at him with what must be a look of utter agony.

"You're cute when you're miserable," he teases.

"You would know."

I feel his hands on my hips. They're unzipping me.

"Don't get any ideas," he orders as he lifts my ass and pulls my jeans to my feet.

I still have all sorts of ideas.

I open my eyes, meeting his gaze.

There's always something sincere about him, but it's heightened today. It's like he's desperate to prove we really can make this work.

Or I'm projecting.

My chest tightens. I'm getting ahead of myself. The two of us are in a gorgeous hotel room in the middle of paradise. We can discuss these kinds of awful matters later, when we're free from aching heads.

"I have a few ideas," I murmur, pushing everything else away.

He smirks, swinging his knees around my hips so he's straddling me. I arch into him, pressing my crotch against his.

"You're dreaming," he says.

But he places his arms alongside my body, leans down, and presses his lips into mine.

His kiss is hot and sweet, a wonderful spark igniting everything inside me. A gentle warmth floods my body.

We've barely touched in the last two weeks. God, we need to touch.

I dig my hands into his hair, pulling him closer. The sweetness slips away, his kiss becoming hungry and desperate. I'm pouring need into him, just like I have a million times before.

He breaks our kiss. "This isn't what I meant by a hangover cure." His voice is heavy and strained.

And he's hard. He wants this as much as I do.

"You couldn't have meant anything better than this."

He leans closer, his fingertips on my shoulders. "Not better. Just different." He runs his fingers over my skin, until they're on my neck, my chin, my cheek.

"What was it?" I turn my head away from the window, my eyes fluttering closed.

His breath is on my ear, his hands back on my shoulders. "I can show you."

The whisper sends shivers all the way to my fingers and toes. He brings his mouth closer to my ear, sliding his tongue over the lobe.

I dig my hands into the cotton sheets, shifting my body into his. He sucks on my ear lobe with the gentlest pressure.

"Was this your plan?" I ask again. I swear I had a sassy follow-up, but it's impossible to think with his mouth on me.

He runs his finger along the neckline of my t-shirt, pressing the fabric against my skin. He traces from one shoulder to the other and back again.

"Luke..." I groan. That always gets a response.

He releases my ear and presses his lips into my neck. They're so soft and sweet and wet. It's only a hint of pressure, as soft as it could possibly be. I dig my hands into his thick hair, tugging at the roots.

He scrapes his teeth against my neck. It's harder, sharp even. The tiniest hint of pain.

My sex clenches, my body filling with pleasure. I need more, harder, rougher. I need him to mark me, to use me, to lose himself in me.

He nibbles on my neck again, a little harder, a little sharper. I groan, tugging at his hair, bucking into him.

His hands slip under my shirt, skimming my bra. Dammit, they're so close but so far away. I need him to touch me properly. I need those expert fingers on my chest, playing with my nipples until I'm so fucking wet I can't take it anymore.

Luke sinks his teeth into my neck. It's a proper bite-- hard, desperate, needy.

His fingertips are on my skin, sliding over my breasts but not quite touching my nipples.

My sex clenches. My body is on fire. Every place he touches is electric, amazing, perfect.

He bites me again, ever so slightly harder. He's testing, careful. Too careful.

I wrap my legs around him, pulling his body towards mine. His cock is straining against his jeans, and I arch my pelvis, rubbing my crotch against his--my underwear against his jeans.

Jesus Christ.

Luke pulls his lips off my neck, his hands from my bra. He runs his fingers over my t-shirt, pressing it against my skin. It's so soft I can barely feel it.

He explores every inch of that damn t-shirt, pressing it against the skin on my neck, shoulders, stomach. Tracing the outline of my bra, his fingers so, so close to my nipples, so, so close to my fucking skin.

I groan, my legs shaking, my hands digging harder and harder into his hair.

He's evil.

He retraces all of his steps with two fingers. The fabric of my shirt scrapes against my skin, the gentlest bit of friction. Up and down and left and right and back and forth.

Finally, he cups my breasts over my shirt. He rubs gently, three fingers making circles over my nipples.

There's an ache between my legs. I'm empty and, my God, I need him to fill me. I squeeze my legs together, as if to somehow contain the want pouring out of me.

He brings his hands to the bottom of my shirt. His fingertips slip onto my stomach. Jesus. Every touch sends tingles to my sex.

I force my eyes open and look into his. His attention is foggy, like he's already slipped deep into lust. He kisses me, his soft, full lips sucking on mine.

When our kiss breaks, he pulls my shirt over my head. His eyes pass over my body, slowly taking in every inch.

"Get on your stomach."

The order sends a shiver of anticipation through me.

He shifts his body off mine, watching as I roll onto my stomach. My body is on fire, waiting to be touched, caressed, filled.

He straddles me again, his knees pressed against my thighs, his crotch against my ass. He brings his mouth to my ear and scrapes his teeth against my lobe.

"I was going to give you a massage," he finally tells me.

His fingers slide down my neck, around my shoulders. He traces my spine. It's slow and gentle and light. He stops at my lower back, his fingertips pressed against the top of my panties.

He runs his fingertips over the edge of my panties.

I swallow hard, digging my hands into the sheets. "And what will you do instead?"

He slides his hands back up my back, stopping to unhook my bra and press the back off my back.

"Well," he says, bringing his body onto mine. "I'm going to have to touch you everywhere." He kisses my shoulders, his teeth gently scrapping against my skin. "Until you're so desperate to come that you're shaking."

"Luke..."

He runs his hands over my sides, along my chest, stomach, hips. "Do you object?"

I shake my head.

"Good," he says.

He drags his fingertips back up my side, moving closer and closer to my breasts. My body hums, tingling everywhere. I bite my tongue to keep from screaming.

He slides his hands under me, onto my chest.

Jesus. My sex clenches, my body filling with want. I try to roll over, but he squeezes his knees around me to hold me in place.

"Not yet," he says.

He cups my breasts as he brings his mouth to my neck. He bites me, gently at first. Then harder. And harder.

I push my legs against his, trying to push him off me, to force him into a position where I can feel his cock against my sex. But he holds strong, biting me harder and harder.

The pain sends shivers down my spine, heightening the feeling of his touch. The ache inside me grows.

I need him now. I need him inside me.

He brings his hands back to my hips, digging his fingers under my panties. Fuck. He's so, so close, but he's not touching me properly. Not yet.

He shifts his body lower, so he's straddling my thighs. I

lift my ass, and he slides my panties down, shifting his body along with them, until both are at my feet.

My legs start to shake. I hold onto the bed for dear life, my body tingling from anticipation.

Luke slides his fingers over my calves, grabbing my knees and pushing them apart like he's prying me open.

I swallow hard. He can see every inch of me.

He trails his fingers over my upper thighs until they're so, so close. Almost there. Almost...

"Fuck, you're so wet," he says.

I feel his fingertip, soft and fleshy, against my clit. He strokes me, slowly and gently. Every second of his touch sends another round of shivers through my body. I'm already so keyed up. There's already so much pressure, so much ache inside me.

He grabs my hips and shifts me to my side. Our eyes catch, just for a moment. It's electric. It's amazing. It's perfect.

He moves towards me, pressing his lips into mine. His tongue slides into my mouth, and I dig my nails into his back, trying to claim him the way he claims me.

He maneuvers my body, placing a pillow under my stomach, so my ass and crotch are lifted in the air for his viewing pleasure.

Fuck.

He brings his lips to my inner thigh, kissing and sucking and nibbling. I can't see anything he's doing. I can only hear him and feel him.

His teeth catch the skin on my inner thigh. He's so damn close. My clit is aching for his tongue. For him to lick me until I come, until the edge is taken off.

He moves closer and closer, until he's barely a centimeter away. His brings his mouth to my lips, sucking gently.

I groan, digging my hands into the sheets. He sucks a little harder. A little harder. A little harder.

He licks me up and down, his tongue soft and wet against my lips. He passes over my clit gently, barely a touch, barely more than a hint of pressure.

His hands find my thighs and push my legs apart. He licks me back and forth with slow zig zags.

I shudder, groaning to release some of the wonderfully agonizing tension.

He brings his tongue to the very tip of my clit. Just a touch. A taste. But it's enough to make my whole damn body shake. To make me scream his name.

He slides his tongue over my clit, from top to bottom, with long, slow strokes. The tension inside me builds, tighter and tighter. He licks me again and again. It's almost too much to bear. Almost too much.

He licks faster, harder. Again and again and again. Quick flicks of his tongue against me.

My legs shake. I reach for anything I can grab onto.

His tongue is soft, wet, perfect. He brings his mouth to my clit, sucking gently. He licks me all over again, faster this time. I slide my knees apart, opening myself to him.

Almost. Almost.

Another lick, long and slow. I groan, tearing at the sheets. My sex clenches, tighter and tighter, almost there.

He licks me again. Again. Again.

The tension builds. A little more. A little tighter. Everything unleashes, an orgasm ripping through me.

He pulls back, for a moment, as if to give me time to catch my breath. Then, his tongue is back on me, licking me again, harder and faster.

My sex clenches, the tension inside me building quickly. Fuck. My legs shake, all the way down to my damn feet.

The pressure builds and builds and builds, until I can't

take it anymore. I come again, my body flooding with pleasure.

I push myself off the bed, starting to move. But his hands close around my hips, gripping me tightly.

"Back on your stomach," he says hoarsely.

Fuck. I return my arms to the bed, spreading my legs apart for him.

He presses his palms into my ass, pressing me against the bed. His hands find my knees and he shoves them apart.

The tip of his cock strains against me, teasing me.

"Luke," I groan.

I throw away any resolve not to beg. I need to make him feel as good as I did. I need to make him come.

I slide my legs apart, arching my body into his.

He grabs my thighs, bring my body towards his.

His tip slips inside me. Fuck.

I savor the feeling for a moment. Pleasure courses through my body, to my nipples, my fingers, my lips, my toes. I arch into him, and he squeezes my thighs, sliding his cock deeper inside me, filling me.

He groans, digging his hands into my hips. "Fuck, Alyssa."

His grip firm, he guides me. Slowly, back and forth, back and forth. I slide over his cock, feeling it against every inch of my sex.

His groans, his nails on my skin, his breath heavy. No more playing around. He moves faster, thrusting into me, again and again and again.

Fuck. I'm close already. Every nerve in my body is turned on. Every one of his thrusts feels damn intense. I sink my teeth into my lip, gripping the sheets for dear life.

He goes deeper. Harder. His nails dig into my skin, another sharp hint of pain.

He groans louder.

My face flushes as a shiver runs to my toes. I close my eyes, soaking in the sounds of his groans, his breath, his ecstasy.

"Mhmm." His nails are sharp against my hips.

He's almost there.

My sex clenches, desperate to come with him.

The tension inside me builds. More and more and more, and tighter and tighter and tighter. I squeeze him with my thighs to keep from coming. Not yet. Not until it's with him.

"Fuck." He moans, thrusting into me one last time. His cock is pulsing inside me, and my sex responds in kind; tightening more and more, until everything releases. And we come together.

Pleasure floods through me, drowning my senses. I close my eyes and flop onto my stomach. He collapses next to me, his arm curled around my waist, his chest against my back.

Chapter Twenty-Six

LUKE

It doesn't take much to coax Alyssa into a joint shower. She's tired and giggly, gripping onto my shoulders to help herself stay upright. I lather her with soap and she returns the favor.

There's such a sweetness to it. It's the two of us, in this tiny steamy glass room. Nothing but the sound of rushing water, the slick feel of soap and shampoo, the heat rising off the tile floor.

We finish the shower and linger naked in the hotel room for far longer than we should. It's quiet here, no sounds except the ocean crashing some two hundred feet outside the window.

Alyssa explores the nooks and crannies of the room, marveling at its grandness. It is an amazing room--tall ceilings, bright furniture, huge windows--but I'm mostly interested in the wide bed and the private balcony.

I bring my gaze back to Alyssa. Now that is something to marvel at.

Her wet hair sticks to her head and neck, and the light streaming through the blinds surrounds her with a soft glow. She's so damn beautiful--clear eyes, lush curves, perfect skin.

She catches me looking at her and blushes.

Damn. I could never get tired of that blush.

"I suppose," she says, stretching her arms over her head, "That I should put on some clothes."

I offer my hand. She moves towards me, into my grasp. I slide my arm around her waist and pull her onto my lap. "That's not necessary."

She rubs my shoulders. Her touch is sweet and gentle. An I love you, not a fuck me now.

"Don't get any ideas," she teases.

"That's my line." I pull her closer, wrapping my arms around her. It's been hell being away from her. I need to soak in every damn second I can be in her presence. I bring my gaze back to her eyes. "How's your headache?"

She laughs. Her expression is sweet, but there's an intensity to it. A need. "Cured mysteriously."

"I have many skills."

She shakes her head and pushes away from me. "Enough bragging."

Alyssa scans the room, no doubt looking for her clothes. I point to a small heap on the floor. She groans in irritation and moves to her suitcase instead.

"And did I also wipe all your energy?" I ask.

She turns back to me, rolling her eyes. "Where do you get this endless confidence?"

I smirk.

"From the sounds you make when you come."

She shakes her head, blushing a little. "My energy is decent. I couldn't go for a run, but... why?"

"We're in paradise. If you're going to put on clothes, there's nothing worth seeing in the room."

She brings her eyes back to mine, her lips curling into a smile. "Not if you're naked."

"I'm getting dressed."

I make my way to my suitcase and pull on my boxers. Alyssa pouts in mock irritation, but she watches me dress with an expression of pure delight.

When I finish, I move closer to her, wrapping my arms around her waist. "Have you ever been on a horse?"

Her eyes go wide. "I don't... I guess not."

I smile. "You're in for a treat then."

———

"You rich asshole." Alyssa stares at the pair of horses in shock, even though she knew what we were doing. She turns to me, a hint of trepidation in her expression. "What if it tries to kill me?"

I stifle a laugh.

"It's a guided trail," I say, keeping my tone even. I point to the guide slowly meandering towards us. "You'll be fine."

"But in *Gone with the Wind*-"

"Let me guess--you read that whole, eight-billion-page book?"

"I'm sure you've seen the film," she retorts, with special emphasis on the word film, as if she's mocking me.

Okay, she's absolutely mocking me. But, before I have a chance to tease her mercilessly, the guide arrives.

He's a short, bald man. About thirty.

We go through introductions. Steve is going to take us on a guided horseback ride.

"Is this your first time on the island?" he asks.

"It is," I confirm.

"You're in for a treat then." He nods to a stable and motions for us to follow him. "You know, Hawaii is not only the most beautiful state in the country. We're also number one in weddings."

I grin at the off-hand remark, turning to Alyssa.

"What do you say? Want to fuck the planning and do it while we're here?"

She bites her lip. "Horses first, then your nonsense."

I sigh silently.

Not a surprising response at this point, though it's still disappointing.

Steve opens the doors to the stable. It's divided into half a dozen stalls, each one housing a horse.

Alyssa's jaw drops open. "They're huge."

The horses we saw outside were a good bit of distance away, milling around in a fenced in area.

He points Alyssa to the brown horse in the corner. "This is Mabel. She's been doing this trail for years and she's very comfortable with people."

Alyssa nods, taking a deep breath. "Okay."

I frown. I want her to enjoy this, not dread it.

"We don't have to, Ally."

She shakes her head. She's determined. Steve helps lead her horse outside then does the same with me.

Alyssa stares at her horse. She's transfixed.

"It's very safe," Steve reassures her. "Do you need some help getting on?"

She nods, accepting his words, and allows him to help her onto the horse. She looks back at me for reassurance and I give her a thumbs up.

She's an adorable, nervous wreck on that damn horse.

I mount the horse and take the reins. I'm not exactly an expert, but I've gone horseback riding enough times to know what I'm doing.

Alyssa is clutching the reins with a slightly sick but

mostly excited look on her face. When she catches me watching her, she smiles as if to say she's okay.

"The scenery on this trail is beautiful," Steve tells us.

He climbs onto his horse and leads us down a beaten dirt trail. The horses move without any prompting--they shuttle tourists down this road day in, day out. They've got it under control.

The scenery is gorgeous. The crystal blue ocean is to our right. A lush tropical forest is to our left. Palm trees and tall grasses sway gently on the breeze.

But they don't hold a candle to Alyssa. She digs her fingers into the leather reins, squeezing her thighs against the saddle tightly. But there's a smile on her face and it's gorgeous, bright. Hell, it's the widest smile I've seen on her in ages.

"You're doing great," I offer.

She shakes her head. "I bet you played polo when you were a kid."

"My family isn't that rich."

"You don't deny it." She turns her gaze towards me. Her expression is so bright, so happy. It's like she's finally shrugged some of the tension off her shoulders, finally relaxed.

"I've never played polo. Only Marco Polo."

She laughs. "Such lies."

"I recall playing with you."

"You may have to remind me. I have so many vivid memories of you in that pool." She frowns but shakes the look off her face. "Mostly good."

We round a corner and come onto a clearing. It's gorgeous--a field of bright wildflowers as far as the eye can see.

Alyssa's drinks it in.

God damn. It's good to see her this taken with something.

It's good to see her this happy.

———

THE AFTERNOON PASSES PEACEFULLY. WE WANDER AROUND the beach, dipping our toes in the ocean until the sun sets. The sky is a rainbow of colors--the bright yellow sun sinking into the ocean, bleeding into a soft orange, a bright pink, a cool purple.

Alyssa is here. She's next to me. But I can't tell if I have her attention, if she's lost in the sky or if she's lost in her head.

I squeeze her hand as the sun dips all the way below the water. The color bleeds from the sky, first the red, then the orange. Then, it's all purple and blue and black.

I look back at Alyssa. Her eyes are on the sky, on the silver light of the moon. It casts a soft glow on her face, bringing a brightness to her gorgeous blue eyes.

She takes a deep breath and turns her attention to me. "This place is perfect."

I'm tempted to add something, to bring up the distance that's been growing between us for the last three months, but I stay silent.

I don't want to ruin the moment.

"What's wrong?" she asks.

I'm clearly not hiding my thoughts very well.

"Nothing," I murmur.

I lean towards her and brush my lips against hers. We have four more days in paradise. Whatever happens, I'm making the most of these four days.

She slides her hand around my neck. It's soft, sweet, perfect. That's my Alyssa.

For now at least.

The kiss breaks. I push aside the empty feeling in my gut.

The sky is full of stars. They're bight, brilliant, perfect.

I squeeze her hand, tighter, trying to soak in every damn ounce of this moment.

After a while, she lets go and gets to her feet. She looks down at me, a small smile on her lips. "Let's go to dinner."

"I have to do something first." I stand and slide my hands around her waist.

She raises a brow.

"And what is that?"

"This."

I press my lips into hers, pulling her body into mine. I kiss her until she melts into me, until she's putty, until I'm sure she'll remember this moment for ever.

The rest of the night is perfect. Fantastic food. Fantastic drinks. Not a word from either of us about what Alyssa is or isn't eating. Honestly, it barely crosses my mind. She did okay on her own in New York City.

We talk and joke during dinner, but it does nothing to ease the dread in my gut. We can't keep going on like this, leaving everything unsaid.

Chapter Twenty-Seven

ALYSSA

I 'm a kid in a damn candy store.

Sure, I've been treated to the finest things before. But not like this.

The gorgeous hotel room is only the tip of the iceberg. This whole damn island is amazing. Indulgent, expensive, perfect.

Our morning starts with Kona coffee. Real Kona coffee--creamy, smooth, sweet even without globs of honey. I am in coffee nirvana, and I drink cup after cup after cup. Luke teases me, licking honey off his spoon every time I order another cup.

There are no comments about proper breakfast food. No comments about caffeine in moderation. Actually, he hasn't said a thing about my eating since... since forever. That's what I wanted. It's a sign he respects my wishes. That he trusts me. Not that he stopped caring. Not that he's closing off so he can cut ties.

I shake the thought away, focusing on another sip of perfect, creamy coffee. Focusing on Luke's big, brown eyes. His million-dollar grin. His messy hair.

We talk about little things. TV. Movies. Gossip about Laurie. From the sound of it, he's spent most of his free time in front of the TV or the theater screen. Not that I'd expect anything else from him.

But... there's something missing in the conversation. Some place where we aren't quite connecting.

As soon as I think it, I push it aside, push it down as deep as it can go.

We're in paradise. We may as well enjoy it.

Our day is too full for dwelling on whatever it is that's wrong. There's a surf lesson, a hike at a volcano park, dinner at a little seafood restaurant under the stars. We spend our evening at a quiet bar, staring into each other's eyes, whispering sweet nothings that promise only the immediate future.

No "I'll always love you." No forever. No "you fill me with so much joy that I must make you my wife."

Only now. Only tonight.

We take a long, slow walk along the beach on our way back to the hotel. The air is warm, salty, sweet. I squeeze the soft sand with my feet, letting it creep between my toes. Luke presses his hand against mine, but there's a coldness to it. Something is missing.

I swallow hard. The last few months have been miserable. It's not like we can carry on ignoring it. It's not like we're both going to forget it.

But I'm not ready to broach the subject.

So I squeeze his hand a little tighter, and I press my feet into the soft sand. It gives just enough. It's just hard enough. Just wet enough.

The waves roll onto the beach with a gentle roar. It's so quiet here. So peaceful.

I turn to Luke. I can just make out his expression in the darkness. There's something on his face. He's not here.

He's somewhere else. Probably trying to figure out how to tell me he can't put up with me anymore.

I push the thought down as far as it will go. It's so pretty here. The sky is a glorious shade of purple, and it's filled with stars. The water is so calm, so peaceful, so damn blue.

He stops and brings his eyes to mine. They're still so earnest, so full of life.

"Hey." He pushes a lock of hair behind my ear. His touch is soft, sweet, electric.

"Hey yourself." I lean into him, soaking in the feeling of his body. There's something so safe about it, even if he is...

Even if we're nearing the end.

"You having a nice trip?"

I nod, pressing my palm into his back. There's something in his eyes, something off.

"Are you okay?" I ask.

"Perfect."

"You sure there's nothing you want to talk about?"

He smirks and wraps his arms around me. "You sound like me." His eyes stay on mine even as his expression grows more and more intense. "We can talk later. Right now, I want to be with you under the stars."

"Now, you sound like me."

He nods. "I learned from the best."

I swallow, again, turning my head away from him. I can't bear to hold his gaze, not now, not like this. But I feel his fingers on my chin. His touch is so soft, so sweet, so here. Maybe I was wrong and he's not a million miles away.

He nudges me gently, tilting my chin so our eyes meet. "I mean it. I love being here with you."

Our lips meet. It's soft and sweet, and I can't bear to

resist him. I press my palms firmly into his back, arching into him.

He sucks on my lower lip, his hands sliding to my ass. It still feels so good to touch him, to taste him, to just be near him.

Our kiss breaks and he brings his gaze back to me. "We're in a pretty secluded area."

"Is that right?"

He nods, steps back, and pulls his shirt over his head. "It's been a while since we've done any skinny dipping."

He unzips his jeans and slides his boxers to his knees. Jesus. He's not wasting any time waiting for an answer.

I soak in the sight of him. He's sheer perfection.

"Always objectifying me." He smiles, his eyes dark. Tempting. "You coming?"

I nod and slip out of my dress. He looks at me with an intent focus that makes me feel more naked than I am.

"You're still a little over dressed," he rumbles, his voice deeper.

My body hums. I squeeze my thighs together to maintain my composure. "I need help."

He moves towards me. "I may be able to provide some help."

I look up at him, into his eyes. Right now, he's mine. I rise to my tip toes, wrap my arms around his neck, and kiss him. Kiss him like the ship is going down.

His hands are on my back, pushing my body into his. His touch is so hot, so electric. I can barely take it.

My body is buzzing, begging for more.

He slides his hands over my back, until they're at my bra. But he doesn't unhook it. Not yet. He traces its edges with his fingertips.

I groan, digging my nails into his skin, arching into

him. He slips his hands into my bra and rubs my nipples gently.

He moves his free hand to my ass and slides it under my panties. Damn. This is so much better than what I had in mind.

I melt into him. He sucks on my bottom lip, scraping his teeth against it. Then, he slides his tongue into my mouth.

He circles my nipple with his fingers. It's light, soft, perfect.

"Why are you always ruining my plans?" His voice is hoarse, heavy with desire.

He slides his hands up my back, unhooks my bra and flings it onto the sand. His eyes pass over me, a look that says I'm the best thing he's ever seen.

When he looks at me like that, I believe it.

Then his lips are on mine. He kisses me, hard and deep, his fingertips skimming my back, stomach, shoulders. They settle on my chest, and he rubs my nipples with his thumbs.

Electricity surges through me, down to my fingers and toes. I grab his ass and pull his body into mine. He's hard, and I need him here. I need him no matter what might happen tomorrow.

"Please don't tell me you want to wait until we're back at the hotel," I groan.

He laughs softly.

"Turn around," he orders.

I do, and he places his body behind mine. He presses his lips into my neck as he kneads my breasts. He kisses me softly, then harder and harder. Then it's teeth, gently scraping against my neck.

I try and reach back, to touch him, but he grabs my

arms and places them at my sides. He slides my panties to my knees, and I step out of them.

Now there's nothing between us.

He grabs my hips, bringing my body into his. I can feel him, hard, against me, but he doesn't enter me. Not yet. He drags his fingers over my thighs, so, so close. I feel his teeth on my neck again. It's harder this time. Like he's claiming me. Like he's hoping to leave a mark.

I arch my back, rubbing against him. I need him to claim me, to make me his, to show me how much he wants me.

I grab his hand and place it on my sex. He rubs me gently, sinking his teeth into my neck again and again. My body is swimming with desire, desperate for him to move faster, to fuck me.

But he moves slowly, stroking me with one hand, teasing my nipple with the other. He plants kisses on my neck and shoulders.

I groan, and he moves a little faster, strokes me a little harder. My sex clenches, my body filling with pleasure.

He rubs his thumbs against my nipples again. It's so soft I can barely feel it, but it sends sparks down my spine. I tilt my head back, turning to him.

I kiss him, plunging my tongue into his mouth. It's desperate and needy and proof that he wants me as badly as I want him.

He moves his hands to my chest and traces circles around my nipples. I turn back, pressing my ass into him, arching my back as far as it will go.

"Luke," I groan. "Please..."

He sinks his teeth into my neck. His hands find my thighs and he pries my legs apart. His cock strains against my, almost. He kisses me, one more time.

Then he slides inside me.

My body floods with relief. I'm exactly where I need to be.

He grabs my hips and shifts into me with slow, tiny movements. My body hums, filling with pleasure. I arch into him, try and feel as much of him as I can, try to give him space to go deeper.

He squeezes my hips, pulling me closer as he thrusts into me. He groans, his breathy heavy. He's almost shaking. He wants this. Badly.

I close my eyes, soaking in the feeling of him inside me, his body against mine, his hands on me. There's a pressure between my legs and it's getting tighter and tighter, deeper and deeper.

I turn back to Luke, kissing him hard, sliding my tongue over his. He squeezes my chest, rubbing my nipples with his thumbs again.

His hands move to my hips and he brings his mouth to my ear. "Touch the ground."

I bend over and press my hands into the sand for support. I can barely stand. He can do whatever he wants to me.

The thought only makes me hotter.

I can feel every movement deep in my core. I'm so close, almost there...

He thrusts into me, slow and steady. He groans. "Fuck, Alyssa..."

He's close.

He squeezes my hips as he moves deeper, filling every inch of me. I moan, squeezing the sand and biting my lip. Fuck, I'm so close.

He thrusts into me, again, and again, and again. The pressure inside me grows, more and more and more.

He groans, diggings his fingers into my hips. Damn he's so deep in me, and I'm so close and...

One more thrust, a little deeper, a little further. I bite my lip to keep from screaming. I dig my fingers into the sand. I clench my sex.

A torrent of pleasure washes over me, from my fingertips to my toes.

He holds me tightly, thrusting into me a little deeper, his breath harsh.

His nails sink into my skin, and he releases everything, coming deep inside me.

For a long moment, we just stay in that position.

It's a struggle. My body is almost limp in the aftermath.

He reaches for me, pulling me back to a standing position. He slides his arms around me, squeezing me tight.

We catch our breath, our bodies pressed together, nothing around us but the glow of the moon.

He presses his lips into my neck. "Now... how about that skinny dipping?"

I let out a small laugh, nodding.

Grinning in response, he leads me to the water.

————

WE SPEND FOREVER IN THE WATER, SWIMMING AND KISSING under the stars.

Everything is warm and sweet and perfect. We don't discuss the last three months or the next three months. Hell, we don't discuss anything at all.

We swim until we're both exhausted.

When we get back to the hotel, Luke crashes. I've never seen him fall asleep so easily. Hell, I almost never see him asleep. But, there he is, asleep.

I try and get comfortable. I read on the couch. I brush my teeth and change into pajamas. I even flip through TV channels with the volume turned way down.

But I don't get anywhere near tired enough to sleep.

I try for a while, but it's in vain. Even next to Luke, with his body warming the bed, I still can't get comfortable.

The time difference is wonky. I'd be waking up in New York. But it's more than that.

Something is wrong, something is missing.

I can't stop thinking about Nicholas's words. *We've spent so much time together, but I still feel like I haven't even scratched the surface with you.*

Luke has been backing off. He's been afraid. And I've pushed away all his attempts to reach me.

I need to break this cycle somehow.

I just... don't know how, don't know where to start. I could call Laurie, use her as a sounding board.

And I would. In any other situation. In this case... as wonderful as she is, she doesn't know all of me. Not really. There's a lot of dark corners I like to keep buried.

But there's someone who does. Someone who might be able to shed some light on the situation.

Ryan was my friend for years before he was my boyfriend. If anyone knows how hard it is to put up with me, it's him.

I push off the couch and look for my phone. It's still early in Los Angeles, really early, but this might be my only chance before Luke is awake.

I deleted Ryan's contact a long time ago, but he's had the same number since high school. I punch it into the phone and then just stare at the digital display.

I can't quite bring myself to hit "dial."

Luke will be jealous if he finds out. He'll misunderstand. He'll think it's something different than it is.

I move to the bathroom and lock the door behind me.

It's not a secret. I'll tell him later. But I can't deal with an inquisition right now. Not after dodging sleep all night.

I dial.

A few rings and Ryan answers. "I hope it's you and not your jealous boyfriend."

So he's not wasting any time with pleasantries.

"It's me. And he's my fiancé."

"Ah." His voice is steady, like he's remembering a pasta dish has mushrooms. Like this means nothing to him. "Do you have any clue what time it is in Los Angeles?"

"Later than it is in Hawaii. And I'm sure you're in the office by now."

He doesn't respond to that, which tells me I'm on the money.

"Hawaii? If you're calling me at five A.M., that vacation must be going well," he says, his voice sly.

"It's... complicated."

"It's never complicated, Alyssa. That's just a convenient excuse for behaving inappropriately."

Jesus, I've heard some bit of that lecture at least a hundred times. I take a deep breath, trying to fight off a rush of memories. Ryan has always been a condescending asshole, but he was well-intentioned once upon a time.

"I'm only calling to talk."

"And what are you calling to talk about?" He asks. It's not impatient or harsh, but there's a certain immediacy to it. A demand that I explain myself right away.

"Us."

"Don't be vague. It irritates me." It's still flat, like he's expressing a distaste for those mushrooms. Not like he's mocking my apprehension.

I take a deep breath and hold it in my lungs for as long as I can. "I have to ask you something and I want you to be honest."

"Okay." He's still so calm and collected. So Ryan.

"Why did you ever want anything to do with me?"

A pause. He didn't expect that question.

"Back in high school or after?"

"Both." I press my nails into my thumb until I can't take the pinch.

There's a lot of painful history between Ryan and me, and I'm not too keen on reliving it.

"I wanted to help you."

"Why?"

"Because no one else would."

I bite my lip. It's not like I ever doubted Ryan started a friendship with me out of pity. I was pitiful back in high school. No prospects. No friends. Nothing but guys who wanted to get their hands up my shirt.

"And what if someone else had helped me?"

"I still would have helped you. I saw something in you. A potential."

"To be your trophy girlfriend?"

"Alyssa, if I wanted to make you my girlfriend when we were in high school, I would have done it."

"Why didn't you want to?"

"We were from two different worlds. My family wouldn't have approved." He almost sounds like he regrets it. "Maybe if you hadn't been-"

"Such a pathetic mess?"

"Don't do this to yourself," he says. It's almost kind. Like he really cares about my mental health.

"So you were waiting until I'd blossom into a good trophy wife?"

"Partially," he admits. "But I did care about you. I'd be an idiot not to realize you're beautiful and a bigger idiot not to realize you'd make an excellent wife."

"What kind of 16-year-old thinks about his future wife?"

"I told you. I wanted to help you. I didn't think about marrying you until we were both in L.A. It only seemed natural then. You needed my help, and I needed someone too."

"Someone to show off."

"So what? You needed someone to take care of you. I needed someone to show off. It was a mutually beneficial relationship."

I take a deep breath. "I'm not hearing a lot about how you truly loved me."

"I'm not going to insult your intelligence. I loved you, yes, but our relationship was never about love."

The room is spinning around me, but I'm sure it's because it's so damn early, because I've barely slept. "Would you have been with me if I wasn't beautiful?"

There's a pause. Finally, a question Ryan doesn't have the answer to. I almost forgot how hard he is to rattle.

"No. I did care for you, but I have expectations to live up to."

My stomach drops, but it's not like this is a revelation. Ryan always made it clear I needed to look a certain way, that I needed to play my part.

"Alyssa, you're torturing yourself. I cared about more than your looks."

"Oh, like my career? You were so supportive there."

"I was trying to help you. I pushed too hard, yes, but you must understand why. You must understand how scary it was to watch you destroy yourself."

Help. Like getting me to do everything he wanted. Like putting his career ahead of mine. Like ordering me to stay in the cocoon of our apartment so nothing would hurt me.

Nothing but him.

"I did love you."

"I heard you the first time," I mutter.

I press my hand against the marble counter. It's so cold. It's warm and sticky outside, but the marble is so damn cold.

Ryan sighs.

"Do you really love Luke?" he asks impatiently. "Are you really happy?"

"Yes."

"Then talk to him about whatever it is that's really bothering you."

Chapter Twenty-Eight

LUKE

Alyssa isn't in bed. It's early--light enough outside that the sun is just rising--and she's nowhere to be seen.

The light in the bathroom is on. It's probably nothing, but, still, I roll out of bed and move towards the closed door.

There's sound in there, a conversation. She's on the phone. In the bathroom.

It's not *that* unusual. This room is huge and open. The sound travels. She probably doesn't want to wake me.

I press my ear against the door, but I can't quite make out what she's saying, or who she's talking to.

"Are you okay?" I knock on the door.

"Fine," she calls out. She mumbles something into the phone and opens the door.

Her eyes find mine. There's something in her expression--guilt or concern or embarrassment.

"What was that?" I ask.

"It's not important." She moves out of the bathroom and takes a step towards me. "It's really not."

"Humor me."

Her eyes turn towards the windows. It is gorgeous outside--the purple sky is streaked with yellow light.

Alyssa brings her gaze back to me. "Can we talk about it after I've had some coffee?"

I want to refuse, but then I look at her a little closer. There are dark circles under her eyes and she's pale. I know that look.

"Did you sleep last night?" I ask.

She shakes her head. "Too many time zones. But it's fine. I just need coffee. A lot of coffee."

"You sure you don't want to spend a few hours in bed?"

She nods. "I'd much prefer coffee."

———

WE HAVE A SLOW BREAKFAST. ALYSSA DRINKS CUP AFTER cup of coffee, but none of them bring her any closer to explaining what the fuck happened this morning.

I want to push her, but I know from experience she might just shut down completely if I do that.

If I'm honest, I'm tired of having to wear kid gloves with her so often.

But I also want answers.

So I talk about last night. I talk about work. I talk about the Oscar bait movies that are playing in every theater in Los Angeles.

She's responsive, even though it's obvious she's tired. I suggest we opt out of our original plan for the day--we're taking a long, difficult hike--to do something that won't exhaust her. But she refuses.

"You haven't slept in 24 hours."

"I'm fine," she says. "Great even."

Bullshit.

She certainly doesn't look great. She looks ragged, though it's unclear if her exhaustion is from lack of sleep or from whatever it is she's hiding.

"You're going to pass out from dehydration after all that coffee."

She gives me a look.

"Are you a lawyer or a doctor?"

"Technically, a law degree is a doctorate."

She rolls her eyes.

"I'll laugh my way to the bathroom," she says, smiling despite herself as she pushes out of the table and makes her way to the restaurant's bathroom.

A thought crosses my mind for a split second--what if she's purging--but I shake it away. She's been doing better for a long time. And she'd tell me if she was struggling.

We've been together for the last two weeks. There's no way she'd be able to hide a relapse.

I take a long sip of my tea. I'm getting worked up over nothing. I need to calm down, so she'll feel comfortable talking to me.

Alyssa returns to the table. She looks at me as she slides into her seat. She's really studying my expression.

"Don't tell me..." She shakes her head like she's disappointed in me. "And here I thought you finally trusted me."

Really?

"Fuck, Alyssa. You're not talking to me."

"I was not in the bathroom throwing up. That's what you wanted to hear, isn't it?"

"Stop projecting." I take a deep breath. I can stay calm here.

She didn't sleep last night. She's tired.

"If I didn't trust you, I'd be chewing your ass out about that phone call."

She bites her lip. She knows I'm right.

She packs her purse and takes one last sip of coffee, dropping the subject like it's caught fire in her hands. "Let's go."

I nod. Hiking while exhausted seems like a terrible idea, but if that's what she wants to do, fine.

If at any point she looks like she can't handle it, I'll just drag her ass back to the room.

———

OUR MORNING HIKE IS SUPPOSED TO BE DIFFICULT. IT'S 2.5 very steep miles. I explain the path to Alyssa on the drive, but she doesn't balk.

She rolls her eyes at me. "I thought you were in shape with all that tactical body weight training." It's my turn to give her a look. "You look like you're about to jump off a bridge." Alyssa pokes my shoulder. "I really am okay."

"Alright."

She shifts, pulling her legs to her seat and crossing them. "It doesn't seem like you believe me."

I focus on the narrow road. We're almost there. "I do. I'm just... I worry about you."

She says nothing, but I can feel her reaction. She hates that I'm worried about her. She hates when anyone is worried about her.

"People worry about each other, Ally. It's normal."

"I didn't say anything."

"I know what you were thinking."

I pull into the parking area of the hiking trail. This whole place is beautiful--lush green everywhere and a view of the ocean for miles. There's no reason why this won't be a nice morning.

"Do you know what I'm thinking right now?" It's a challenge, her irritation clear.

I park the car, unbuckle my seatbelt, and turn to Alyssa. "Knowing you, it's probably NC-17."

"Very funny."

"You have to admit I look sexy as hell in my shorts."

She shakes her head, but she's grinning despite herself. "I care about things besides fucking you senselessly."

"Fucking me sense-fully?"

"Smug bastard." She laughs, shaking her head. "Sorry. I guess I'm a little cranky."

"It's alright. You're cute cranky."

She leans towards me until she's only a few inches away. Her eyes find mine. Damn, those are such gorgeous eyes.

She smiles, the tiniest thing, and slides her arm behind my neck. I lean into her, pressing my lips against hers.

When she pulls back, she brings her eyes back to mine. She looks at me for what feels like forever. It's like she's finding something in me, figuring something out.

"I do appreciate the concern," she finally says. "But I'm not going to break."

"I know."

She nods, reassured, and gets out of the car. I follow suit.

The scenery is even more gorgeous without a window in the way. There's blue sky and ocean for miles, and the hiking trail is something straight out of paradise. It's the most vibrant shade of green over mountains and valleys. It's life, everywhere.

I take Alyssa's hand and we make our way up the steep trail. It starts off simple enough--a straight dirt path going up a mountain. We walk slowly at first, taking in the sights, the warm breeze, the feeling of being ensconced by nature.

Alyssa stops at the peak of this curve of trail. She turns back to look at me. There's such a joy in her expression. For a minute, I forget that we've spent the last few months falling apart, that she's having secret conversations on the phone at the crack of dawn, that we're going to have to deal with this impossible distance.

The trail slopes down and starts to wind. There's a mountain to the left, and it's covered with layers and layers of vines. It's so green and so overgrown, it nearly blocks out the sky. To our right is a long valley. Tiny green bushes and tall, thick trees with deep, knotty roots.

"Come on, Grandpa. I don't have all day." Alyssa rushes ahead.

She's moving fast, almost running. I pick up the pace and catch up to her. She's tired, a little out of breath, but she is holding up fine.

I was worrying for nothing.

We hike for a long time. There's so much to take in. This place is so different from anywhere we've ever been together. Hell, anywhere I've ever been. It's pure, untouched jungle. It's secluded.

It's perfect.

The morning turns to afternoon. The sun rises, until it casts a soft glow over everything.

We don't stop until we come to a sharp batch of rocks. The only way up the rest of the trail is climbing. Alyssa eyes them with trepidation, but she won't admit she's scared.

I'll have to give her an easy out.

"How about we take a break?" I suggest.

"I'm fine."

"Yes, but I'm in the middle of paradise. There's beauty everywhere I look." I turn to her. "Especially in front of me."

"Cheesy." She smiles.

I grin.

"Sometimes a little cheese is a good thing. And I want to absorb everything."

Alyssa shakes her head. "You don't fool me for a second. But fine." She takes a seat on a short rock.

I find a place to sit near her, watching her take in the scenery. The look of amazement in her eyes is really nice to see.

She's happy.

I'd hate to destroy that.

She brings her gaze back to me. "What are you thinking?"

"How lucky I am to have you."

"Cute answer, but what are you really thinking?" She props her chin on her hand.

"How lucky I am to be here with you." I shift, but I keep my eyes on her.

"That's very sweet."

"I mean it."

She nods. "I feel that too you know. Lucky that you put up with me."

"Ally... it's not like that."

"Never?" Her eyes turn towards the expanse of sky. Like there's an answer somewhere in the clouds.

I choose my words carefully. I don't want to lie.

"Everyone gets frustrated sometimes."

She shakes her head like she accepts the answer, but she's doesn't. There's something off about her posture.

"Are you frustrated I haven't told you about the phone call?"

"Yes. You say it isn't important, but..."

"We don't always agree about what is or isn't important." She looks at me for a second, then her gaze is back on the ground.

Whatever this is, she's afraid to tell me.

"I do trust you." I slide to my feet and kneel in front of her. "I mean it."

She looks down at me and nods. I offer my hand and she takes it. She squeezes it so tightly she nearly cuts off my circulation.

"Tell me, Alyssa."

She nods. "Give me a second." She takes her hands back and runs them through her hair. She adjusts her tank top, her shorts, anything that can serve as an excuse. Then she brings her eyes back to me. "Are you sure you won't get upset?"

I laugh. "I know we've had this conversation before."

She nods and looks away again. I bring my hand to her cheek, turning her back to face me.

"Tell me."

She takes a deep breath. "It was Ryan. I was on the phone with Ryan."

My stomach drops.

Alyssa was on the phone with Ryan. At the ass crack of dawn. My fiancée locked herself in her bathroom to call her ex-boyfriend.

And she insists this conversation wasn't important.

"You look like you're going to throw up."

I stand up, raking a hand through my hair.

"I feel great. Peachy fucking keen."

She winces at my tone.

"It didn't mean anything."

"Would you swear on that?"

She holds my gaze for a moment but breaks to shake her head. "It didn't mean what you think it means."

I'm a reasonable man. I know she wasn't calling him to have hot phone sex. Or to profess her undying love.

But they were friends for a long time. There might be something there.

It's possible this has been going on for a long time.

"What are you thinking?" she asks.

"I'm thinking you should put me out of my misery and tell me why you were talking to Ryan."

She nods, turning her gaze to the sky again. Squinting to block out the sun. "I should put my sunglasses back on."

"Alyssa."

"I can't explain it exactly," she hedges.

"Did you call him?"

"What's the difference?" She crosses her legs. She's still looking at the sky.

"You did, didn't you?"

She shakes her head, but she still won't look at me.

"Why?"

"Well." She takes a long breath. "Nicholas visited me in New York. After a show."

I have a flashback to them walking into the bar at the same time.

"When was this?"

"On the last night."

"So, while I was listening to your friends get drunk, you were having a private chat with another guy in your dressing room? After you told me not to come?"

There's no way to keep the anger out of my tone at this point.

"I knew you'd take it the wrong way." She shrinks back, just a little bit, still looking anywhere but my eyes.

"Okay. Explain to me how I should fucking take it. And what the hell does this have to do with Ryan?"

"Nicholas said something... he said that we'd spent a lot

of time together, but he still didn't really know me. That he felt like he'd barely scratched the surface. Nothing happened in the dressing room, but what he said... it got to me." Her expression, her voice, all of it is so earnest.

I'm pretty fucking sure if that Nicholas asshole showed up at her dressing room and started having a conversation like this, it wasn't because he wanted to touch base with a platonic friend.

But if Alyssa says nothing happened, I believe her.

I take a deep breath, trying my best not to get angry.

But, fuck. She's giving me a lot to be angry about.

"And so you decided to round things out by calling Ryan?"

She folds her arms in irritation. "Do you want to hear this?"

No.

Yes.

"I'm guessing you weren't calling him this morning begging for more forgiveness."

Her eyes find mine. There's shame in her expression. She's ashamed of whatever it is she was doing with Ryan that wasn't sex.

"Ally, you're killing me here."

"What Nicholas said got to me. I know I can be difficult to reach... anyway." Her voice gets low and soft. "The last three months... you weren't exactly trying to reach me."

She's right.

"I know. I'm sorry."

She shifts out of the sun, so she's turned away from me. "I had to know if Ryan felt the same way. If he really thought being with me was that miserable. He's the only other man I've been with. I thought maybe he'd have some insight on what's going wrong with us."

She called her ex to get insight into our relationship.

I'd laugh if I didn't feel like grabbing Ryan's perfectly coiffed hair and slamming his head against any hard surface within reach.

"And?"

"He said he'd never manipulate me. On purpose."

"I doubt he would call it manipulation."

"Can we not start about Ryan?" She asks. She shifts off the rock and unfurls on the ground.

"I'm pretty sure you started this." I lay down next to her, my anger tempered slightly as I take in her demeanor.

She looks more tired than anything.

"But I need to know why you didn't tell me about Ryan. Or Nicholas for that matter."

"Honestly... I didn't think there was anything to say about Nicholas before he showed up in my dressing room. And I knew you would overreact about Ryan."

"You know everything. Don't you?"

"Luke... Don't start."

"Don't start? Seriously? Then tell me what the fuck is going on. Why are you talking to Ryan about our relationship?"

"I wasn't," she insists. "I was talking to him about my relationship to him." She opens her eyes and looks straight at me. "As I recall, you spent a lot of time talking to Samantha, your ex-fiancée, about your relationship with her. In fact, I recall her trying to kill herself and you rushing to her hospital room. You were with her for weeks! What high horse do you think you're on?"

One week. My ex-fiancée tried to kill herself, and I spent a week with her. To make sure she was okay. Eventually, she overstepped the boundaries of our friendship. Hell, she begged me to leave Alyssa for her.

But I ended her friendship over it.

"And?" I ask.

"I deserve a little bit of the same leeway."

I scrub at my face, stubble scraping my fingers.

Maybe she's right, and she deserves a bit of leeway. She wanted closure with her ex, fine.

But she should be talking to me about this.

"Okay. But if you're afraid I can't reach you, that I'm not willing to try—why aren't you talking to me about that?"

She leans back, her eyes on the sky. "I don't know."

Chapter Twenty-Nine

ALYSSA

Luke makes a few stabs at prying my feelings out of me, but I'm too damn tired to talk about it anymore.

Yes, I have doubts, but doubts are normal. Yes, I neglected to tell him about Ryan, but...

I was right. He did overreact.

And, yes, I called Ryan secretly and I had no real intentions of telling Luke about it. But it wasn't really about Luke. It was about me and Ryan. And I should be allowed to talk to the person who was my best friend for my entire adolescence.

So, I ask if we can save the conversation for when I've had more sleep, and I fall into a fitful nap on the top of a mountain. Luke holds me the entire time, probably terrified I'll roll off a cliff into oblivion.

But we're already so close to oblivion. What's really the worst that could happen at this point?

After a quiet walk back to the car--mostly downhill, thank God--we drive in silence. It's well into the afternoon at this point, but I have no clue where we're going, what our plan is.

The narrow, windy roads seem to stretch forever. Thank God Luke is driving. I'd probably steer right off the side of the road. If I could even manage to keep my eyes open for long enough to drive.

Once we're back in civilization, Luke pulls into the parking lot of a mall. Of course, even in paradise, there are plentiful malls.

He looks me over, carefully, like I really am about to break. I'm sure I look like shit, like I'm really about to explode into a million pieces. But it's irritating.

"How about an early dinner?" he offers.

I nod, okay, and I don't bother to make a comment about how we're skipping lunch. The sarcasm would do nothing to convince him I'm healthy. That I'm worth reaching. That I'm really going to talk to him when my energy is better.

We stop at a Vietnamese noodle shop. It's a tiny place in a strip mall, packed with plastic tables and chairs. There are mirrors all over the walls, but I try to avoid them. I'm not at my best at the moment.

We take a seat at a table by the door. We're the only customers in the whole shop, but the server hangs back by the kitchen, chatting with one of the cooks.

Luke scans the menu. "They have Vietnamese iced coffee."

"I thought I was over-caffeinated and dehydrated."

He shrugs.

"Has that ever stopped you before?"

We pour over our menus for a while. I pick out something that won't overwhelm me--chicken and vegetables in some kind of white sauce.

When I look up, Luke's eyes are on mine. There's so

much concern in his expression, but he keeps his mouth shut.

The server stops by and we place our orders. My main concern is water. Lots and lots of water. I squint my eyes closed until we have our drinks.

Luke has a Vietnamese iced coffee. It's in a parfait glass and it's swimming in whipped cream. Not something I would ever order. But, still, when he offers me a sip, I take one.

It's sickeningly sweet, but there is something satisfying about it. Like it could chase away every inch of pain in my body. I nod, thank you, and pass the drink back to him.

I focus on my water. After half a dozen glasses, I finally regain my senses. Whatever happens, it's nice to be here with Luke in the middle of paradise. It's nice to sit across from him at an empty ethnic restaurant, trying out some food I've never had before.

We talk a little about the trip, about Hawaii, about life back in Los Angeles. But we're still dodging everything important. Even Luke is careful not to tread on any subject that could be a damn land mine.

I have half a mind to let everything out. To say fuck it and demand a better explanation for why things have been so difficult.

But I don't.

I talk about the weather, about movies, about the mystery I'm reading on my Kindle. I'm certain the ex-husband did it, but there's no telling, really.

After lunch, we duck into the mall's movie theater. Nothing good is playing, but it's nice to sit in the air-conditioned room with Luke's arms around me. I fall asleep in his lap. When I wake up the credits are rolling.

Back in the car, he asks how I'm feeling. "Do you think you're ready to talk yet?"

I shake my head. "Maybe later."

He nods, but there's a resignation to it.

Like I am just too damn difficult to reach.

———

BACK IN THE HOTEL ROOM, WE SHOWER, DRESS, AND RETIRE to the balcony.

We're on the second floor, surrounded by nothing but stars. The ocean is a few hundred feet away and gentle waves roll onto the beach in a soft rhythm. It's dark and breezy, but it's warm and humid and sweet all the same.

Still, I shiver in my skimpy pajamas, leaning against Luke for warmth. He wraps his arms around me, presses his lips into my cheek. He leans towards me, his breath on my ear.

"I love you," he whispers.

He means it. I know he means it. I know he loves me, wants me, needs me as desperately as I need him.

He loves me.

But he's not convinced that will be enough.

I meet his gaze. His eyes are sincere.

But when his lips curl into a smile, it doesn't light up his face. Not the way it usually does. He brushes his fingers against my chin, holding my gaze.

"I'm tempted to repeat myself." His voice is soft.

There's a heaviness in my chest, like the weight of all this is going to crush me into a million tiny pieces.

But I say nothing. He moves closer, wrapping me in a hug, squeezing me so tight I think I might burst.

But he says nothing.

I pull back. I'm tempted to apologize, to convince him to find someone who will be what he needs, to convince him that I'm that someone, that everything will be better, easier.

But I say nothing.

He meets my eyes again. For once, he knows what I'm thinking. I can see it in his eyes, in the sad resignation in his expression.

"I love you too." My voice is tiny, a whisper. It's nothing, because it's not enough.

It's never going to be enough.

I bite my lip. "Maybe we should-"

"Don't," he cuts me off. "Don't say it."

"We can't keep running away from it."

"I know." He smooths my hair back, his eyes not leaving mine.

It's like he can see straight through me.

This should be enough. I love him and he loves me. Sure, we have problems. But we can work through them.

My throat goes dry again.

Or maybe we can't.

I blink back a tear. The same hot sting as last time. And this is the same. Worse, even. Nothing has changed. Nothing will. Not like this.

I close my eyes, pressing my nails into my palms. There's no reason to hide. Not anymore.

"You're not happy with me," he murmurs.

There's salt on my lips. I wipe my eyes, turning away so he won't see. "That's only a matter of circumstance."

A small pause.

His voice is gentle when he speaks.

"What if it's not?"

"You're the one..." My voice breaks. My throat is too ragged and dry to make any of this fit. "You're the one who wants more."

He shakes his head. "I want you to be happy."

"Please..." I clear my throat. "Please don't do this."

"I don't want to," he says, his voice rough. He takes my hand, squeezing it with both of his. "But, Ally—do you really want to marry me?"

His eyes are on me and his gaze is laser focused on me. He wants to know the truth. Not bullshit that will placate him. The actual truth.

I swallow hard. "I think so."

He runs his thumb over my index finger. His eyes don't waver. "It's a 'yes' or 'no' question--do you want to marry me?"

Chapter Thirty

LUKE

lyssa bites her lip. She looks anywhere but in my
eyes.

"That's not fair," she says. She turns her gaze
to her engagement ring. Runs her fingers over it.

A tear rolls down her cheek.

"Ally..."

I reach for her, to touch her, offer some hint of
comfort. She pushes my hand away, turning her gaze back
to the ocean.

"Don't pretend," she says.

"This isn't even the first time this month I've made you
cry."

She shakes her head as if to protest, as if to suggest
that she's not crying.

"It's okay," I say. "You'll be happier."

I move closer to her, but she pushes me away. Harder
this time.

"Don't tell me how I'll feel."

"Okay." I hold up my hands. "You tell me."

Tears roll down her cheeks. She hugs her knees into her chest. "You really did give up on me, didn't you?"

"Of course not."

I reach for her. This time, she doesn't push me away. I rub her shoulders. Brush her hair back behind her ears. Her eyes are still on the floor. Her nails are still digging into her shins.

"Then why don't you... why do you want to break up with me?"

"I don't."

"But you are anyway?"

My heart sinks. I love Alyssa. I want to be with her.

But, whatever she needs, I'm not giving it to her. She's not happy. She's distant, she's angry, she's miserable.

And I'm not getting what I need either. Not if I'm thinking like this.

She meets my gaze. Her eyes are red and filled with tears.

"I'm not going to be another person who drags you down," I say.

She shakes her head, squeezing her knees tighter. "You're not."

"You're crying."

"We're going through a rough patch. It will get better."

"How?"

She looks back at the floor. Damn. I was hoping she had the secret answer. The one little thing that would make all this easier.

I wrap my hands around her wrists and pry them off her shins. She lowers her knees, shifting into me so that I can wrap my arms around her.

The feel of her body against mine is still magic.

I bite my tongue. This hurts so fucking bad, but I can't fight it. She deserves better than settling. We deserve better.

I have to be strong for both of us.

Even though it hurts so fucking bad.

She presses her palms against my back.

I can't drag this out. It will only hurt her more.

And it's killing me.

"You never answered the question," I murmur.

She still doesn't answer it. She just rests her head against my chest, hugging me tighter.

"I love you," she says in a low voice.

"But you don't want to marry me." The words are acid in my throat. But it's the truth. It's the only possible conclusion.

"I do... I... don't know."

"The problem is... I do, Ally. When I look at you, I see forever. I see our wedding day. Our honeymoon. I see us getting old and crotchety and bemoaning the kids and their terrible taste in TV." My stomach drops. This is terrible. It's awful. But it's what I have to do. "When you look at me... you don't see any of that."

"I..."

She shakes her head.

It fucking hurts. It's not a surprise, but it still fucking hurts.

"It's okay," I reassure her, my heart breaking. I absorb everything I can about this moment--the smell of her hair, the softness of her skin, the feeling of her body against mine. "You've spared my feelings for long enough. I want the truth. Not platitudes."

She chokes back another sob.

I swallow past the knot in my own throat.

"So that's it? Engagement's off, I'm moving out. Everything is over?"

"You're miserable with me."

She breaks our embrace and moves back. Her arms

tighten around her chest and she looks into my eyes. It's angry. "Don't pin this on me. That's a cowardly move."

I clench my fists. "Fine. Neither of us is fully happy." She flinches. I soften my tone, but I don't stop. This has to come out. "I love you so much, Alyssa. When I'm with you, I feel like my heart could burst. But every time you put me off, every time you don't talk to me about what's going on, every time you can't make a simple commitment to our future together... a little part of me feels like it's dying. I can't do it anymore. I don't like feeling like I'm fucking forcing you into marriage."

A tear rolls down her cheek. I want to go to her, to hold her, to kiss all that pain away. But I have to be strong here.

"I still remember seeing you with Ryan, thinking how tragic it was that someone so smart and sure of herself was willing to settle for someone who didn't make her happy. And I wanted so much to convince you that you deserved better. And, now, here I am. I'm the asshole fiancé who isn't making you happy. And I can't live with that."

She shakes her head, wiping at her face.

"But you're not... you're nothing like him."

"I'm not going to tell you how you feel," I say. "But I can't be with you unless we're both happy." I look at her, into those clear, blue eyes. "Are you happy?"

She shakes her head. "I don't know."

"Neither do I."

There's a long silence. The waves roll onto the beach, a slow, steady rhythm. They'll be there, rolling in and out, forever.

A warm breeze passes over me, pressing my T-shirt against my skin.

This will hurt a little less tomorrow.

We'll both hurt a little less tomorrow.

"I should get to decide who makes me happy," she mutters. It's barely a protest, but it's something.

"You do," I say. "But so do I. And I can't be with you like this--with the two of us 3,000 miles apart no matter how close together we are."

A tear rolls down her cheek. I tell myself not to hold her, not to stroke her hair, not to do something to ease the agony she's feeling in this moment.

But I can't. I take her into my arms, holding her tightly, soaking in the warmth of her body.

"I don't want to put any more demands on you," I say. "But I can't keep fighting all your defenses."

She squeezes me. "If you're breaking up with me, do it. Say it."

She's right. I have to pull the band-aid.

"I'm breaking up with you."

She chokes back a sob. Her fingers dig into my shirt as she squeezes me tighter.

I want to take it back. I want to tell her I changed my mind, that I'll do whatever she says, be whatever she wants. I love her so damn much.

But that's all bullshit.

She doesn't want to be my wife. She doesn't even want to tell me how she feels.

I hold Alyssa for what seems like forever. Her sobs fade to gentle cries, to choppy breaths, to slow, steady inhalations. She doesn't protest.

She must agree she'll be happier with someone else.

Chapter Thirty-One

ALYSSA

Luke offers me the rest of the vacation. Like spending the next four days in Hawaii by myself is some kind of consolation prize.

Sorry I'm dumping you. Here's some time in paradise to really let that sink in.

Fucking wonderful.

He retreats to the living room of the suite, leaving the bedroom to me. He calls someone, making some kind of arrangements. Probably some woman who actually talks to him.

I pull my knees into my chest and bury myself under the covers. It's dimmer, darker, quieter. It's warm, too warm, but the suffocating feeling is comforting somehow. Something is wrapped around me. It's not Luke's arms. It's not his undying devotion or even his damn patience.

But it's something.

I stifle a sob. I don't want to cry too loudly, don't want to tempt him to console me. A hug from him, the sweet smell of his body, the taste of his lips...

It would be too much. I'd fall apart.

I hug my knees tighter.

He's tired of fighting me.

I squeeze my eyes closed, willing the darkness into my brain. I need black. I need nothing. I need to be empty, again, to be filled with anything except this.

This is it. The end.

I can't blame him. I'm tired of fighting me too. If I had the choice, I'd walk away.

Tears sting my eyes. Okay. Fine. This is one thing I can't fight.

A sob wells in my throat. I clutch the blanket around me. Here, alone, in this dark room, I can really fall apart.

———

"ALYSSA."

Luke's voice is so gentle and sweet. For a moment, I'm convinced this was all a nightmare. Another premonition of the awful I might face.

I open my eyes.

Luke is sitting on the bed with that look on his face that says I'm sorry I'm getting out of here.

We're in the room where we were supposed to fix everything, where we were supposed to erase how much the last six months hurt.

Not a nightmare. Just real fucking life.

I feel his hands on my hair. I close my eyes, fighting another round of stupid tears. There's an emptiness inside of me, starting at my throat and going all the way into my gut.

He strokes my hair gently. He should stop. He shouldn't do this. It hurts too much. It's too awful. I should tell him to stop.

But I need the comfort too much.

"I talked to Laurie. She's taking a red eye. She'll be here in the morning."

Oddly enough, that's what cuts through the haze.

Now he's calling my friends to console me?

"No."

He frowns, clearly concerned.

"What?" There's mostly concern in his eyes. Even when he's desperate to get the hell out of dodge, he's still concerned for me.

"No," I repeat, sitting up. "I don't want you to call someone else in to take care of me. I can take care of myself."

He searches my eyes for a long moment before nodding.

"Okay. If you're sure..."

"I'm sure."

He nods again, looking away.

"I'm leaving in a few minutes."

I swallow hard, willing my eyes to stay dry. "Okay."

It's not. But what else can I say?

He reaches out to stroke my hair but catches himself before touching me.

It hurts so fucking bad.

"I'm sorry," he says. "I don't want to drag you around."

I clear my throat, looking down at the bedspread.

"What now?" I ask.

"You have a few days in Hawaii. I'll be back at the house. You're still welcome there." He looks to the far corner of the room.

What a shitty consolation prize.

He brings his gaze back to me. There's love in his eyes. I can see it. He still loves me. He still wants me. He's frustrated, but that's it. There's still a chance... he could be convinced.

But not by a bunch of empty promises.

"I'm not going to abandon you," he says.

I'm sure he means it, but right now, it's just another shitty consolation prize.

I nod, okay. I'm still welcome in his house, in the spare room, to be around him but not with him. So I can watch him move on to some girl who will actually talk to him, some girl who won't frustrate him, some girl who is everything he really wants.

He squeezes my hand, looking into my eyes one last time. "Call me if you need anything."

If I need anything. What a joke. He's everything I need and he's leaving and he's being so damn sweet about it.

But, I nod, okay, and I turn my back to him. The sky is still dark. The stars are still bright. The waves are still crashing onto the beach.

And I'm still empty.

———

THE PHONE RINGS.

I ignore it.

But whoever is calling only tries again. Which tells me exactly who it is.

I stick my arm out from the blob of blankets, searching the nightstand blindly.

The familiar shape of the phone hits my palm on the third ring.

I pull it back into my blanket cocoon.

I clear my throat, knowing it won't help.

I'll still sound like I'm having a breakdown.

"Hello?"

"What a dick, huh?" Laurie mutters.

A laugh--the tiniest damn laugh in the world--catches

in my throat. Maybe, one day a million years from now, I'll manage something close to happiness again.

"I mean. What kind of asshole calls you at six and begs you to fly, first class, on his dime, to spend half a week in Hawaii with your best friend?"

"It's worse that he's being considerate," I mutter. "He should have slapped me and told me he never wanted to see me again."

"Hmm. I'll hire someone to kill him."

"He deserves it."

"No, what he deserves is slow, painful torture. How could he invite you to God damn paradise then break up with you?"

I laugh again, but it's heavy in my chest. "I don't want to talk about Luke right now. Why don't you talk to me about what's going on with you?"

"Whatever you want. Let's see...oh, I ran into..."

———

I MANAGE TO DRAG MYSELF OUT OF BED FOR THE REST OF the trip.

For the most part I sit at little cafes, pounding cup after cup of coffee.

I don't do any amazing Hawaii things. There's no scuba diving, no happy hour cruises, no romantic dinners under the stars.

I eat, I drink, I call Laurie sporadically to talk about anything except Luke.

But the weight of it grows in my chest, refusing to be pushed away.

On the last night, I pack carelessly. There isn't much that matters here. Only clothes.

I sit on the balcony, staring at the waves, trying not to

replay the moment where everything broke into a million little pieces.

It's another warm, humid night and there's something so refreshing about the light breeze.

Laurie calls as I'm taking a deep breath.

"Hey. What are you doing?"

I lean back.

"Sitting on the balcony. Drinking amaretto." I tilt my head back to take another sip from the bottle of liquor. The sweet taste of licorice coats my tongue and throat.

It's the kind of thing Luke would drink.

The heaviness builds in my chest. I blink back a tear.

Laurie sighs.

"Do you want to talk about it now?"

"I miss him so much already," I admit. I press my fingers into my thighs. This whole thing makes me dizzy. I don't know what he wants, what I want, what the hell I'm going to do here.

"Do you think it's really over?" she asks, her tone careful.

"Maybe," I mutter. I shake my head to keep from crying. "He's trying to protect me. Protect us."

"From what--too many great orgasms?"

"You're a pervert." It almost hurts to smile, but I can't help it. I swallow the lump in my throat. "He said something about how he doesn't make me happy. That neither of us are happy."

"Oh." Her voice lowers, like she sees the merit in this horrible idea.

"You really think..." I bite my lip. I can't keep hiding from this. I have to confront it. "Do you really think he's right?"

"Alyssa... there is a lot of conflict between you two."

I can hear the hesitation in her voice. She doesn't want to hurt me, but she wants to tell me the truth.

I can appreciate the sentiment even though I don't agree with her.

"You're both wrong," I insist. "I've never been as happy as I am with him."

"Well. Did you tell him that?"

"I... no."

I shake my head. Of course not. That's been the whole problem all along.

"Maybe, if you talk to him, if you really tell him how you feel... maybe you'll work it out," she offers.

I nod, even though she can't see it.

"But, Alyssa... you're going to have to do a lot better than what you just told me. You're going to have to really open up, really let him see inside your brain. It's all or nothing."

I exhale, pushing all the air out of my lungs. "I know," I say. "I have an idea."

Chapter Thirty-Two

LUKE

The last year or so, the world was bright, vivid, colorful.

Full of promise.

I had someone I loved, someone who loved me back.

Without her...

I knew it would fucking hurt, but I couldn't anticipate how much.

But, even through the pain, I know it was the right thing to do.

Alyssa deserves to be as in love with someone as I am in love with her.

And I deserve the same.

The days pass slowly. Usually, at times like these, I'd work until I was too numb to feel anything. After my mother died, after my father died, after every fight with my damn ex, I'd fill every waking moment with whatever semi-productive activity I could find.

But I can't bring myself to put in an extra 20 hours at the office. I love my job. I love helping people in miserable marriages get divorced.

But there's so much more to life than working.

Even the painful moments with Alyssa made me feel alive, connected.

I don't think I can ever look at work the same again.

And I don't think I want to.

So I make plans to go back to my old schedule, the one I kept when I was convinced I could make things work with Samantha if only I had more time. I arrive at nine every morning and leave at six every night.

The house is lonely without Alyssa.

It's going to take some adjusting. Well, a lot of adjusting.

I do my best to clean up--to put aside anything I know she'll need immediately. There isn't much, really. She has her clothes, her plays, her coffee maker.

Really, the only thing she'll care about is her pour over coffee maker.

Every Sunday morning, she measures her water and coffee carefully, so she can make the perfect cup of coffee. I'm sure she does it every morning. But, for so long, we weren't spending the mornings together. She had an early call time, or she was off, and I wanted her to sleep in.

I place the appliance in a paper bag. I bought it for her eight or nine months ago.

Packing it up... isn't easy.

But what the fuck is going to be?

I rub at my chest, but it doesn't do anything to alleviate the heaviness.

Doesn't matter if it hurts. I have to do what I have to do.

Late that night, Alyssa leaves a message. Her voice is soft, tired.

"Hey, Luke. I hope you're doing well. I miss you, but... I won't get into that. I'm going to stop by for my things tomorrow morning. Around ten or so. Let me know if you'll be there." The message ends with a long stretch of silence.

She sounds miserable, defeated.

But this is a necessary step, a necessary moment of pain.

Alyssa is going to move on. She's going to be happier in the end.

I'm too deep in the dark to think the same of myself quite yet.

Chapter Thirty-Three

ALYSSA

y hands are shaking too damn much to pick up any of these notebooks.

They're all the same. It doesn't matter if I grab a ninety-nine-cent notebook in an awful shade of yellow or if I spring for the fifteen-dollar leather bound journal. Or even if I buy one of those hot pink things with a high heel on the cover.

The notebook isn't what matters.

But picking one of these books makes this plan so real. It's the first step towards opening myself up and spilling my guts on the page. The first step towards showing Luke I'm willing to let him in, showing him how ugly things really get.

I scan the notebooks again. They're a mess, loosely organized by how much they prefer form over function. The cheap, plain, college-ruled things are together. The ridiculously girl things are together. The classy, I'm a damn executive, look at my fancy notebook...

I take a deep breath. It doesn't matter what the notebook looks like. I can't delay this any longer. Not when it's my best chance of convincing Luke we can do this.

There.

I pick up a little, black notebook with a slick faux leather cover. It's simple enough. Not something that screams *these are all my horribly dramatic thoughts. That's what you wanted, right?*

The girl at the register gives me an aren't-you-that-girl kind of look. I pay cash so she can't check the name on my credit card and start some conversation about my career.

I feel a pang of guilt about it, but I just don't have the energy right now.

"Thank you," I murmur before hightailing out of there to my car.

It's cool outside, as cool as it gets in the evening in L.A., and all my hairs stand on end.

Not that the weather matters either. I'm not going to be out in it.

I have to get home and fill this damn notebook.

I drive back to Laurie's place. The streets are quiet at this time, her neighborhood pleasantly calm.

She's not home, but I still lock myself inside the guest room, pull the curtains closed, and curl up on the bed.

The cover of the notebook has a slight softness to it, and it's filled with pages upon pages. The label says 80 pages, but it seems more like 800. It seems endless.

There's no way I can fill all these pages.

But I have to try.

I scribble my greeting--Dear Luke--then I let my thoughts pour onto the page. Every ugly thing inside my brain. Everything that he'd beg to know, even if it might crush him.

I don't censor anything. Don't let myself think about any thought too long before it comes out onto the paper.

And hope it will be enough.

————

I ARRIVE TO LUKE'S EARLY AND I LET MYSELF IN WITH my key.

He's sitting on the couch, in his blue pajama pants and a V-neck, watching *The African Queen.* His mom's favorite movie.

The movie he busts out whenever he feels like his life is falling apart.

"You're early," he says.

He smiles. It's not his usual million-dollar grin, but I appreciate the effort.

He leads me to the kitchen and points me to a hot pink thermos. "I figured you'd like the color."

There's a matching blue Thermos next to it. Normally, he'd mock such obvious gender divides in coffee cups. But I do love hot pink.

He hands me the mug and our hands touch, just for a moment. The spark is enough to make my knees weak.

Dammit, this is even harder than I thought it would be.

"Thank you." I push the lid open and take a sip without asking for clarification.

It's the Kona coffee we were drinking all morning in Hawaii. A strike against it.

But it is damn good coffee.

He meets my eyes, not shying away. "There's oatmeal in the microwave," he offers. "In case you're hungry."

"You want me to eat oatmeal?"

He shrugs.

"If you say you like oatmeal, I believe you."

"You'll be the first," I mutter.

I dig my fingers into my purse, feeling for the notebook in it.

No, I'll call it what it is. It's a diary. A year or so worth of thoughts collected over a single night.

A very, very long night.

Luke holds my gaze. There's something sweet about it, sincere. Like maybe he's about to say he made a mistake, that he loves me too much to let me go, even if he foolishly believes I'll be happier without him.

"Do you need help with anything?" he asks.

I shake my head. "Just some clothes for the week."

"Oh." It's a happy oh, an oh, so does that mean you expect to be back here in a week.

The tension in my chest eases. He still loves me. That might be enough.

"You have a suitcase?" he asks.

I shake my head. A suitcase is too much, too permanent.

"You're usually more prepared." It's sweet, a joke, like he knows I can't bring myself to remove anything from our house.

He grabs a paper bag from the kitchen. "Is that enough?"

I nod. It's too much, really. I don't want to take anything from here. I don't want to set up shop at Laurie's. "I only want a few clothes."

"Ally... I did mean what I said in Hawaii."

I don't want to ask which thing he meant. It could have been that I'm always welcome here. Or it could be that he's intent on staying broken up.

I set the bag on the table and place my coffee next to it. "Hey, Luke..."

I don't know why I say it. It isn't like his attention hasn't been laser focused on me since I stepped inside. "Yes?"

"I... have something for you."

Any hint of joy drops off his face as he looks at the ring. "I'm not taking it back."

"It's your mom's."

"Yes. And I want you to have it."

My heart breaks a little more as I shake my head. "I wasn't talking about the ring, actually."

"Good. Because I'm not giving up on that."

I swallow, hard. The leather of my purse is smooth and supple against my fingertips, but I have to let go. I have to pry that notebook out and hand it to him.

I take a deep breath, trying to ease the knot of tension in my chest.

It will be easier once I give this to him. I'll be done.

I reach into the purse, running my fingers against the slick cover of the notebook. There's no more hiding after I give him this.

I suck in another deep breath. Any more of them and I might make myself pass out.

This might turn out okay. I have to believe it.

I pull the notebook from my purse and hand it to him. He presses his fingers into the cover, staring at it like it's the greatest work of American literature.

He offers a tiny smile. He must be relieved I'm not insisting he keep the ring. But why? If he's really dead set on breaking up, he should take it back.

That's more than something.

He turns the cover, his eyes passing over the first page. My stomach twists in knots.

"Don't read it yet," I blurt out. "Please."

He nods, closing the cover. "Okay."

"I, uh, I made some plans. For this weekend. I know you made yourself clear in Hawaii. And maybe that whole thing about making me happy was sparing my feelings, but..." My head spins. God damn. It really is bright in here. "Just, well, if you change your mind. If you decide you want to be with me, then meet me at the Marina at 11 A.M."

He laughs. "Bright and early at 11 A.M.?"

I nod.

He meets my gaze. His eyes are still so fucking gorgeous.

A long silence passes.

Like we could stare into each other's eyes forever.

"Okay," he finally says, gripping the notebook tightly.

A lightness floods my body.

This really might turn out okay.

Chapter Thirty-Four

LUKE

I hug Alyssa goodbye, doing my best not to hold her too tightly.

It takes all of my strength to shut the door behind her, to stay put instead of dragging her to bed and holding her all fucking day.

It's so hard to see her while having to maintain this distance.

I flip through the pages of the notebook. Every one starts the same--Dear Luke.

There must be two dozen letters in here.

I feel my stomach turn a little.

It's entirely possible every one of these letters come to the same conclusion--that they are all "fuck you, asshole."

But I have to read it to find out.

There's a message scribbled on the inside of the cover:

Here you go, Luke. Exactly what you asked for. This is every thought in my damn brain, the good, the bad, and the ugly. It's really, really damn ugly, but it's not like I've got anything to lose.

So here we go.

I pore over the pages. This is everything Alyssa's kept locked inside her for so long.

And she's finally sharing it with me.

Dear Luke,

God, I don't know where to start. I don't know if I want to hit you or kiss you or take Laurie up on her offer to have you killed. I don't know which would be more painful--living without you in my life at all or watching you move on with someone else.

I don't even know how I'm going to get through today.

I hate you so much right now. Haven't you ever heard the phrase "you have to be cruel to be kind?" A.K.A. you don't dump a girl in paradise then sweetly offer to make sure she's okay. You have to make sure she fucking hates you, damn it.

This is... awful.

Dear Luke,

Speaking of awful. Those last three months, huh? I'm still not sure what happened, why I wasn't strong enough to reach out to you. I know it made you give up on me.

Things were hard. We were far apart. I needed you, but you were also done dealing with my bullshit. It's not like I blame you. I'd do the same thing in your place. I don't mean to be so distant, so difficult. I really want to let you in. Hell, this is some sad attempt to do that. It's really more of a promise than anything, proof that I'm willing to try.

I was sure you were going to end things in New York, that you were waiting until after my show. You're so polite in my head, aren't you?

I wasn't all that wrong. You ended things shortly after my show. Was that your plan all along? If so, maybe skip the romantic vacation next time. I'd appreciate that. Or some other woman will appreciate it.

Shit, I can't stomach the thought.

DEAR LUKE,

Here's the truth.

Part of me thinks we're better off starting over. I'm less broken than I was a year ago. Maybe you are too. Maybe it would be easier with other people.

But I don't want that. I don't want easy. I want you.

Nicholas or Ryan didn't even put the idea on my head. I was already thinking it, that you weren't willing to be patient with me, that you're too damn romantic to deal with the day to day bullshit of all my baggage. I should have talked to you about it a long time ago. I should have done more therapy, stayed more vigilant about all my recovery work (don't worry. I haven't veered towards a relapse). I should have done a lot.

But it's better late than never.

I want to be with you, Luke. You make me happy. Maybe you don't see it, but you do. Sure, when things are off with us, I'm miserable. But I can't have the highs without the lows. Everyone gets mad. Every couple gets into fights.

I'm tired of running from it. I don't want to keep running from what I feel. Every time I make progress, I stumble backwards. But I can't have you living and dying by how well I'm functioning. If you don't want to be with me because you're sure I'm too much work, then fine. But don't bullshit me about how it's because I don't love you the way you love me.

That's a lie, and it's a cheap one. I love you so much. Like I've never loved anyone. You're better than a perfect cup of coffee and a "bullshit English major novel" on my Kindle. Hell, you're better than just about anything I can think of.

So, fuck you for trying to squirm out of this breakup. But *I* forgive you for it.

Because *I* really do love you, and *I* really do want to marry you, and *I* really want to do whatever *I* can to make this work.

Please let me do what it takes.

Chapter Thirty-Five

ALYSSA

L aurie takes a long sip of her coffee. She nods like she's confident, but she's not fooling me.

She's a nervous wreck.

She looks at the clock. It's almost ten. "Why did you give him so much time to think anyway?"

"It seemed fair."

She sets her coffee cup on the counter and paces around the kitchen, her chaotic energy not doing a whole lot to calm me down. "This is a ridiculous 180, Alyssa. Are you sure you know what you're doing?"

"I'm positive." I run my fingers along the engagement ring. Pretty sure. At least eighty percent.

"It's rather dramatic for you."

"I could use some dramatics."

"Are you really going to drive yourself to the Marina. Shouldn't you take a limo or something?" Laurie stops at the counter. She pushes against it, turning back to me. She shakes her head. "It's stupid. He lives like five minutes from here. Why are you going 10 miles south?"

"Because that's where we..." I can't explain it exactly.

It's not the first place we kissed--that was at his old house. Or where we met--at the office he used to share with Ryan. It's not even where we had our first kind of but not really a date thing.

I want to say that's where we fell in love, but that's not quite right either.

It's where... it's where I found him lying on the grass, reading a dog-eared paperback.

It was the paperback that got me. It was falling apart, like he'd read it a hundred times but still wanted more.

It was our secret place to meet. Where we'd hide in plain sight. And it was like he was there every time I wanted to see him. Like he could read my mind.

"It's important," I say, settling for that vague statement. I gather my purse, doing a mental check. I have everything I need for this. And it's warm enough that I shouldn't need a coat.

"You can't leave yet," Laurie says.

I give her a look.

Because you'll miss me?"

She rolls her eyes.

"What if he doesn't show? Are you really going to wait alone?"

I bite my lip. It's not like I've been replaying that possibility in my head all week, imagining myself standing at the marina like an idiot, waiting until the sun sets.

"How about you call at noon? If I don't pick up-"

"Assume you're having crazy hot sex?"

I laugh, and a bit of my tension releases. "Exactly."

Laurie looks at me like I'm her kid sister. "I'm so fucking worried about you."

"Whatever happens, I'll be okay."

She nods, wraps me in a hug. I repeat the mantra in my head. Whatever happens, I'll be okay.

I'll be okay.

———————

IT'S TEN FORTY-FIVE WHEN I FINALLY SET FOOT ON THE concrete path surrounding the Marina.

Maybe Laurie was right. This is all too melodramatic and I should have just called Luke and demanded some response to my heartfelt confession.

It's still possible he won't show.

But it's unlikely.

If he wasn't going to show, he would have called me, texted me, sent me a damn messenger pigeon--something to let me down easy.

I hope so, anyway.

I make my way to the oversized tree behind our old apartment complex.

For a while, we both lived here. I lived with Ryan. Luke was renting a condo, so he wouldn't have to stay in the house he'd shared with his ex.

It was all terribly complicated.

But this spot is where I found him with that book. He was waiting for me. I'm sure of it.

He'd arranged the whole thing perfectly. He was wearing only running shorts and he was splayed over the grass so casually, like he was waiting for someone to come along and mount him.

I press my hand into the tree. It's smooth and hard, like it can withstand anything.

It's bright already, and I'm certain that everything around me is spinning. I lean against the tree, squinting my eyes to block out the sun.

Whatever happens, I'll be okay.

I'll be okay.

I'm sure I'll be okay.

There are footsteps behind me. They're steady and determined. I tell myself it's nothing. It's still too early to get excited.

"I didn't think you'd move on so quickly."

Oh, God, what if he's here to ask for the ring back, to tell me how pathetic I am, to tell me he's so glad he broke up with me?

Everything is spinning around me.

So, I open my eyes and spin around too.

He's standing there, on the grass, in a black suit. He looks damn good with his hair slicked back. His eyes are full of that life I haven't seen in so damn long.

He's wearing a suit. It's not like he'd wear a suit to give me a brush off.

It's not like he'd wear a suit to break my heart.

My mouth is dry. I try to open it to speak, but nothing comes out.

"I'll take that as hello." His voice is smooth, calm. But there's a hint of amusement, of... brightness there.

It's a good sign.

"Did you, um..." My legs are shaking, but I hold onto the tree to stay upright.

Luke swoops in, catching me before I can hit the ground. His hands are on my waist, firm and supportive.

I meet his eyes. "Did you... Did you read everything?"

I feel like my heart is going to beat out of my chest.

He nods. "Every word."

That's a good sign. Right?

"And...?"

"It's everything I wanted."

My legs want to buckle, but he squeezes me tighter, pressing my body against his.

He wouldn't be holding me if he was about to dump me. Right?

God, I'm going crazy here!

I take a deep breath and exhale slowly. I need to be clear here, put all the chips out on the table. "I want to make this work. No matter how hard it is."

His hand finds my lower back and he presses my body into his. I close my eyes, rising up onto my tip toes to meet him.

Our lips connect and it's the sweetest, softest kiss we've ever shared. Everything is in this kiss--everything we've finally managed to say, every bit of hurt, of joy, of need.

Of love.

The kiss breaks and he looks into my eyes. "I want to be with you. Even if you're scared. Fuck. Even if you'll never be ready to marry me."

I take a deep breath, squeezing him to keep from crumbling. "Then prepare to be pleasantly surprised."

I reach into my purse for the ring box and attempt to lower myself to one knee. I only barely manage not to fall over, but I do it.

I take Luke's hand and look into his eyes.

That's the man I want to be with forever.

I've never been more sure of anything.

"I know this isn't really traditional," I start.

He nods, looking a little mystified.

I peel open the ring box, displaying it for him.

It's a men's wedding band. Simple. White gold. Exactly the kind of thing he'd pick for himself.

I hope.

"I've done a lot of thinking." God, I feel like I might pass out. Is this how every guy feels when he does this? "And I realized that there's no one I'd rather share my life with. Luke...

you fill me with so much. Not just happiness, but also laughter, excitement, passion. Hell, you fill me with this renewed will to make every day better than the one before. To try as hard as I can to stay on the path of recovery. To be a better version of myself." I stare up into those beautiful eyes of his and squeeze his hand tightly. "I would be honored if you would marry me."

He doesn't wait to answer, doesn't keep me in suspense.

He smiles, the expression lighting his eyes. "Ally, you know that's what I want."

"That's not exactly a yes."

His smile widens into a grin.

"Yes."

I slide the ring onto his finger.

I'm so happy I wonder why I don't just float away.

Luke laughs and pulls me back to my feet. His hands slide around my waist and he pulls me close, so close I can barely breathe.

Breathing is overrated anyway.

We kiss. Everything else fades away.

We have each other. That's all that matters.

Chapter Thirty-Six

LUKE

I t's a warm day in June. Of course, seasons are nearly meaningless in the great state of Hawaii. Every day is warm and humid with a pleasant breeze.

We're on a gorgeous beach with clean sand and clear blue ocean for miles. The setting sun casts a soft glow over everything.

It's breathtakingly beautiful.

But I can't take my eyes off Alyssa.

She looks so fucking gorgeous in that flowing silk dress. It's not a traditional wedding gown, but it suits her perfectly.

This whole thing is perfect.

She's beaming, brighter than the damn sun.

I wasn't sure about her idea to get married in Hawaii so we could fix our past mistakes. But she was right.

It's just us and the officiant.

The two of us against the world.

She bites her lip and whispers "I love you."

I squeeze her hands and whisper it back.

I was sure I wouldn't be nervous, but there's a lightness

in my chest. But, when I look into her eyes, at the joy that radiates from her, all that tension melts away.

Alyssa is about to become my wife.

This is the best day of my life.

The officiant clasps his hands together. "We're here today to celebrate the union of Alyssa Summers and Luke Lawrence. Today, you will promise your lives to each other." He looks at me. "I understand that you have written your own vows."

I nod.

"Alyssa, I love you more than I thought I could ever love anyone." I look into her eyes. Everything about this moment is perfect. "I don't know where life will lead us, but I promise to stay by your side on this journey. I promise to love you forever. I promise my life to you."

She smiles, a tear rolling down her cheek. She shakes her head, wiping it away and mouthing a curse.

It makes me grin as I wait.

The officiant turns to her. She nods, taking a moment to catch her breath.

She looks me straight in the eye. "This isn't a vow. It's a privilege. I have the privilege of spending my life with you, of growing old with you, of sharing every bit of joy with you. For that, I'm the luckiest girl in the world." She smiles, the edges a little shaky. "I promise to share every day with you. I promise to love you until the end."

The officiant turns to me.

"Do you take Alyssa to be your lawfully wedded wife?"

Fuck yes.

I smile. "I do."

"And do you take Luke to be your lawfully wedded husband?"

Alyssa nods. "I do."

Alyssa squeezes my hands.

He opens the ring box and hands Alyssa's wedding band to me. "Please place this ring on her finger and repeat after me: I give you this ring as a daily reminder of our love."

I nod and slide the ring onto Alyssa's finger. "I give you this ring as a daily reminder of our love."

The officiant hands Alyssa my wedding band. "Please place this ring on his finger and repeat after me: I give you this ring as a daily reminder of our love."

She slides the ring onto my finger, her hand lingering on mine. "I give you this ring as a daily reminder of our love."

I hold her gaze. I can see everything inside her, and she can see everything inside me.

I know we're going to be happy for the rest of our lives.

The officiant nods. "You have made your vows as promises to each other and sealed your promises by exchanging rings. So, now, with the power invested in me by the great state of Hawaii, I pronounce you man and wife. And invite you to kiss each other."

I lean in before he's finished talking, pulling Alyssa close.

She smells so good, looks so good, feels so fucking good.

I press my lips to hers.

There's no more doubt.

She loves me, and I love her.

As long as we're together, everything is going to be more than okay.

Stay In Touch

Sign up for <u>my mailing list</u>. (You'll get first notice on cover reveals, teasers, and new releases, and a bunch of awesome bonus content like a free copy of *Sing for Me*).

You can also <u>like my page on Facebook</u>, <u>join my fangroup</u>, <u>follow me on Instagram</u>, <u>follow me on Twitter</u>, or <u>friend me on Facebook</u>.

Turn the page for a taste of sexy alpha hero Blake Sterling in the first chapter of <u>*Dirty Deal*</u>, a modern day Cinderella story.

Dirty Deal - Special Preview

Get *Dirty Deal* Now

The manager takes one look at my discount heels and my loose pencil skirt and shakes his head.

"Sorry, but the position is already filled." He leers at my chest. Raises a brow. *Maybe you'd like to fill a different position.*

I swallow the insult rising in my throat. "Do you know when you'll be hiring again?"

"It might be awhile."

"Keep me in mind. I have a lot of experience." Not so much the kind he's looking for. But I do know how to wait tables.

He takes my résumé but keeps his eyes on my chest. "Sorry, honey, but we're looking for something specific."

Yeah, I bet.

I take a not-at-all-calming breath. This guy is nothing. He's not going to make me lose it. I've dealt with a thousand entitled jerks worse than him.

I'll deal with plenty more tonight.

It comes with working at a nice place.

I nod a *thank you* and walk out of the restaurant slowly.

I keep my steps casual. Easy. Well, as easy as I can in these shitty heels.

The air outside is freezing. Even by March in New York standards. The white sky is heavy with grey rainclouds.

Usually, I like the drizzle. I like the temperamental weather—the snowy winters, the rainy spring, the humid summer, the crisp fall.

Right now, not so much.

I dig into my purse for my phone. Lizzy will cheer me up. She always does.

With my next step, I bump into something solid.

No. Someone. Soft wool wraps over a hard body.

My leg catches on his. I think it's a his.

My ankle shifts.

Shit.

I throw my hands in front of my face to catch my fall.

Ow. The concrete smarts. And it's fucking cold.

"Are you okay?" a deep voice asks.

So that's a him. Very him. His voice is masculine. There's something about the steady timbre. Something that makes me forget I'm splayed out on the ground, damp concrete wetting my skirt.

"I'm fine."

His shoes are nice. Leather. Designer. Expensive. His slacks fall at exactly the right place. They're grey. Wool. And they're covering long legs.

His black wool coat falls at mid-thigh. It's buttoned. It's hiding his torso. It's hanging off his strong shoulders.

He's looking down at me, his blue eyes filled with… with something. I'm not sure. It's hard to do anything but stare back at those eyes.

They're beautiful.

And he has this square jaw. The kind of jaw that belongs on a sculpture.

Or a Disney prince.

He's the hottest guy I've seen in months.

And I'm splayed out on the concrete staring dumbstruck.

Awesome.

"I… Um… You should watch where you're going." I pick up my purse and slide it onto my shoulder.

He leans down and offers his hand.

Okay.

I guess he's a gentleman.

That's weird, but it fits him, what with the whole Disney prince vibe.

I take his hand. It does something to me. Makes the air sharper, more electric. Sends heat from my palm, down my arm, through my torso.

It's a strong hand, but it's smooth.

And that suit—

And that *I get what I want* look in his eyes.

I know this guy. Well, I know his type.

He's pure money.

The kind of guy who has the world at his fingertips.

"I really am fine." I pull myself to my feet. Or maybe he pulls me. Either way, I take a step towards the corner— the subway is only a few blocks away—but my ankle isn't having it. Fuck. That hurts.

His grip on my hand tightens. "Sit down." He nods to the bench behind us. "If you can walk."

"I don't need your help."

"Oh, really?" He raises an eyebrow and nods to my shoe as if to say *put it on then*.

Oh.

I'm not wearing a shoe.

For some reason, my foot isn't cold.

None of me is cold.

He's just so…

Obnoxious for telling me what to do.

And incredibly, painfully appealing.

I shift my weight to my other ankle, but I can barely balance. "I have to get to work."

"You'll get to work. Trust me." He slides his arm under mine, like a human crutch, and he sets me on the bench.

His touch is comforting.

It should be scary—this guy is a stranger. I don't even know his name.

But it's not.

It's soothing.

Tender.

But that doesn't mean anything.

It's just that it's been so long since anyone has touched me with any care or attention.

I take a deep breath. It does nothing to slow my heart-beat. "What's your name?"

"Blake. You?"

"Kat."

Those piercing eyes find mine. He presses his fingers against my ankle. "It's sprained."

"I've dealt with worse."

His stare is penetrating. It demands an explanation.

But why?

He doesn't know me.

He doesn't have any obligation to help.

He's someone and I'm no one.

He's not even going to remember me tomorrow.

Still, I want to wipe away the worry in his eyes. "I ran cross-country in high school."

He nods with understanding.

"I can't work on a sprained ankle."

"What do you do?"

"I'm a waitress." And I can't afford to not work.

I stare back at Money Guy. Blake. His expression is still streaked with concern. He's not going to leave me alone until he's sure I'm fine.

And I can't exactly make a quick exit. Not with my ankle this fucked up.

"I'll ice it when I get home. I promise." Ibuprofen will have to get me through my shift tonight. I've played through the pain before, back when I ran all the time instead of every so often.

"I'd feel better if you went to the E.R."

I press my lips into a customer-service smile. "Not happening."

"Where do you work?"

"It's not far. I can walk."

"I'll walk you." He slides my shoe onto my foot.

His fingers graze my ankle.

His touch is soft. Tender. Sweet. Like we're old lovers, not strangers.

It wakes up all my nerves.

I want those hands on my skin.

Under my skirt.

Tearing off my blouse.

Sliding my panties to my knees.

I swallow hard.

I don't think about sex like this. And certainly not with strange, rich men who insist on walking me to work.

Blake.

Money Guy.

He certainly has the tall and handsome thing covered.

If things were different, if Lizzy wasn't home, if I

didn't have to work, maybe I'd invite myself out with him.

We could have dinner. Drinks. A night at a hotel. The kind with security. So it's safe.

I could finally punch my v-card.

But things aren't different.

I can't waste time with strange men.

Even rich ones.

I rise to my feet. "I can walk myself." I take a step to prove it. The first is fine, but the second makes me wince. Maybe I can't work on this. Fuck.

He slides his arms under mine, offering himself as a crutch again.

This time, I take his help without protest.

"You really shouldn't work on that." His voice is steady. Impossible to read.

"It's really none of your business."

He nods and walks with me. "It was my fault. I wasn't paying attention."

"You can admit that?"

"Should I not?"

"No." I take a few more steps. It's not so bad. I'm off tomorrow. With rest, ice, and plenty of over the counter painkillers, I'll be okay. "Just… I serve a lot of guys like you."

"Handsome?"

He… he's joking. I think.

I try to find the meaning in his expression, but I get lost in his beautiful eyes.

"Business types," I say. "Guys who are used to getting what they want."

"And they want you as dessert?"

"Sometimes." I get a lot of phone numbers. But that's normal. All the girls at the restaurant do. "They don't usually take no for an answer."

"And I?"

"I guess you're the same." I manage to put my full weight on my foot. It hurts, but it's tolerable. We turn the corner. It's not too far now. "Those guys… they don't like to admit anything is their fault. Even if they order the wrong entree. Or forget to say 'hold the onions.'"

"I know the type." He raises a brow.

We cross the street. I'm moving faster now. New Yorker fast. I nod to the restaurant two blocks down. "I'm there. I've got it." I step away from him.

He pulls his arms back to his sides. "I'm not different."

He pulls something from his back pocket and hands it to me.

It's a business card.

His voice is that same steady tone. "Give it a few days and let me know how you're doing."

"You mean how my ankle is doing?"

He holds my gaze. There's something in his eyes— some tiny hint of vulnerability. I look at the pavement, then back to his eyes. That vulnerability is gone. Replaced by pure determination.

"That's my personal number. Text or call anytime." He takes a step back. "Be careful."

I nod. "Thanks."

He turns, walks around the corner, and he's gone.

I look at the business card.

Blake Sterling. CEO of Sterling Tech. They're huge. Lizzy is obsessed with them. Uses their web services exclusively.

Blake is the CEO of one of the biggest tech companies in New York.

And he wants to know how I'm doing.

Get *Dirty Deal* Now

Also by Crystal Kaswell

Come Undone Trilogy

Come Undone

Come Apart

Come To Me

Dirty Rich

Dirty Deal - Blake

Dirty Boss - Nick

Dirty Husband - Shep

Dirty Desires - Ian

Dirty Wedding - Ty

Dirty Secret - Cam

Pierce Family

Broken Beast - Adam

Playboy Prince - Liam

Ruthless Rival - Simon - coming soon

Inked Hearts

Tempting - Brendon

Hooking Up - Walker

Pretend You're Mine - Ryan

Hating You, Loving You - Dean

Breaking the Rules - Hunter

Losing It - Wes

Accidental Husband - Griffin

The Baby Bargain - Chase

Inked Love

The Best Friend Bargain - Forest

The First Taste - Holden

The Roomie Rulebook - Oliver

Sinful Serenade

Sing Your Heart Out - Miles

Strum Your Heart Out - Drew

Rock Your Heart Out - Tom

Play Your Heart Out - Pete

Sinful Ever After – series sequel

Just a Taste - Miles's POV

Dangerous Noise

Dangerous Kiss - Ethan

Dangerous Crush – Kit

Dangerous Rock – Joel

Dangerous Fling – Mal

Dangerous Encore - series sequel

Standalones

Broken - Trent & Delilah

Sign up for the Crystal Kaswell mailing list

Printed in Great Britain
by Amazon

10199947R00192